SOUTHERN BRED
AND DEAD

ANGIE FOX

Also by Angie Fox

SHORT STORY COLLECTIONS:

A Little Night Magic: A collection of Southern Ghost Hunter and Accidental Demon Slayer short stories

Southern Bred and Dead

The Southern Ghost Hunter Mysteries

Book 9

NEW YORK TIMES BESTSELLING AUTHOR

ANGIE FOX

SOUTHERN BRED AND DEAD

ISBN: 978-1-939661-68-5

Moose Island Books

Chapter One

I t isn't every day you walk into the parlor and find a skunk in your purse. But there she was, nestled in the pink leather bag my sister had lent me this morning. My skunk snuggled in so tightly that the side of the bag smushed up the fur on her face and sent one ear poking sideways in a manner that made me want to smooth it down and tell her she was adorable.

Still, I was raising her to be polite, and this just wouldn't do.

"Lucille Désirée Long," I said, using her full name to let her know I was serious. Truly, she owned a perfectly good bed, a brand-new one my boyfriend Ellis bought as a present for her. It was pink and white and fit for a Disney princess, complete with a canopy. "You should try to sleep in your fancy bed."

The little skunk leveled an appraising eye in my direction before she closed them both and snuggled deeper into the purse.

She was a Southern girl, which meant she had a stubborn streak.

My heels clicked on the hardwood as I approached her to deliver the sad truth. "Taking a nap in my handbag won't keep me from leaving." I was due at a somewhat dressy gathering, and it wouldn't do to arrive with a skunk in my purse. At least not today in front of the ladies from the Sugarland Heritage Society.

Lucy flicked her bushy white-striped tail and wedged it into the bag with the rest of her. Poor thing. I smoothed the flowing skirt of my magnolia-patterned dress and crouched down in front of my skunk-in-a-purse. "You know I'd take you along if I could."

She twitched her nose but made no move to leave the bag. I leaned in to stroke her on the head, my thumb skimming the little stripe of white between her eyes. "How about you come out of there, and we can have a Cinnamon Banana Skunk Crumble before I leave?"

Lucy's ears perked up and she lunged forward, dragging the purse with her a few feet. That didn't last long before she gave it a kick with her back foot and sent the bag spinning across the floor without a second thought.

Her little claws pitter-pattered as she about ran me over on her way to the kitchen. Not that I could blame her. Cinnamon Banana Skunk Crumbles were heaven on a plate. They were also the perfect way to slip Lucy some extra vitamins. I'd gotten the recipe online from a skunk owner in Alabama, and yes, I'd tried them. They'd smelled so amazing when I'd taken the cookie sheets out of the oven, I couldn't resist a nibble.

"Here you go, sweetie," I said, drawing one out of the cookie jar on my kitchen island, grinning at my little girl as she snorted and danced in circles. She whipped the treat from my outstretched hand like she was afraid I'd eat it myself and dashed straight for her princess bed.

"Look at you, trying out your bed!" I said, savoring the small victory.

A distinct chill seeped through the air, and I suddenly understood why my skunk had sought out a safe place.

We were about to have company.

Lucy hunkered over her treat, her gaze fixed on the empty space she'd just vacated.

My pet had strong opinions about the ghost of the 1920s gangster who haunted our property. Frankie "The German" was a particularly cantankerous spirit Lucy snubbed on a good day and outright feared on a bad one.

He shimmered into view decked out in the clothes he'd died in—a depression-era gray pinstripe suit over a white French-cuffed shirt. He wore a white Panama hat pulled low to hide the bullet hole smack in the middle of his forehead. It was the shot that had killed him, and he was sensitive about it.

Today, Frankie also wielded an ugly black tommy gun in one hand, his finger poised on the trigger.

"Ohmyheavens, no," I exclaimed. It was one thing to belong to a ghostly criminal syndicate, but it was quite another to bring his work home with him. "You are not allowed to bring that gun into my house."

He gave me a long look, his lip twitching into a snarl under his hooklike nose. To my relief, he held the weapon out and let it dissolve into nothingness. "You do realize I'm packing heat every day," he said, not at all contrite. "I have a shoulder holster, a belt holster, a sock holster. If I could put a Luger in my under-wear, I'd do it."

"A pistol in your pants would certainly get you some atten-tion from the ladies," I reasoned.

The tips of his ears reddened. "Anyone ever tell you to mind your manners?" he asked, watching me retrieve the purse from the floor.

Not that I recalled.

"You scared Lucy," I said, plunking the purse onto my kitchen island and gesturing to the skunk, who kept one eye on the ghost while hunting for cinnamon treat crumbs in the tufted pillows of her bed.

"You're scaring *me*," Frankie countered, giving me the once-over as I fished a lipstick from the bottom of the purse and applied a coat of Revlon Fire & Ice. "Heels and a dress? You said you'd take me on a manhunt today."

"I certainly did," I assured him before rubbing my lips together then adding a coat of gloss. I always kept my promises.

"I didn't mean the blonde-bombshell type of manhunt," he clarified.

"I'll take that as a compliment," I said, tossing the gloss into the bag.

Frankie not only lived here; he was stuck on my property. Or as he would put it, "unavoidably detained." I'd grounded his spirit to my land, quite unintentionally, and he couldn't leave unless I took his burial urn off the property with me.

It wasn't always fun for either of us.

"This," I said, smoothing the blooming magnolias at my waist, "is my going-out dress." I directed a firm, yet reassuring smile at the frowning ghost. "I told you last night, I'll be more than happy to drive you to meet your mafia buddies." He couldn't exactly take off without me, and I owed him some sort of afterlife. "I'll even read a book in the car while you stake out that other gang's speakeasy, but you said yourself the raid doesn't start until dusk, and it's barely noon. We have plenty of time to go to the Sugarland Heritage Society fundraiser first."

His eyes bugged. "I thought you were joking."

Hardly. "I assure you the yearly church fundraiser is a serious responsibility. It's the only thing that keeps the doors open at the Three Angels of the Tabernacle Blessed Reform Church of Sugarland. They barely have a congregation anymore."

"That's because nothing good ever happens at the Three Angels," he warned.

"This fundraiser is good," I countered. "The work they do in the community is good."

He ran a hand over his face. "Can you for once, just once,

stop trying to boost up every cause, charity, fundraiser, man, woman, child, circus, and stray dog in town?"

"Sure," I said sweetly, "but then I'd be sitting at home tonight reading a book instead of helping you."

He shot me a withering look. He was in such a mood today.

I moved Lucy's skunk treats to the cabinet lest she be tempted to scale the kitchen island in my absence. "Jorie Davis called last night," I said, changing the subject, hoping it would help. "Jorie was very close friends with my late grandmother. I believe they met in grammar school." He ran a hand down his face, and I tried to deliver the happy news over his groan. "Jorie is moving to a suite in the old Sugarland Grand Hotel on the north side of town. They've turned the whole place into luxury senior apartments. I hear it's amazing. Anyhow, while she was cleaning out her bungalow, she found a few things of my grand-mother's she'd like to give me. She's bringing them to the fundraiser."

Frankie looked to the ceiling. "Just shoot me now."

"Someone already did," I said, with a pointed glance toward the jagged bullet hole in his forehead.

He caught me looking and quickly straightened his hat. "All I ask is for one simple clip on a gin joint, and instead you have to drag me to a church ladies' event and remind me about my death."

Heavens. His raid would go much better if he could relax and shake that awful mood. Although I didn't think telling him so would help. I headed to the parlor to fetch his urn.

"How about we get to the stakeout two hours early instead of six?" He'd still have a few hours to sulk and ruminate. I'd get my fundraiser in. Just as important, an afternoon's diversion might give him a new perspective on his raid. "Keep an open mind," I called. "I daresay you'll enjoy visiting the historic church. There's an old graveyard outside."

5

"I'm aware." He stood in the arched entryway to the parlor, glaring at me.

"You might make a new friend," I added.

Frankie reared back so fast you'd have thought I took his Popsicle and called him ugly. "What? Just because we're all dead, I'm supposed to get along with random strangers?"

Lucy leapt out of her bed near the doorway and toddled into the front room. She had no patience for ghostly sass.

"I didn't mean it that way," I told him. Being dead was a very broad thing to have in common, but it didn't mean he wouldn't find something else to talk about. "Never mind."

Any other time, I might not have put up with his attitude, but I knew why the gangster had wound himself so tight. Today was a big day, and it had everything to do with that bullet hole in his forehead.

Frankie had gone his entire afterlife not knowing who killed him. On our last adventure, we'd learned it had been Frankie's own brother who had pulled the trigger.

I couldn't imagine his pain or his shock.

Frankie hadn't seen his brother, Lou, since the revelation, despite the fact they were in the same gang and ran with the same crowd. Lou had been lying low, avoiding a confrontation. But Frankie had learned the location of his brother's hideout and would face him tonight.

I lifted Frankie's urn from underneath the rosebush I kept next to the mantel. The heirloom red had lived outside until that fateful day when I'd mistaken Frankie's urn for a vase. I'd found the dusty old thing stashed in my attic, and it had been in need of a fine and thorough rinsing. So I'd taken a hose to it and washed the dirt—I mean his ashes—into the soil under my favorite rosebush.

Of course, it was only after Frankie had appeared and scared me to death, I'd learned those ashes were his earthly remains and I'd mixed him in good. So I dug up the bush and the soil underneath and planted the entire kit and caboodle in an oversized plastic trash bin. Even better, I gave it a place of honor in my parlor. Frankie had been satisfied, mostly. Although he'd resisted my every attempt to replace the ugly trash can with a pretty painted pot or whimsical planter box.

I held the urn over the trash can and carefully brushed the dirt from the bottom. "What are you going to say to your brother when you see him?" I asked quietly.

Frankie stood silently for a long moment, motionless under the arched entryway to the parlor. The morning sun streamed through him.

"I'm going to ask him *why*," he said, his tone even, his eyes dead. "I'm not going to forgive him. I only want to know why he did it."

I clutched his urn to my chest, wishing I could make it better. "I realize this is hard." In Frankie's case, it was a big step for him to even talk about his death. "I know you don't like to think about that night."

He cast an uncertain gaze at me, then down at the floor. "I think about it plenty, I just don't tell you. Believe it or not, sometimes it's better not to talk about every thought and emotion the second it enters your brain."

"It can be equally harmful to block things out," I reminded him.

"Not when it's the kind of messed-up stuff I'm used to dealing with." He raised his eyes, looking past me. "Just because I couldn't remember doesn't mean I didn't care." He ran a hand along the back of his neck. "I didn't want to get my hopes up that we'd ever figure this out."

Yet we had.

"And now I learn it was my brother." Frankie sighed and dropped his hand. "I mean, things weren't exactly sunshine and roses between Lou and me before we were dead. I hardly saw him." He shoved his hands into his pockets. "But now I know

7

he's avoiding me. So yeah, I kind of feel like shooting something."

"You have every right." Except for the shooting part. But I wouldn't win that debate.

I closed the distance between us. "Try not to drive yourself crazy in the meantime."

"Too late," he groused, retreating into the kitchen. "He's my family—the only family I have left on this earth." He paced the kitchen, walking straight through my kitchen island in the process. "And worse, what if I need to make buddy-buddies with him in order to be free? What if I need to tie up the loose ends, you know?"

Stars. I hadn't considered it. "This could be afterlife changing."

"No pressure there." He turned to face me.

We'd been trying to free Frankie for more than a year now, and nothing else had worked. Our first attempt had been science-based—a middle-school lab experiment I'd found on YouTube. We used it to try to separate Frankie's ashes from my garden soil. It had resulted in a mess, along with the trash can full of garden dirt and ashes, topped with a rosebush, that now resided in my parlor.

We'd called in a psychic. She'd proceeded to give Frankie a complex he'd soothed by opening an illegal racetrack in my backyard.

We'd attempted to reunite Frankie with the only thing he'd claimed to love: a long-lost favorite revolver. It had led to a gangland shoot-out I'd barely survived, and to the beat-up, empty revolver now gathering dust in the trash can under the rosebush.

Yet he remained stuck.

So we were working on a new theory. Frankie was so attached to his ashes and the life they represented that he'd created a sort of prison for himself. I hoped if he could come to

SOUTHERN BRED AND DEAD

terms with what had happened to him, if he could make peace
with his sudden death, then maybe Frankie could be free.

Making peace with his brother could be a huge part of it.

I mean, Frankie had made an enormous step even deciding
to pursue closure. He was growing as a person, although I
wouldn't tell him that. It would only upset him.

"You can do this," I assured him. "I'm here for you."

Frankie's face hardened at my reassurance, and he pointed at
me. "Don't start."

And we were back to the ghost having trouble facing his
feelings. He was going through some heavy emotions, but he
didn't have to face them alone. He needed to understand that.

He had a hard time letting me or anyone—even his ghost
girlfriend—help him cope. Just last week, I'd gotten him a book
from the library on dealing with his emotions. I probably
shouldn't have pushed it on him, and I'd definitely made a
mistake when I'd sat outside his shed and read it out loud to
him. I'd thought it might help him understand what he was
feeling.

Until Frankie had insisted he didn't have emotions.

"I'm sorry if I'm doing this wrong, but I'll do everything I
can to support you," I insisted. "I know I don't always say the
right thing, but I care," I added when he clenched his jaw and
stared at me. "And I know you're hurting."

We'd been through too much together for him to shut down
on me like this. Since he'd been trapped on my property, we'd
learned he could lend me some of his ghostly power and I'd
become a ghost hunter. Seeing the other side had become more
than a career for me—it was a calling. Frankie had given me a
new way to look at the world. That was about as intimate as you
could get.

As ghost hunters, Frankie and I were partners. I'd shown him
that angry spirits weren't necessarily bad spirits, just ones who
needed to get over their hurt. He'd taught me that sometimes it's

better to bluff a little than to show the entire world your poker hand. I was still perfecting that one. Together, we'd talked our way into a Great Gatsby–era house party and had the time of our lives. We'd narrowly escaped, but, oh—it had been worth it.

He could certainly count on me to listen to what he was going through.

Frankie glanced behind him. "Enough talk."

But we still hadn't worked anything out. "I know it makes you sad a lot of your friends won't talk with you about your death," I said, watching his eyes widen.

He looked over his shoulder like the police were onto him. The air went cold, and goose bumps scattered across my skin. "Ix-nay on the death talk," he gritted out.

"But you told me that yourself last week when I made you do that worksheet," I reminded him, watching his eyes bug out. Was that a sign of denial? I'd have to check the book. In any case, he had to talk about his feelings with someone—a safe person, like me. "Are you lonely?" I asked.

"Who says I'm lonely!" he squawked as if he were being strangled.

"See? This is what I'm talking about." He needed to deal with his emotions, and he needed to know I cared. I'd listen to what he needed to say, no matter what. It was the least I could do.

Living with me had separated him from the old gang. He couldn't carouse unless I sat on a bench outside knitting. He couldn't go on runs to Chicago unless I drove him, which was one thing I refused to do. Why, at one point, he'd tried to tunnel under the vault of the First Bank of Sugarland just to let off some steam.

He deserved the kind of cheering that went with a bottle of wine and a bit of girl talk, although I didn't think he'd go for it quite that way.

"You have every right to be upset about your afterlife right now," I assured him, rubbing a fresh scattering of goose bumps from my arms.

Frankie tended to use cold spots to express his discomfort. We must be really digging deep.

"You're making it worse," he said through clenched teeth.

"I'm helping you grow." As long as he didn't freeze me out of the room. His refusal to talk about his death had kept him trapped for years. It was time to move forward. "Your feelings are valid, and you should deconstruct them so you can process this."

Frankie glided straight at me as if I were tap-dancing on his last nerve. "I am going to die—again—unless you shut it."

"Would it kill you to let a friend help you find peace?" Dare I say we'd become friends over the course of our adventures. "Have you at least let yourself cry?"

I met his jaw-clenched, bug-eyed stare. Then he said something I could barely hear through gritted teeth. "Some of the South Town Boys dropped by. They are right behind me, and they are listening to every word!"

"Oh," I managed before Frankie hit me with his power. The cold, wet sting of a thousand tiny pricks of energy radiated through my skin and settled in my bones. It doubled me over, stung me to the core.

It never felt particularly pleasant, but when he did it without warning, it was worse. My teeth vibrated like I'd chomped down on tinfoil. As I recovered, a trio of gangsters shimmered into view behind Frankie, laughing.

They poked each other with the butts of their tommy guns as they took turns doing impressions of Frankie crying, which wasn't fair because Frankie hadn't admitted to anything. Or gotten in touch much with his emotions. And so much for my rule about no machine guns in the house.

"Don't you dare make fun of him," I said to the gangsters,

shaking out my tingling hands. Frankie's power vibrated all the way to my fingertips.

"Can you please stop defending me?" Frankie said, his voice going high.

"Frankie has feelings," crooned a guy with a jagged scar running up his cheek and over his eye.

"I wish I had a girl to cry with," added a skinny guy riddled with bullet holes.

"Go cry with your mother," Frankie shot back half-heartedly.

These jerks were probably the reason he was afraid to share. "You'd better watch it, or Frankie's going to make you beg for mercy like he did that biker gang from Tulsa," I said to his testosterone-soaked buddies.

Frankie shot me a warning glance. "That's enough, Verity."

But I had the guys' attention. The least I could do was use it to help rebuild my friend's gangster cred. I stood straighter, planting my hands on my hips. "Frankie was manly, very tough," I said, making it up as I went. Frankie should be glad I was a solid friend who supported him instead of a person who would hold a grudge over an unwanted power transfer. "You should have seen Frankie in Tulsa. Karate chopping and all that," I managed, giving the best demonstration I could come up with on the fly based on tough-as-nails movie heroes. Perhaps *Charlie's Angels* wasn't the best inspiration.

The guys stared at me, Frankie included.

"He whipped them single-handedly," I added. In for a penny, in for a pound. "I was terrified."

"Enough," Frankie ordered. He'd reverted back to gangster mode. "Meet me at the Lucky Dime at dusk," he commanded the trio. "Bring extra ammo. Don't shoot nobody unless I give the signal." The wiseguys filed out of the house in front of us. "Tell anybody what you heard here, and I'll use your eyeballs for fish bait," he added after them.

Frankie let them get out the door before leveling an accusing stare at me. "There are no gangsters in Tulsa."

"There could be," I offered, hurrying to grab my purse. He was upset, and I certainly hadn't helped. If he really needed to wait around with his friends, or even start his raid early, I'd skip my event. "We can go to the Lucky Dime now if it makes you feel better."

"Nah." Frankie sighed wearily and adjusted his hat over the hole in his forehead. "I'd rather avoid those mugs until the job goes down, or I might be tempted to shoot a couple of 'em myself." He looked at me appraisingly, almost amused. "I can't believe I'm saying this, but let's go to the church fundraiser."

"Oh, let's," I said, with an enthusiasm that made him stiffen. Well, I couldn't help it. The yearly event at the Three Angels of the Tabernacle Blessed Reform Church of Sugarland might be exactly what he needed to take his mind off his troubles. "You haven't been to anything like it," I promised.

Chapter Two

The Three Angels of the Tabernacle Blessed Reform
Church of Sugarland stood near the north edge of
town, past the town square and the old, established
neighborhoods surrounding it.

Gatherings of cows grazed with their calves in the pastures
scattered along the highway as we exited on Jackson Boulevard
and continued on, traveling past the Sugarland Fair grounds,
which were no more than a gravel parking lot and a field this
time of year.

Despite the fact you could get almost anywhere in Sugarland
in ten minutes, most folks considered this church too far out to
bother. There were so many other places to find the Lord these
days, with livelier congregations, choirs, potlucks, and bingo
nights.

That, and the place had kind of an odd feel. Every time I'd
ever set foot on that property felt like a cloudy day.

We came upon a deserted crossroads surrounded by green
fields. Even though we were still somewhat close to town, this
particular place felt like the edge of the earth.

Despite the absence of any traffic for miles, I stopped

ANGIE FOX

because there was a sign, and that was the law. I ignored Frankie's muttered plea to his maker.

"It would do you good to learn a little patience," I said, turning left at the crossroads after a thorough look in all directions.

"You're always talking about what other people need to learn," Frankie said, sticking his arm straight through my window and flicking the ghostly ash from his cigarette with his thumb.

"Dare I ask what you mean by that?" I countered, wishing the gangster were a bit more shy with his opinions.

He took another drag. "You always want other people to look at life—or the afterlife—the way you do."

Wasn't that human nature? We all had our blind spots. I'd keep an eye out, I vowed, as I caught the first glimpse of the church steeple past a copse of trees at the crest of a hill.

The church was a gorgeous white clapboard structure, built in 1832. Sure, it had seen better days, I decided wistfully as we climbed the hill and reached the low iron gate surrounding the property. Layers upon layers of black paint clung to the spindles like moss.

"I'm gonna cut your power," Frankie announced.

I gripped the wheel. The tingle of energy slid down my arms and legs as it left me. At least he'd been gentle about it this time. "Why'd you do that?" Not that I minded. I'd kind of forgotten I had it.

Frankie stared at the approaching cemetery gates. "This business with Lou has me feeling zapped."

"I'm sorry to hear it," I said. Ever since he'd fallen in love with a ghost named Molly, he'd had power to spare. I found myself doubly glad he'd be facing Lou tonight. "I appreciate you sharing your energy issues with me."

"Better than my other issues," he smirked.

Although the way he watched the cemetery gates as we

passed made me wonder if he'd told the whole truth. I had a hunch we'd come across something he didn't want me to see.

"What is it?" I asked.

"Nothing," Frankie murmured, drawing his arm back inside the car.

"I'm not going to melt if you show me what's lurking around in this place," I reminded him. Truth be told, I was curious.

"Nah. You're here for happy times, remember?" he said, and I had the distinct impression he was mocking me. "I also need to save my energy for tonight."

"Good point." I let it slide. I'd come here to relax, and Frankie could stand to take a break as well.

At the same time, I tried not to think about the uneasy feeling trickling down my back. Perhaps I'd let Frankie's anxiety rub off on me.

The cemetery appeared serene enough. Weathered graves dotted with lichen leaned to-and-fro under a smattering of towering oaks.

"Look at that," I said, pointing up the long drive toward the historic gem of a church, trying to focus on the positive.

Paint flaked from the white clapboard walls, but it didn't mar the simple beauty of the modest rectangular main building or the small square reception area jutting from the front. The steeple rose front and center, and even from this distance I could see a woman waving excitedly from one of the tall windows at the top.

"She's going to fall out if she doesn't watch it," Frankie warned.

"She's excited," I said, grinning at her enthusiasm. It was Kelli Kaiser, a woman I'd met while solving a murder at the Sugarland Heritage Society. She and her group of well-to-do friends volunteered for the heritage society mainly as a social outlet, but they did do a fine job, and that was all that mattered.

"There's a ghost behind her," Frankie said. "From the shovel he's hefting, I'd say he's a gravedigger."

"Charming," I said, chancing a wave back at Kelli, although she was probably too far away to notice.

Kelli liked me because her archrival—the town matriarch, Virginia Wydell—did not. I'd been on Virginia's list ever since I broke off my engagement to her youngest son. Then she'd gotten truly frosty when I started dating my current boyfriend, who also happened to be her middle son, Ellis. I had to admit it sounded a little reality-show crazy unless you knew the whole story. Maybe even then.

No doubt Virginia lurked somewhere up ahead. I'd cross that bridge when I came to it.

For the time being, I concentrated on what a blessing it was to do my part to preserve the nice things our ancestors had left in our care. I admired how each church window came to a point at the top, with trim painted the same green as the slanted roof. A craftsman had fashioned those windows by hand, every last one of them.

"They don't make buildings like this anymore," I told Frankie as I slowed to navigate a series of potholes in the road. Maybe he'd be impressed when he saw the inside. "You should see the three angels carving behind the altar. We're raising money to restore it. They've already redone the old bell tower, which is why Kelli is up there. We get to take tours today."

As if on cue, the bell rang, a long, low bong.

"Ask not for whom the bell tolls," Frankie said, his attention fixed on a spot on the side of the road. "Is that...Easy Eddie?" he marveled, leaning forward.

"A friend of yours?" I asked, slowing down.

"A politician. Always on the take," he said, rubbernecking as we passed.

"You should talk to him," I said.

"I have my standards." Frankie scoffed.

He did?

"Ooh..." I strained to see what lay ahead. "It looks like they set up a tent with balloons next to the church. How festive!"

"I thought I taught you how to party." Frankie groaned.

So much for him keeping an open mind. "You can either come with me, or you can find your own friends." I cringed as the car lurched over a craterlike pothole. Tombstones rose on either side of us, some leaning precariously, others worn to stubs.

"Huh," Frankie said, doing a double take.

"What do you see now?" I asked, slowing to a crawl. As much as I sometimes regretted having his power, I felt a little left out now that I didn't have it.

"That's the shoeshine kid from Third Street." Frankie said, rubbernecking. "He didn't have folks. I always tipped extra."

"How sweet." Maybe Frankie did have a heart.

He grinned. "Davey saw everything that happened outside the Dubliner bar on Third. The Irish ran numbers out the side door."

Lovely. "Maybe Davey grew up to be a member of the Three Angels Church."

Frankie snorted. "If you didn't keep an eye on him, that kid would steal your shoelaces."

People changed. "Go talk to him," I pressed. "Or you could always go to the party tent with me and check out the balloons."

"I'm out of here," Frankie said, passing straight through the car door.

That had worked better than I'd hoped.

It would do the gangster some good to reconnect with an acquaintance from the old neighborhood.

My Cadillac lurched over another large pothole in the road. Yes, this place definitely needed a fundraiser.

I parked in one of the last spaces left in the lot, glad to see the event had drawn a crowd. Grabbing my bag, I fished past

Frankie's urn and located my donation envelope. It wasn't as fat as some of the other envelopes would be, but it was generous for me. I sighed and put on my best smile. It would be fine.

I made my way to the bustling tent at the side of the church.

Several ladies clustered together, talking around a lemonade station decorated with a tablecloth and streamers. Nearby stood the cookie station—for show only. Most of these society ladies would rather eat a garden slug than touch a cookie.

To the left of it all, nearest the church, stood a special round table topped with a vase full of pink and white lilies. There sat Emily Proctor, looking pretty as a peach next to the donation basket. She had gone to high school a year behind my mom and ran the Twinkle Toes Dance Studio, where I'd been a star pupil from age four to ten.

"I do declare," Emily said, her ruddy face beaming as I approached, "aren't you just a diamond in a rhinestone world. Did you do something with your hair?"

She would notice I'd added a sprig of baby's breath to the barrettes holding it back. "This is from a bouquet Ellis brought over."

"Aww," she clucked, "I'm so glad you found a good one, sweetie."

I smiled. "Me too."

I was pleased to see the basket on the table full to near bursting with envelopes, most of which had the names of the donors scrawled on the front.

"Oh, I didn't write my name," I said, searching the table for a pen, as if that were my concern and not the icy breeze at my back, or the tickling sense someone was sneaking up behind me.

I glanced over my shoulder, expecting Frankie, but I saw no one.

"Oh, don't bother printing your name on the outside," Emily said. "It's the richest ones showing off, making one hundred percent sure the pastor knows how charitable they are." She leaned closer as I added my envelope to the stack. "Times like this, I really wish the Bible would let me judge." Emily pushed past the unopened box of name tags—it wasn't like anyone from Sugarland needed one—and picked up a roll of pink raffle tickets. "We're also selling these today. You can win dinner with the very handsome and available Pastor Clemens. Hosted at the winner's house. Only fifty dollars each."

"Ha," I said, trying to sound as if I could afford it. "I think I'll save my dinners for the gorgeous and not-available-anymore Ellis Wydell."

She grinned and fanned herself playfully as my boyfriend walked up from the side of the church, right on cue.

"Music to my ears, darlin'," he said, brushing a kiss across my cheek.

Ellis was the most handsome man in three counties, and no, I wasn't exaggerating a bit. He had the broad-shouldered strength a man could only earn through real-life labor and not in a gym. Better still, he possessed a rugged lean-on-me quality. He watched out for the people he cared about. He had a soft spot for kids and animals. And he topped that with a devilish grin that undid me every time.

"You look like you've been working," I said, running my hands down his broad arms. His dress shirt was damp with perspiration and his hair mussed.

"I was clearing some brush out from around some of the tombstones out back. My mom has me running a security station at the rear of the church," he said, clearly enjoying my attention.

"Why does she think she needs security?" I asked. "Have the deer been getting out of hand?"

Ellis laughed. "I think she likes organizing things, and I'm always ready to be of service," he said. The corner of his mouth hitched up. "So, yes, I'm manning a completely unnecessary 'command station' in case of emergency because we need a full police presence at each and every society fundraiser," he added with no shortage of irony.

"I do always feel safe in Sugarland," I teased.

He tipped his hat. "I allowed myself to take a break when I heard your car coming."

"Ah, yes. The distinct rattle of an old transmission. You never miss a clue."

"Or an opportunity to see you," he said, making me go a little melty. "Listen, I have to head back, but I wanted to mention I saw your grandmother's friend Jorie. She brought me a cookie." At least someone was eating the cookies. "She said she'd be inside by the bell tower stairs. She has something for you."

"Thanks," I said, kissing him on the cheek, holding his hand a second too long before he winked and made his way back through the side graveyard toward the rear of the church.

"I promise I'm not looking at his butt, but I think my ovaries just clenched," Emily said under her breath to me.

"I've never kicked him out of bed for eating crackers," I teased.

"I'd let him crack open some crab legs and pour a beer," she vowed before we said our goodbyes and I headed inside to see what Jorie had for me.

I took cover behind the ladies drinking lemonade and deftly ducked past a welcome banner, barely avoiding Virginia Wydell as she charged down the main stairs. She wore an icy, professional smile, and her youngest son—my ex—Beau Wydell, followed her closely, snapping pictures with his professional-grade camera.

Beau saw me and waved. I was a tad embarrassed to be caught between a Kinko's banner and a forsythia bush, but it didn't matter. The bone-thin, steel-spined Virginia was too busy greeting Myrna Jackson, one of the richest women in Sugarland, to notice me brushing a few leaves out of my belt.

I slipped up the stairs behind Virginia and into the cool, dark interior of the church, breathing in the scent of lemon furniture polish and old wood.

"Would you like a tour of the steeple?" asked longtime volunteer Fiera Marlow. She'd wound her long gray hair into a braided bun with an accent braid framing her face, which proved she was way better at YouTube tutorials than I'd ever be.

Fiera might be older than me, but she'd also worked a farm for sixty years and would no doubt enjoy besting me in a trip up to the top of the tower. "The stairs are small and steep, so we're taking it one at a time," Fiera said, "but the view is amazing, and we'll even let you ring the bell."

"I'd like to, but first, have you seen Jorie?"

"She's somewhere around here," Fiera said, her focus turning to a woman walking down from the front of the church. "Hello, Bree. Care to tour the tower? There's no line right now," she added, sweetening the pot.

"Hey, Bree," I said, brightening. I hadn't seen her since I'd helped her solve a ghost-dog haunting. Bree, an African American girl with natural hair and cat-eye glasses, worked at our local animal shelter. The honey badger tattoo on her arm never failed to tickle me.

"Verity!" She gave me a big hug. "It's so nice to see you. A tour sounds great, Fiera," Bree added, smoothing her orange and green daisy print dress. "Will you be around?" she asked me.

"Sure." I waved her off. "Go explore."

I'd find Jorie in the meantime. The church wasn't that big. I ran a hand along the wooden benches, as old as the church itself, as I walked down the center aisle.

My friend Maisie Hatcher crowded up front behind the altar with several others, listening in rapt attention to Pastor

Clemens as he gestured to the large wood carving of the three angels.

The ladies fawned over him, which didn't surprise me in the least. Pastor Clemens was a handsome man.

He resembled a younger Harrison Ford, his gestures and manner both grand and down-to-earth. I watched as he murmured a joke that caused the group to titter.

It wasn't immediately clear if Jorie stood with them, and I didn't want to interrupt. Instead, I slipped into a pew a few rows back to wait for the tour to end.

Pastor Mike Clemens descended from one of the eight sons of the legendary Pastor Delmore Clemens, who led the church through the Great Depression and remained in charge until he died at the pulpit, mid-sermon, in 1957.

Each of the eight sons of the esteemed pastor were pillars of Sugarland society in their own right and had made it very fashionable to donate to the upkeep of the old church.

Frankie shimmered into the seat next to me.

"How'd it go with Davey?" I murmured.

The corners of his mouth turned down. "He stole my shoelaces."

I tried to hide my smile. "Can't say you didn't see that coming."

"I was distracted," Frankie said defensively, straightening his suit jacket and settling back. "The kid was acting strange."

"How so?" I asked.

"It's hard to explain," he said, leaving it at that.

"Well...death." It could be tough on anybody.

"It's more than that," he said, and I could see the wheels turning.

On the bright side, Frankie wasn't thinking about the stakeout anymore.

"Why don't you try finding another old friend?" I suggested. "They can't all be like Davey."

The gangster snorted. "The former members of the Three Angels Church aren't exactly the people I hung out with." I geared myself up for another pep talk, and he must have seen it coming because he cut me off at the pass. "Why don't you take a look and see for yourself?"

"I hardly think—oh," I murmured as his power trickled over me. He'd taken care to be gentle this time, and still it felt like a thousand hot needles prickling over my skin.

I straightened as the ghostly side of the historic church began to appear. When I had Frankie's power, I could see the other side in black and white, almost like a sheer layer over the real-world version. I could smell the things they smelled, hear the things they did.

And if things turned bad, I could be shot by ghostly bullets or struck by ghostly blows. They were as real to me as the wooden bench under me and the antique chandelier above.

And as the last of Frankie's power settled over me, I tuned in to the low, rich tones of organ music floating from the front, a somber, haunting hymn.

The ghostly stage reflected the vision of the strongest ghost present. I called it the dominant ghost. And as I took in the altered state of the church, I tried to locate him or her.

"Do you know who's in charge here?" I murmured.

"Not sure." Frankie shrugged. "Maybe her."

I followed his gaze to the serious-looking spirit of a woman playing the organ.

The song ended on a long, lingering note.

"That was lovely." I resisted the urge to clap for a performance no one living could hear. The figure remained seated at the bench, unmoving, her fingers lingering on the keys. "Is she okay?"

"How should I know?" Frankie glanced behind us. "I was trying to show you this crazy-eyed golfer holding a nine iron, but now I don't know where he went."

"It's just as well, I'd probably try to talk to him," I teased.

"I did," Frankie countered. "He don't talk back."

"You're not the easiest person to get to know," I reminded him. Frankie tended to be as friendly as a fire ant. I'd only broken through to him because he couldn't get rid of me.

"Let's go," Frankie prodded. "I'm bored stiff and I don't like the vibe."

"Not yet." I still had to talk to Jorie. And I felt bad for the poor organist. She stared straight ahead, her mop of hair limp, the chains of her glasses dangling, her hands frozen on the keyboard.

She seemed out of sorts.

And as long as I had a few moments to spare... "I'll be right back," I told him.

"I tuned you in to get you out of here," he hollered after me, "not to make friends."

Too late. It would only take a minute to make sure everything was okay.

I approached the organist slowly. "That was a lovely song," I said gently to avoid startling her or disrespecting this holy place. "You play so well."

She didn't speak, but I saw her pinkie finger twitch.

Perhaps she wasn't used to conversation. Especially with the living. "Are you okay?"

She didn't move.

"I'm only visiting," I continued, keeping it light. "And I don't mean to intrude if it's none of my business." She could be perfectly alright, merely shy. "I wonder. Do you play all the time here, or are you just visiting, too?"

She straightened and looked directly at me. That was when I noticed a knife buried in her chest. Poor thing!

No wonder she seemed distressed.

I tried not to stare. It wasn't her fault she'd been stabbed.

I made myself smile at her, never mind her gray-rimmed,

SOUTHERN BRED AND DEAD

wild eyes or the blood dripping from the knife. "What's your name?" I asked.

I didn't let it bother me when she didn't respond. "My name is Verity Long, and I live a few miles from here."

She looked to her chest and slowly tugged the bloody knife free.

"Oh, ouch," I stammered.

Blood bubbled out of the wound, soaking her dress.

"Oh, goodness. My." Truly, I hadn't meant for her to do that. "Maybe put that back."

It had to hurt either way.

She looked up at me. "You," she rasped wetly, holding up the bloody, gleaming butcher knife.

"Come here," she hissed, surging straight at me.

Chapter Three

❦

I dashed out of the church and into the yard. I ran past the parking lot and kept going. I didn't stop until I nearly collided with the ghost of a bloody golfer wandering trancelike across the front drive. I dodged him and dared a glance over my shoulder.

"Now can we leave?" Frankie's voice sounded in my ear.

The church doors hung open. Kelli and Bree stood on the steps, looking at me like I was ten shades of crazy. I didn't care. The doorway behind them remained dark. The ghost with the knife hadn't given chase.

Thank goodness and hallelujah. I bent over, hands on my knees, breathing hard.

I heard the next thing before I saw it, glancing up through my disheveled hair. A posse of society ladies gathered around the lemonade, snickering at me. Myrna Jackson stood behind them, glaring at me as if this scene were my fault.

My stomach dipped a little. Sure, my calling was a bit unusual. It would have been nice to get through the afternoon without a scene, but I didn't always have control over that.

"If you've got time to gossip, you've got time to sell raffle tickets," Emily called, waving her roll of pink tickets, earning a few sour looks herself.

I directed a small smile Emily's way. Thank heaven for small favors and kindly dance instructors. *Shake it off.* I straightened. I was used to the talk. And glad the ghost hadn't chased me because I'd blown clear past my car. Where did I think I was running? Home?

I smoothed my skirt and took a deep breath to calm my racing pulse, not in any hurry to face the music.

"It's fine," Bree announced, trying to usher them all back inside. "Come on. Verity just needs a little space."

It only made them dig in more. It was like they sensed a show coming.

Two seconds later, they had it. The growing crowd on the steps directed their attention to Ellis striding down the left side of the church, past Emily's tent, and right for me.

"Hey," I said, meeting him halfway in the parking lot. I offered him a sheepish wave as he scooped me into his arms.

I thought I'd been doing all right, but as soon as I buried my head in his chest, a shudder ran through me and I had to fight to keep it together. I clung to his shoulders and forced myself to steady my breath.

"What happened?" he asked, drawing a lock of hair out of my eyes, shielding me from the crowd with his body and the back of a GMC Canyon Denali. "My mom saw you talking to nobody by the organ, so I turned on my ghost app." Ellis's app was a work-in-progress, invented by ghost hunters we'd met on our last adventure. The technology interpreted spiritual energy into words, but it wasn't always accurate. "My app said, 'Knife. Stab.'"

Oh, okay. Well, in this case, the technology worked perfectly.

I swallowed the lump in my throat and told Ellis about the organist who seemed to have it out for me.

"That's it," he said, his jaw tightening. "I'm taking you home. I'll fix you a late lunch and we can relax."

"That's not necessary," I said, and not just because Ellis couldn't boil water. "I've been threatened by ghosts before. I'm fine." Many of those situations had been even more terrifying than this, although I tended to keep that sort of thing to myself.

The best and worst thing about Ellis was his protective nature. He'd gone into law enforcement to protect people, and that included keeping a keen eye on me. Still, he couldn't help me deal with the other side when he couldn't see it.

That part drove him crazy.

"Look," I said, running a hand down his arm, trying to calm us both down. "Truth is, I think this one got to me because I wasn't expecting it." The ghost worked as a church organist, for goodness' sake. And once I'd stopped to take a breath, it really hit me how strange the haunting on this property felt, especially since I'd tuned in.

The sky was blue, the breeze lovely. Yet my pulse raced. I'd come here to relax and have a nice afternoon out, to connect with my grandma's old friend. Why did I feel inexplicably angry?

"When did people abandon this church?" I asked.

"It doesn't matter," Ellis stated, trying to move on. "We need to talk about what's going on now."

But it did matter. I could feel it in my gut. "Something happened here. I can feel the anger in the air like a living thing."

"There's a lot bothering me, and it's not the air." Ellis ran his hands through his hair, his jaw tight and his manner stiff. Whatever had me on edge appeared to be affecting him, too. "Verity, we need to talk about this ghost-hunting thing."

On our last adventure, I'd overheard Ellis spilling his troubles to Frankie, not that he could even see my ghost. But Ellis had confided that he didn't like me taking the kind of chances I did while ghost hunting and how he wished I'd stop. How he found it impossible to protect me when I opened myself to an entirely different plane of existence.

He'd told my ghost and not me. And that hurt. It frustrated me to realize Ellis hadn't trusted me with his worries—that he'd kept his feelings hidden. I'd fully expected to have a rational discussion when the time was right.

I didn't care how long he had been holding it in. This was not the time.

"You're still shaking," Ellis said, like an accusation. "This is crazy. Ghost hunting is taking over your life. You need to stop."

Like I could simply turn it off. Well, technically, Frankie could. But I wasn't sure I wanted him to. "We are not going to have this conversation now," I warned him. Not in this place. Not with these people watching. He'd had every opportunity to tell me how he felt on the last fifty dates we'd had; he didn't need to tell me now.

"I swear to heaven, Verity," he gritted out. "We can't put this off forever."

Maybe not forever, but he could certainly wait a few hours. It wasn't as if I were the only one who'd been putting this off.

A half dozen more ladies had already filed out of the church to watch. No, make that a dozen. It was like they could smell gossip from twenty paces.

This was impossible. To be honest, my relationship troubles might have been the reason I'd gone overboard on self-help books lately. "Look, this is neither the time nor the place to have this talk. You're not the kind of guy who confronts someone in public about a private matter," I reminded him. "Actually, we don't fight at all."

"Maybe that's our problem," he said ruefully.

Oh boy.

As if pulled on a string, Pastor Mike emerged with another gaggle of ladies. The poor man tried to get the other rubber-necking do-gooders back inside, but now we had a grandstand going on the steps of the church.

Virginia Wydell stared down on us from the bell tower. She

gripped the wooden ledge like she wished she could yank it off and toss it at me.

Ellis's neck reddened, but he clenched his fists and remained rooted to the spot.

"I don't want to deal with this right now," I told him, fighting off the anger of this situation...this place.

"Figures," Ellis said under his breath, which I should have let pass. I would have. I never liked to fight, especially when I had an audience, but I couldn't resist pointing one thing out.

"It's not like you wanted to talk about this before. You were the one who told Frankie and not me."

Ellis appeared as shocked as if I'd slapped him. "You knew about that?"

"Yes." I notched my chin up. He should feel terrible for keeping it from me.

"What?" He tossed his hands up. "Did Frankie rat me out?"

"I overheard," I said primly.

"So you knew, and you didn't say anything," he concluded, like this was somehow on me.

"You didn't either," I reminded him.

As much as it angered me that he'd kept his feelings hidden, I was done talking on the driveway of the Three Angels of the Tabernacle Blessed Reform Church with his mother and half the Sugarland Heritage Society watching.

I turned and walked back toward the church and my car.

"You want to hear me say it?" Ellis prodded. "I'll say it. I don't want you talking to ghosts anymore," he announced. Loudly.

Yes, well, not only did I have one living with me, but he had friends. Sometimes I didn't have a choice whether or not I had Frankie's power.

Like now.

I turned to face him. "I have solved murders," I said, closing the distance between us, punctuating every word. I said it sweetly, calmly, keeping a lid on my temper, even though he absolutely, positively did not need to bring this up at this very moment. "I have helped people—alive and dead. I have set history straight and energized the town. I'm good at this. And I haven't died yet."

His expression cooled. "Yet."

He would have to get picky with that last word.

"You ran headlong out of the church just now," he informed me, like I hadn't been there, frightened half out of my mind.

"Ellis, there's something really wrong here," I said. "Slow down for a second and let yourself feel it."

"If there's something bad around here, you need to leave," he insisted, missing the point completely.

He didn't even want to understand.

"If I did that every time things got weird on the other side, then how can I live my life?" I asked him, daring him to answer.

"By tuning out," he insisted. Ellis's expression went hard. "I'm getting notes on my phone that say *stab* and *knife*. I hate to break it to you, but this isn't teatime with grandma."

It never was. But that didn't mean I could ignore it, either. "If you're going to trivialize what I do, I'm not having this conversation."

If he had any sort of sense, he'd have stopped right there. But of course, he didn't.

"Listen to me and listen good," he said, pulling out his holier-than-thou police officer tone. "I'm trained to go into dicey situations, and I'm well aware of what's out there. You are a graphic designer who one day decided to be the savior of Sugarland."

"You've seen me in action. You know how careful I am," I reminded him.

His jaw clenched so hard I thought he'd spit teeth. "Yet you walked straight into trouble today when you didn't need to, and I see you hightailing it out of the fundraiser, scared out of your mind."

"What? Did I embarrass you?" I bit out.

"Yes," he shot back. "No!" He threw up his hands. "You need to realize the world is not going to be sunshine and roses just because that's how you think. A ghost pulled a knife on you back there. A knife that could kill you, and I can't do anything about it. I can't help you. I can't save you. Nobody can do a thing about it but you, and you think it's all fine!" He was shouting by the end. I'd never seen him so angry, and it made me want to yell back because he was wrong to tell me what to do, even though he was sort of right about the danger.

Worse, he should be able to see it scared me too.

But he was beyond reason at the moment, so I threw my shoulders back, jutted out my chin, and told it to him plain. "I am not taking orders from you, and we are not having this discussion." When he started to speak, I raised a finger. "That's it," I gritted out, watching Virginia cross her arms over her chest and grin from her tower. Ellis stood resolute, glaring at me, and I wished I'd never gotten out of bed that morning.

"Ah, so you'd rather bury the issue," Ellis said, in a move he must have known would get my goat.

It worked.

Too bad for him, I was a lady. "There is an appropriate time and place for everything, and this isn't it," I informed him before breezing straight for my car.

He didn't stop me.

I had my keys out and was about to slip into my avocado green Cadillac when I spotted my grandmother's friend Jorie fifty feet ahead, past the parking lot, alone in the churchyard.

I glanced back to Ellis, who looked ready to spit nails. Still, he hadn't followed.

Wise man.

I treated him to an icy glare before stuffing my keys back into my bag. He and his preachy attitude and his little scene back there wouldn't keep me from seeing Jorie today. Nor would the stares of the ladies of the Sugarland Heritage Society.

Let them look, I decided as I walked past my car, out onto the uneven ground of the old graveyard. I had more important things to do.

Jorie stood a fair ways out. She hadn't spotted me yet.

She was the only one.

My grandmother's treasured friend seemed oblivious to anyone and everyone as she stood talking to a moss-dotted tombstone in the shape of an Irish cross.

Oh, to be able to ignore the gathering of gawkers behind me.

This must be her husband's grave. I'd attended the funeral a few years ago.

She'd planted dwarf rosebushes on either side, and a brass vase on the ground in front of the stone held gorgeous dried chrysanthemums in white and yellow.

I drew nearer but stopped a few feet away. I took a deep breath and collected my thoughts.

"Hi," I said, hoping I wasn't interrupting anything.

"Oh," she said, turning. "Verity, sweetheart, I didn't see you there."

She was the same age my grandmother would have been, still spry and pleasantly plump, with short curly gray hair set off by a chunky beaded glass necklace in bright yellow and cerulean blue.

"I'm sorry," I said, closing the distance between us and folding her into a hug. "I didn't mean to disturb you."

"I'm always glad to see you, sweetheart. Anywhere, anytime," she said, turning back to her husband's grave. The stone read:

Raymond Earl Davis

1932 – 2018

The shell is here, but the nut is gone.

"Of course that's what Ray's tombstone would say," I said, feeling my humor return. The man had walked around with a grape taped to his navel at the town picnic one year.

"His request, even before he'd been admitted to hospice. I

tried to talk him out of it. Fat lot of good that did. He ordered the stone before he died." Her smile melted into a sigh. "We had so much fun together." She brushed a bit of imaginary dust off the top of the stone. "I stop out here every Saturday, just to talk and let him know how I'm doing. It's like I can feel him listening. I know it sounds silly."

"It doesn't." It sounded beautiful to me.

I didn't see Ray, but that didn't mean he didn't drop by from time to time, even if he spent most of his time in the light.

She patted my arm. "Ray grew up out here going to this church. He bought this plot along with a diamond pendant for our first wedding anniversary." She gave me a sidelong look. "He joked I had to stay with him until one of us died or we paid off the necklace, whichever came last."

They didn't make them like that anymore. "I remember the time he dressed up as Ursula from *The Little Mermaid* for Halloween," I said. You haven't lived until you've seen a three-hundred-pound man with a beard wearing purple face paint and a ball gown.

She lit up. "Remember that autumn picnic by the river when he snuck a turtle into the hood of your jacket?"

"Yes. I loved that turtle." I'd played with it all day and fed it half the lettuce my mom had cut for the burgers.

She touched my arm. "When I left town with your grandma for that church trip in '86, Ray ordered so much pizza from Joe's To Go that Joe sent him a Christmas card that year."

"I've missed you," I told her. I should have checked on her before now.

"That is so sweet of you to say," she said, giving me a pat on the arm. "Now before I forget, I have to give you something. Your grandma Delia would want you to have it," she added. Jorie dug into the large needlepoint purse slung over her shoulder. "I was sorting pictures to give to the kids when I found this." She pulled out a large manila envelope and handed it to me.

I drew out a photograph in black and white.

Jorie, a fresh-faced young bride, stood next to my grandmother, who couldn't have been more than twenty years old. Grandma wore a poufy 1950s-style pleated-skirt dress and carried her bridesmaid flowers, a rose bouquet. Framed by the embellished V-neck of her gown, she wore the delicate filigree cross I so cherished, the one she'd passed on to me.

My fingers touched the pendant at my neck as I took in every detail of the photograph, of my grandmother and her dear friend smiling in the churchyard on such a happy day.

"We posed right over there," Jorie said, pointing to a gorgeous sprawling oak tree on the other side of the road. I recognized the same thick trunk, the aged branches spread wide like fingers.

"What a treasure." Truly, I was grateful to have another link to my grandma.

"There's more," Jorie said, taking the envelope from my distracted grasp and drawing out a flat wax-paper packet with a pressed red rose inside.

"Delia made my bouquet using roses from her cutting garden. I pressed this one in my Bible, and I want you to have it."

"Thank you," I said, touched. "I still tend to Grandma's roses." Even the bush I'd accidentally fertilized with Frankie's ashes, currently housed in a trash can in my parlor.

Jorie pressed the envelope back into my hands. "There's also a letter in here that Delia sent me when Ray and I were living in San Diego, helping our daughter with our very first grandbaby. Her husband was on a ship with the navy then. Anyhow," Jorie said, waving away her story, "the letter talks about you being born and how excited Delia was. She knew you'd be special from the start."

"I don't know what to say." It was really too much.

"There's also some town gossip in there that promises to be a fun read. Some things never change around here."

"You know how I love a little slice of Sugarland history," I gushed. And this slice held a bit of my own personal history as well. "Thank you so much for thinking of me."

"I'm glad you treasure the memories as much as I do," she told me. "But be careful with that rose. It's so fragile."

She was right. I'd loosened a petal already.

"Can you keep this for a minute?" I asked, handing her the envelope. "I'm going to press this rose."

I had a library book in the back seat of my car, all ready to go for the stakeout tonight: a thick treatise on gardening with native wildflowers, perfect for killing time and preserving precious mementos.

"I didn't mean now," Jorie jokingly called after me as I made my way to the car.

If Ray's wife thought I was overly enthusiastic, I probably needed to take it easy—but I didn't think she truly understood what she'd done for me. Two years ago, when I'd called off my wedding, when I'd been under siege by Virginia Wydell and had to sell almost everything I owned in order to keep my house, I'd lost almost all my family history. The tangible parts, at least.

Jorie's gift would help me rebuild my legacy with things that made a difference. Perhaps I'd frame the rose along with the vintage photo.

And so it was with a grateful heart I slipped into the back seat of my car and pressed the rose. I breathed a sigh of relief. Safe.

It had only taken a minute, maybe two because I did say a quick prayer of thanks. Still, it surprised me when I returned to Ray's grave site and found myself alone.

"Jorie?" I called, searching the immediate area.

She had to know I was coming back.

"I'll go find her, Ray," I said, brushing a hand over his tombstone.

But I didn't spot her in that part of the churchyard.

Strange. I returned to the parking lot, more confused than anything, to find a tense, yet sheepish Ellis.

He wound a thumb into the loop of his khakis. "I saw you in your car," he said. "I was hoping you wouldn't leave without saying goodbye."

"I'm not leaving." Not yet, anyway. "Have you seen Jorie?"

"I think she went inside the church," he said, "but I'm sure she'll be out soon," he added hastily when I started heading that way.

"Believe me, I'll avoid the ghost at the organ," I told him.

"And you think the ghost will avoid you?" he challenged as if that was what we'd been talking about all along.

I really didn't want to fight again. "Chances are she haunts the organ," I said, hoping I was right. "She seemed very protective of that spot."

If I let it destroy me every time a ghost threatened me, I'd never get out of bed in the morning.

"I don't know what came over me a few minutes ago. You're right. I'm not one to argue in front of a crowd."

Yet he had.

"I'm worried about you," he added helplessly.

I understood, but… "I don't know how to fix that," I told him as the old bell rang.

Bong.

Bong.

A woman screamed.

Another shouted.

And Ellis ran for the church as Jorie Davis plunged from the upper window of the bell tower.

Chapter Four

Jorie lay on the grass to the right of the stairs, her needlepoint bag flung open and its contents scattered, her open eyes trained on the blue sky above.

Nothing could have prepared me for the shock of seeing such a vibrant woman so suddenly lifeless.

A stunned crowd began to gather, gasping and staring, before Ellis deftly inserted himself between them and the body.

Not *the body*. Jorie.

"Stay back," he ordered, holding up a firm hand while dialing his cell phone with the other. "In fact, I want everyone inside the church. Now," he announced. "Nobody leaves," he called to the few who'd begun retreating toward their cars.

The ladies dutifully began filing up the stairs to the church.

"Are you coming?" Fiera paused next to me, touching a hand to her braided bun.

"In a minute," I promised. My eye caught something she couldn't see in the space directly above poor Jorie. Flickering streaks of white and yellow energy rose from where she lay.

They were soul traces.

And they were beautiful.

I'd encountered them before when I'd been tuned in to the other side, in places where there had been a recent death, but I'd never experienced them as they appeared.

Jorie's soul had risen up, free. Good for her. I hoped she would stay in the light and be happy. Maybe even now she was reuniting with Ray.

I had to look at the positive, because the reality—that Jorie had left us—was too tragic.

According to Frankie, souls underwent a period of processing after death, and it could be months, more likely years, before they could attempt to return. Still, you could tell a lot from the traces a soul left behind. For instance, pops of red piercing the white and yellow light meant the person had experienced violence or struggle in their final moments. Red and sometimes orange streaks were often found in crimes of passion. I'd seen shadows of anger swirl like smoke.

But Jorie's soul traces only showed love and light.

It made me glad for her, but at the same time, I didn't understand. Falling from a tower wasn't what I'd consider a peaceful, natural death.

Frankie shimmered into view next to me. "Can we leave now?"

"What? No." A woman had been killed. "I don't understand what I'm seeing in the soul traces."

"They could still be forming," he said grimly. "It can take a minute. But that's not an excuse to stay here all day. I've got a stakeout."

"We have plenty of time. I want to stay a bit longer. Keep my power on," I urged him.

"What do I do in the meantime?" Frankie asked, rubbing a hand along the back of his neck. "I'm feeling the energy drain."

"Go make another friend," I suggested.

He groaned and disappeared, hopefully to take my advice.

Ellis, who had been hunkered over the scene, stood and

walked over to me. "Can you tell me more about what happened?"

"It was a terrible fall. Still, her soul traces don't show violence or suffering." Maybe he could make sense of it.

"What does Frankie have to say?" he asked as if he didn't quite believe me.

"He said it may take a minute or two for her soul traces to completely appear. I've never seen soul traces this fresh before," I admitted.

Ellis grunted in frustration. Well, we could agree on that.

"Let's give it some time," I said.

Ellis nodded. "I'll bring you back out. In the meantime, it won't do to have you outside at the crime scene when everyone else is in the church."

"Right." I nodded. He had to secure the area, and for the moment, I had nothing to offer. I won't lie. It wasn't the best feeling.

Good thing I didn't have time to think on it much. I entered the vestibule and ran smack into a crowd of ladies gawking out the church door windows.

"You'd better step back before Ellis sees you," I warned, squeezing inside and closing the door behind me.

"Can't see anything when you're blocking the window." Bobby Sue, married to the school superintendent, inched around me.

I let her reclaim my spot and tried not to step on Fiera's toes. She expertly dodged me while looking out the window. "I stopped giving tours fifteen minutes ago. Why was Jorie even up there?"

"That's a good question," I said to the tour guide, not sure I wanted to ask more in front of so many ladies. Right then, Kelli grabbed my arm, her pink nails digging deep. "What happened?" she asked breathlessly. "I saw you talking to Jorie right before."

"Give her some space," Bree said as I extricated myself from

Kelli's grip, never mind she still stood too close. I was starting to get claustrophobic.

"I left Jorie in the churchyard for only a minute," I told them. "She was supposed to be waiting for me to come back."

"Then why would she climb the bell tower?" Kelli's friend Eudora asked, snaking in behind us.

That was my question.

"Jorie and Ray used to babysit me every weekend my mom worked," Bree said, her voice breaking. "I can't believe she's gone."

"I saw several people leaning out the window too far," Kelli observed as if she hadn't been one of them. "I should have said something," she added, her eyes filling with tears. "Why didn't I say something? I'm a horrible, *horrible* person."

"It's not your fault," I assured her. It couldn't be. "And I refuse to believe it's that easy to fall out a window." She looked at me hopefully, doubtfully. "If it was, somebody would have done it a long time before today," I added.

The church was a century old, after all.

"What if it was a ghost?" Bree gulped. "I mean, this place is old. It has to be haunted, right?" she asked, looking right at me.

"Ghosts aren't usually able to harm the living. A lot of the time, they don't even notice us." The case I'd solved for Bree had been an exception. "Besides, when I'm tuned in, I'm vulnerable, but the rest of you are fine."

What they didn't see couldn't hurt them.

However, it occurred to me that I might have a ghostly witness to Jorie's death. If the gravedigger Frankie had spotted earlier did indeed haunt the tower, or the ground below, he might have seen what had happened.

Bobbi Sue gave a shriek and dodged clear as the door opened behind me and whacked me in the back.

"What—?" Officer Duranja pushed it open more, forcing his way into the very warm, very crowded secondary meeting of the ladies of the Sugarland Heritage Society. He gaped at us like he'd never met a Southern woman before. "What are you all doing in here?"

Kelli flashed him her winningest smile. "Ellis said to wait."

"In the pews. Isolated from other witnesses," Duranja insisted as if he'd walked in on us having a slumber party.

"He did not say that," Eudora stated.

"Go," Duranja said, ushering the lot of us through the vestibule and into the main church. "One to a row," he said over the gaggle of women as each launched into her own theory about what had happened and who might be haunting various places in Sugarland. "Quiet," he ordered, which only resulted in some of them lowering their voices.

We were in a church, after all.

Just then, I spotted Fiera sitting in a pew near the back.

I slipped in behind her, making a respectful sign of the cross as I did. "It's terrible, isn't it?"

Fiera turned around, knuckles white as she gripped the top of the pew. "I keep trying to say a prayer, but I can't get the words out. I feel horrible that I left my post."

"So you didn't see her go up?" I asked.

She shook her head no, a tear slipping down her cheek. "I'd left to take a break. I need a break every hour with all the climbing up and down the stairs. I'm the only one Pastor Mike approved to give tours," she added, her voice breaking. "He trusted me."

"It's not your fault," I assured her.

"I put up the rope barrier in front of the door," she insisted. "People know what that means. It works at the library. I don't know why Jorie would slip the rope. I offered her one of the first tours of the day, and she turned me down, saying she didn't want to take the stairs with an achy hip."

A shadow fell over us as the ladies filed past down the main aisle. I looked up and saw Pastor Mike. "How are you holding up?" he asked Fiera.

"I'm going to miss her so much," the tour guide said, her voice breaking as she accepted a tissue from the kindly pastor.

"Did you see Jorie go up into the tower alone?" I asked him while Fiera blew her nose.

For a moment, I saw his controlled, pastoral demeanor break and the raw pain shine through. He cleared his throat. "I had a group up at the altar, looking at the carvings. I saw Jorie come inside, but I didn't notice her going up to the tower." He directed a sympathetic nod to Fiera. "Maybe I should have assigned you someone to help you keep an eye on our guests."

He might have only been trying to comfort the distraught tour guide, but he didn't need to make it sound like Fiera's fault.

"Maybe she was depressed and I missed the signs." Fiera sniffled, accepting another tissue. "Maybe she killed herself."

"I'm quite sure she didn't," I said, glancing up at the craggy, frowning face of the reverend. The Jorie I'd spoken with minutes before her death had not been suicidal, nor eager to climb the bell tower so quickly—or at all.

She was supposed to be waiting for me. She had a bad hip. I wondered who could have led her up there and what reason they had given for her to abandon me.

The soul traces had shown no violence or struggle. If someone had lured her up to the bell tower, it stood to reason she'd known the person. Of course, that included pretty much everyone here.

"I saw her talking to you," Pastor Mike said, in the kind of gravelly, reassuring voice that made it seem easy to tell him things. "Did you perhaps, without intention, say or do anything to make her upset?"

"Not at all." In fact, just the opposite. "Jorie gave me a lovely surprise. I only stepped away for a moment to put it in my car. She was waiting for me to come back."

"I saw it." Fiera nodded, blowing her nose once more and folding over her tissue. "Jorie showed a few of us before Verity arrived." She gazed at me with red, round eyes. "It was a lovely photo. And those roses"—she clicked her tongue—"your grandma had a special gift."

"I don't understand it," the pastor murmured. "I wish I'd known she was in so much pain."

"Cut the talking. One to a pew," Duranja said, walking up to the pastor. "You too, Mike."

"Of course. But can I speak to you for a minute?" the pastor asked. "I've been meaning to talk to you anyway," he continued to Duranja, and they retreated to the back of the church, then through the open vestibule. I watched them take their hushed conversation out to the front steps as the front door eased shut behind them.

Bree slipped into my pew, startling me. "I'll cover for you if you want to go to the tower and investigate," she whispered.

I wanted to, but... "Ellis would have my head."

Jorie was in good hands with Ellis and the Sugarland Police Department. It would be a literal crime for me to get in the way.

"What you do is important," she insisted. "I've seen it." She folded her hands in her lap. "God gave you a gift so you could use it."

I wouldn't necessarily call Frankie "God's gift."

At the very front of the church, Ellis's mother, Virginia, looked over her shoulder and frowned. It seemed the old guard, the rich and exclusive leading ladies of Sugarland, had retreated to the front of the church from the start.

Bree ignored them. "All I'm saying is that if I were the one who fell, I'd like to think you'd be up there checking it out."

And that was actually what did it for me.

Jorie had loved me and trusted me. She had always believed in me and had never shied away from controversy. If Jorie had been in my shoes, she'd already be up in the tower.

"Wish me luck," I said, slipping from the pew.

At least the old guard way up front had given up on us. Each of them faced staunchly forward. Maybe they were praying for our souls. Virginia would take great delight in reporting me, as would her cronies.

"You can do it," Bree whispered after me.

Ducking down, I scooted out of the pew and hurried down the aisle. I didn't see anyone out the side windows. They were probably all gathered out front.

Faster than a bee-stung stallion, I rushed to the bell tower entrance.

It would have been nice to have Frankie with me. He could be a great help when navigating the other side, and he'd have a gun in case the organist ghost with the knife lurked somewhere up in the tower.

Ghosts couldn't kill each other, since technically they were already dead. But a death blow would knock a ghost out for a time.

I paused at the entrance to the tower. As Fiera had said, the rope barrier stood in front of the door, secure.

Did I dare?

Not until I knew I was alone. I retreated to the front window overlooking the yard and pressed close to the stained glass. Through the swirling reds, blues, and yellows, I saw Ellis speaking with the coroner while another officer took photos of the scene.

Nearby, Duranja talked to Pastor Mike.

And so I casually made my way to the bell tower door and slipped the rope.

It had been startlingly easy to do, I realized, as I climbed the steep wooden stairs to the tower.

Later, I might try to time how swiftly a person could make it to the top, but at the moment, I had to go slowly to avoid touching the railing or the walls. I didn't want to disturb any evidence Ellis or the police might need for their own investigation.

The toes of my shoes scrunched over the sandpapery safety strips on the newly remodeled wooden stairs as they wound steeply up.

I smelled the tang of new wood over old brick and saw the glow of sunlight at the top as I made my way to the square cut in the ceiling. I notched an elbow onto the newly buffed wood floor, not chancing the smudge of my fingers over the entryway as I tried to make a decently graceful go of the last few steps.

A large brass bell hung from thick ropes above. I also detected subtle hints of the spirit who haunted this place—the smell of sweat and earth lingered in the air. A ghostly shovel, rusted at the top and clumped with dirt, leaned against the far corner near the front-facing window.

I suspected I'd found the gravedigger.

Chapter Five

I climbed the rest of the way into the tower. My gaze swept over a plain wooden floor, the wide windows on each wall, and the large church bell hanging from a freshly painted white wood beam. But I didn't see the ghost.

Not yet.

I hesitated in the small empty space. The last place Jorie stood before she died.

There were no other signs of the ghost.

How strange. Most of the time, the ghostly side of a room or building appeared exactly as it had in the past, or at least how the dominant ghost viewed it.

But this ghost had merely focused on an old shovel.

A subtle breeze wafted through the windows.

"Hello?" I asked.

No response. Trees rustled outside, the crackling of branches overtaking the faint voices of the investigators below.

I took a deep breath in an attempt to ease my pounding heart.

My attention shifted to the window and the blue sky overhanging the cemetery below. *Something* must have happened to bring Jorie up here.

Crouching low so as not to be seen by Ellis or the investigators, I peeked out the window facing the front of the church and looked down at Jorie's broken body below.

The pain of the loss shot through me, and I closed my eyes.

I cleared my throat and backed away from the window and the view of Jorie's crumpled body, scanning the small space for a sign of what had brought her up here, or who on earth could have killed her.

The rusty scent of earth grew stronger, along with the stale odor of death.

My heart sped up. "Is anyone here?" I asked, doing my best to show no fear. I sincerely hoped this ghost was friendlier than the organist.

The tip of the shovel wobbled against the wood floor.

"I don't mean to intrude on your privacy," I added, keeping the one-sided conversation civil.

The spirit flickered into view between me and the stairs, a hunched, bearded man in worn coveralls. A dirty bandana slouched around his neck.

"Hi," I said, lifting my hand in a little wave. He seemed to stare right past me. "My name is Verity. I'm sorry to pop up here without permission. Heaven knows you've had your share of visitors today." He didn't respond, so I kept going. "There's been a tragedy, and I'm hoping you could help me."

Slowly, his gaze shifted to stare at me.

I felt myself begin to sweat despite the chill of the ghost. "What's your name?" I asked, trying to keep it casual. I couldn't let him intimidate me. He was a person, just like any other. A dead person, but we could get along. Ghosts liked me. Well, most of the time.

When I was lucky.

At the narrowing of his eyes, I hastened to add, "You don't

SOUTHERN BRED AND DEAD

have to tell me your name if you don't want. I don't mean to pry." His breathing picked up, which made me nervous because ghosts didn't need to breathe.

However, when under stress, some would revert to actions they would have taken while alive. I pasted on a smile and ignored the wild beating of my heart. Most ghosts scared me more than I scared them. I had much more to lose if this encounter went bad. The gravedigger couldn't be hurt or killed, while I certainly could.

I cleared my throat and tried again. "My friend Jorie fell from the window of this tower a little while ago," I said, maintaining my ground. "Did you see what happened?"

He let out a hard, low chuff.

"Can you expand on that?" I asked.

I didn't know why listening to me would stress him or why he hadn't said anything yet. Truly, the ghost had me baffled.

Still, I had to find some way to make him more comfortable.

He was blocking my escape.

Besides, his was the most positive response I'd gotten from a ghost since I'd arrived at this property. For starters, I actually had his attention. On top of that, he hadn't attacked me for it. Those were both pluses in my book.

And he'd voluntarily appeared to me. That had to mean something.

"I like your shovel," I said, pointing to the half-rusted thing in the corner. "It looks like you've put it to good use."

Digging graves, I finished in my mind. But it was a very noble profession. This was a hardworking man. "I have trouble digging down far enough to plant a peach tree," I admitted, instantly wishing I could clap a hand over my mouth.

It wasn't the same.

On the upside, he eyed me with more curiosity now.

Probably wondering how much further I could run my mouth.

The tip of the shovel grated against the floor as it slid sideways an inch or two.

That was when I saw an object behind it, something made of paper and wedged behind his shovel. It lay in the corner to my right, and from what I could tell, it existed on the earthly plane.

Oh my.

"Are you trying to show me something?" I asked, edging casually toward it, keeping my eyes on the gravedigger. I didn't want him to interpret my movement as a threat. With any luck, we were on the same page.

Even so, I refused to turn my back on him when he blocked my only escape route that didn't involve a window. I mean, I'd misinterpreted ghostly intentions before—like downstairs with the organist. And the gravedigger hadn't given me much to go on here.

I grinned at him and tried not to let my smile falter when he frowned.

"If you move your shovel, I can get that paper," I suggested.

The corner of his mouth tipped up into a snarl.

"Okay," I said brightly, chancing a step that way. "No worries," I added as if saying it would make it so. "I'll grab it myself."

Boy, I hoped that paper was worth the risk of upsetting another ghost today.

I'd hate to go to all the trouble for an old Kleenex or a discarded fundraising flier.

Handling objects on the ghostly plane was never pleasant. Usually it gave me a hair-raising shock. Combine it with the fact my touch would make any otherworldly object disappear within a few minutes, and handling the shovel became risky business. I mean, the gravedigger and I had just met. There was no telling how he'd take me fiddling with his tool of the trade or making it fade into thin air.

"I could try to reach around your shovel," I offered, bending down to take a closer look at the object wedged into the corner.

Sweet heaven above. It was an envelope. But not any old envelope. I recognized my grandmother's looping handwriting, and the return address in the corner:

Delia Long
#12 Peach Orchard Lane
Sugarland, Tennessee

Unless Grandma's private correspondence was now falling from the sky, this had to be the letter Jorie had planned to give me.

I glanced up at the ghost, who, to my dismay, had begun to advance on me. I hoped he'd decided to help but couldn't be certain. He wasn't talking.

And from this angle, I was pretty sure I could get it without him.

"I'll save you the trouble," I said, deftly reaching around the ghostly spade to grab the letter. A cold shock seared my thumb as it glanced through a clump of ghostly dirt, but I managed to snag the paper and whip it out.

"There!" I said, holding it up to the ghost as if he'd been cheering me on. "We did it."

He loomed above me, jaw clenched, breathing heavily out his nose. The cold air dusted my shoulders, making me shiver.

I scooted away from him, toward the window, and popped to my feet as gracefully as possible. "See, no harm done," I insisted cheerfully as he advanced on me.

Backing me toward the window.

"Ha. You know, really, you don't have to get so close," I said, trying for nonchalant, my voice pitching way too high. The windowsill hit me mid-hip. "Touching me will give you an awful shock."

But he knew it already if he'd been the one to push Jorie from the tower. Sakes alive, I realized I stood in the very spot where she must have been when she toppled over the edge to her death.

The gravedigger loomed almost on top of me. He opened his mouth to reveal rotten teeth as he reached for me.

"Verity Long, you get down from there this instant," a voice rang out from the bottom of the stairs, one I'd recognize anywhere. It was Officer Duranja of the Sugarland Police Department.

The ghost turned at the sound.

"Coming," I hollered. "Bye," I called back to the ghost, dashing for the opening, not daring to look back and see if he followed.

"Help me, help me, help me," I chanted as I fled down the steep stairs in my fancy dress heels, acutely aware I absolutely could not, must not touch the handrail or the walls. And I didn't want to drop Grandma's letter. I shoved it into my brassiere as I ran down, down, down. I felt the icy chill of the ghost at my back and chanced a glance back at him. He stumbled after me like a living person, lurching down the staircase. I ran for all I was worth.

I saw a pair of shiny shoes first, then his spit-and-polish uniform over a thin runner's frame, and lastly, an entirely unamused countenance as I ran straight into Officer Duranja at the bottom.

"Oof!" he uttered as I took him down to the floor.

"Watch out," I warned, scrambling off him. I took to my feet and spun to face the ghost of the old gravedigger.

But I only saw an empty stairwell.

Nevertheless, I braced for the impact, the chilly wind, the attack.

None came.

To my eternal relief, it seemed the ghost had given up on me.

Of course, that didn't mean I was out of hot water.

"Verity, a word," Duranja said, braced up on his elbows, the rest of him sprawled on the floor where I'd flung him.

Every lady in the church gawked.

Except Bree. She gave me a thumbs-up.

"It's fine," I assured them all, including myself.

"It is most certainly *not* fine," Duranja barked.

Ouch. I smoothed my dress and managed a small smile of contrition. Duranja tried to be fair, but he was an ex-Marine who liked things cut and dry. I didn't quite fit his mold. Despite my charms, he considered me an irksome distraction to his idol, Ellis.

After today, I might be able to see the distraction part.

"Come with me to the vestibule," he ordered.

I spared a glance at Bree, who grimaced for me.

"Of course," I said to Duranja, ignoring the rubbernecking stares from the pews. But I did keep an eye on that stairwell the entire way.

I could handle Duranja. I could. As soon as the vestibule door closed, he turned on me like a snake in the rapture.

"Why did I look up and see you in the bell tower after I left you in a church pew?"

"I wanted to see if I could get any insights on Jorie," I said quickly.

"Talking to a ghost?" he barked, like it wasn't a good reason at all.

"I'm the only one who can," I pointed out sweetly. A fact he'd do well to remember.

"Don't you think Ellis has enough going on?" he demanded.

"You need to halt with the hero worship," I said. Although, I couldn't help but ask, "Did Ellis see me just now?"

Duranja squinted so hard his eyes were like pebbles. "Ellis is the one who sent me after you."

Lovely.

"Believe me, you don't want to be talking to him right now," Duranja said. "I'm the least of your problems, sweetheart."

I had a feeling he was right.

"Look," I said, trying to salvage what was left of the conversation, "so you know, I didn't touch the walls or the ledge or the railing." I'd never intended to out-police the police. "I went up to see if the ghost in the tower had seen Jorie fall."

You know, normal, everyday stuff.

"And?" he asked, escorting me back to my pew.

"And I got chased out."

"Smart ghost," he snorted.

He didn't have to be snotty about it.

"Never mind all the times the police have asked for my help," I said, settling onto the hard wooden seat. Not Duranja, specifically. He was too strait-laced for the likes of me. He tended to think my ghost hunting made Ellis look bad. But Ellis had sought my professional advice on more than one occasion. I shot an icy look at the scowling officer. "Never mind I can talk to witnesses you can't see."

He leaned in so close I could smell his spearmint gum. "Do Jorie a favor and let us handle the investigation."

"Sure," I said.

"Now stay put," he ordered. "For real this time. And stay out of trouble."

"I fix problems, I don't cause them," I declared to his retreating form.

I'd have been better off talking to a fence post.

I settled in for the wait and felt a dry crackling against the tender skin of my chest. That was when I remembered the letter in my bra.

Well, dang.

Chapter Six

I straightened my dress, listening to the paper crumple against my bosom.

With a sinking heart, I realized I'd gotten my finger-prints all over Jorie's letter. Worse, I'd lost my chance to come clean right away.

Not that Duranja would have been civil about it.

I clasped my hands together in my lap. So much for my efforts to mount a seamless investigation. I'd been scared by the gravedigger and off my game. I'd only wanted to help Jorie, but instead I'd thrown a wrench in the investigation.

"What did Alec Duranja say to you to have you looking so glum?" Fiera whispered from the pew in front of me. "You know he's all bark and no bite. I watched him cry when he held his baby niece up to be baptized."

"It's not Duranja," I told her. Well, it was partly. "I made a mistake," I said. I was ashamed and overwhelmed and I didn't know what to do.

I heard the kneeler clunk down on the pew behind me and smelled Bree's peach blossom perfume as she crowded up behind me.

"What'd you find up there?" she asked, scarcely containing her excitement.

"Nothing," I insisted, slapping a hand over my chest.

"It's in her bra," Fiera said. "I see it peeking out."

This was bad. She had to realize it. "I shouldn't have taken it," I said under my breath.

"Show us," Bree urged.

"No," I said, voice hushed, wishing I could sink into the floor.

"Ladies," Duranja cautioned from the back. He could see us talking. I pressed my back against the pew and stared straight ahead.

"Did the ghost give it to you?" Bree pressed.

"No," I whispered back. "It's evidence."

Fiera's eyes widened. "You took evidence? Why did you take evidence?"

"I don't know," I hissed, drawing the envelope out of my bra.

Fiera slapped her hand down so hard on the pew that the pop echoed through the church. Ladies turned to stare, and Fiera's eyes grew big.

"That was a big mosquito," she said to nobody in particular, turning back to face the front. To me, she hissed, "You've got to turn that in right away."

"I know that," I whispered back.

Five pews up, Kelli's head swiveled around. When she realized she was missing the latest, she began to scoot out of her pew.

Oh no.

"Kelli Lee Kaiser," Duranja's voice boomed up the aisle from the back, "I know you don't mean to wander the church when I distinctly told you to stay put."

She slunk back down. "I thought I saw a mouse."

"You are here for questioning," Ellis said, not even looking at me as he, Duranja, and two other Sugarland police officers strolled up from the back. "We're going to be talking to you one-on-one privately. We've set up rooms in the vestibule behind the altar."

"Please cooperate as best you can," Pastor Mike said, trailing the officers. "I know this is a terrible time for all of us."

It would be worse when Ellis found out I had the letter the killer discarded in the bell tower.

I had no doubt in my mind Jorie had been murdered.

While the officers called up the first four potential witnesses from the pews near the altar, I dropped down on my kneeler and drew up close to Fiera. "I know Jorie showed you the letter this morning, along with the rose and the photograph."

She turned toward me, bringing up a hand to fiddle with her bun and help block the view from the front. "Did you read it yet?"

"No. And now I can't." I wasn't going to tamper with it any more than I had. "I was hoping you'd read it." I'd like to know a little more about it before I turned it over.

She blew a frustrated breath out her nose. "I didn't look. I was more interested in the wedding picture."

"That's still missing."

Hopefully, the police had found it.

"Do you know who else saw what Jorie had for me?" Fiera said earlier that there had been a group of women looking at the photograph. Perhaps someone else had read the letter.

Or perhaps one of them had been the killer.

"It was only me and MayBelle Clemens, but neither of us looked too close," Fiera said. "I can't recall her showing anyone else." She shook her head slightly. "It got busy quick, and we needed Jorie and MayBelle to start putting out the cookies, and then we ran into trouble finding enough cups for the lemonade."

"Where is MayBelle now?" I asked, scanning the church. "I don't remember seeing her today." MayBelle had known both

Jorie and my grandmother well, although she had been closer to Jorie on account of them volunteering for the local Meals on Wheels program together.

Fiera's silver charm bracelet jangled as she rested an arm on the pew and leaned back. "MayBelle drove home right as I started my first tour. Her arthritis was acting up, and she didn't want to push it."

So MayBelle probably hadn't been up in the tower pushing Jorie off the ledge.

Never mind she'd been quite spry when I'd seen her at the Cannonball in the Wall event this past spring.

Either way, she wasn't in the church with the rest of us.

"Where does MayBelle live these days?" I asked Fiera. Perhaps I'd pay her a visit on the way home.

"Oh, she's at the old Sugarland Grand Hotel, same as Jorie. She moved in across the hall from MayBelle."

We both caught our breath at the mention of Jorie.

"No talking," Ellis called from the front, and I sincerely hoped he was scolding someone besides me. His expression lacked his usual warmth.

Then again, he was on the job.

I sat back in my pew as Ellis and another officer released two ladies and brought two more up into the vestibule.

Kelli waved again from five rows up. This time, I wasn't in the mood.

We were here because a woman had died, for no reason I could fathom. Still, I felt responsible for her. She was my grandmother's friend. And as far as I knew, I'd been the last person to see her alive. Worse, if I'd just botched part of the investigation in the tower, I felt even more obligated to do…something.

Fiera held out a piece of paper over her shoulder. I took it and saw MayBelle's name and address.

"Thanks." I'd be very interested to hear if MayBelle could shed any light on the events leading up to Jorie's fall.

I'd also come clean with the police and hand over the envelope.

That would go over like a lead balloon, but I couldn't avoid it. I had to do the right thing and help the police in their investigation regardless of how it affected me personally.

I only hoped that in the end, Ellis and his colleagues would understand we were all on the same side. We all wanted the same thing: justice.

Only I was used to being on the same team as Ellis, and after the way we'd butted heads this afternoon, I wasn't sure how we'd manage this time around.

In fact, I felt very much alone.

I closed my eyes and concentrated on the sounds of the church, the harsh whispers of the people in the pews, the faint scent of incense and candle wax. The sturdiness of the pew that supported me and the building that had stood for more than a century.

We were all simply passing through this world, this place.

I wished I could read my grandmother's letter or see the smiling photograph of Grandma and Jorie as I sat alone, waiting.

More police arrived, and they set up another interview station in Ellis's command tent behind the church. I watched my boyfriend studiously avoid me as they processed each group for questioning. The man who'd claimed to love me didn't look my way.

He should be feeling guilty about our very public fight earlier.

Most likely, he was still upset with me.

Ellis let Duranja question me, which made sense. He wouldn't want to show any favoritism.

I accompanied the deputy to a closet-like office crammed with an oversized, outdated computer and walls full of old photographs I wasn't in the mood to enjoy.

Duranja sat stiffly behind the desk while I took the visitor's chair.

"How's your niece?" I asked him, hoping to start off on the right foot. Yes, it was off the subject, but so were most of the conversation starters in Sugarland. I didn't go for so much as an oil change without talking for a few minutes about Bob Stutz's latest fishing trip.

So it did surprise me when Duranja folded his hands on the desk and shot me down cold. "Let's start from the time you arrived at the property."

"All right, then."

He didn't let me deviate. He asked pointed questions about exactly why I thought I should be in the bell tower. And he inexplicably treated me like an irritating younger sister as much as a witness.

We went over and over the details leading up to the event, as Duranja attempted to prod my memory for clues. I disappointed him, and myself, when I admitted I didn't witness anything earth-shattering.

Worse, Duranja didn't care about the envelope Jorie had tried to give me. It seemed inconsequential to him in relation to her death.

That is, until I showed him the letter I'd taken from the bell tower.

I hadn't realized police were allowed to curse during questioning.

He took the envelope and bagged it. He also made me go over my story several more times, which could only help Jorie.

It also meant I didn't make it out of the church until nightfall.

Ellis stood talking with the chief of police while Duranja escorted me out.

So much for a goodbye.

By the time I stepped down into the parking area, the police had finished with the scene and the coroner had removed Jorie's body. The soul traces remained, shining gently in an ethereal light, showing no sign of distress, murder, or even suicide.

They would have turned other colors by now if they were going to. So there we had it, a clean death.

Yet she couldn't have fallen on her own.

Or maybe she had. Maybe I was making this all up because I wanted to believe in my heart of hearts that nothing this terrible could be an accident.

Soft light illuminated the windows of the church, and my gangster ghost stood outside, having a smoke.

"I could have used you in there," I said, telling him about the letter in my bra.

"I'm better at hiding evidence than turning it in," he said, blowing smoke out his nose. "Let's go."

"So did you find a friend?" I asked, walking down the steps next to him.

He scoffed. "I met an angry old lady and her six cats. Of course, they were terrified of me. Why do pets hate me? I like cats. I like skunks."

"I have no idea." I couldn't speak for Lucy.

He stopped at the bottom of the stairs. "The thing about this gal—and I'm not saying it because she didn't like me—but she was odd, like she didn't talk."

I stopped. "I had the same issue with the ghost in the tower." And the organist, come to think of it. "Nobody on the other side is saying much."

Frankie shivered. "It's strange. Everybody walking around like it's the end of the world."

"Why?" I asked. "What possible reason could the ghosts have to remain silent?" Frankie certainly didn't suffer from that affliction.

"I don't know." Frankie shrugged as if the question itself weren't worth asking.

"What about the kid who stole your shoelaces?" I pressed.

He stiffened at the mention. "Davy never did say much even when he was alive. He's got faster hands now, though."

"Well, we both tried to do good," I said, starting toward the car.

"Speak for yourself," Frankie muttered, taking another drag. "Let's make tracks," he said. "I didn't plan on spending all day at church."

"We're leaving," I promised the gangster. "I'm so sorry, Grandma," I added under my breath as I made my way to the car. I didn't know what I could have done to change the events of the day, but I wished it had been something.

My car was one of only about a dozen left in the lot. I spotted the book with the pressed wedding flower in the back seat as I opened the driver's side door. I wished my last words to Jorie had been more heartfelt, that they'd been what she deserved to hear from me.

You never think it's going to be the last time.

I started up the car and turned down the long drive through the cemetery, the Cadillac's bright, overlarge headlights illuminating the tombstones, catching on the ghost of a mechanic with blood streaming into his eyes as he wandered with his humongous wrench.

I gasped. "What happened to him?"

"What happened to the lot of them?" Frankie shifted in his seat. "Just keep driving."

My fingers tightened on the steering wheel. I hoped to heaven that Jorie would go to the light and not come back, no matter how suddenly or tragically she died. After what I'd experienced today, I wanted her far, far away.

I wanted her with Ray.

Lost in thought, I almost drove straight through a dead reverend standing in the road.

"Oh, my goodness!" I swerved, barely missing him.

He didn't notice me. None of them had…at first.

A chill whipped down my spine.

I slowed the car and dared to glance over my shoulder.

It wasn't as if the organist would show up in the back seat of my car, or the gravedigger would appear with his shovel, simply because other ghosts had done so in the past…

The back seat lay empty save for my library book.

"Just drive," Frankie said, crossing an ankle over his knee and settling in. He glanced at the rapidly setting sun. "In fact, do me a favor and hit the gas. In case you haven't noticed, it's dusk, and we're gonna be late to meet the guys if you don't step on it right now."

Heavens. I'd forgotten all about Frankie's manhunt.

This after he'd told me over and over how important it was. Vital.

"We'll make it," I said as we passed the church gates. "I'll even speed," I vowed.

"Downtown. Near the intersection of Fourth and Spring Streets," Frankie said, checking the bullets in his gun.

"We're on our way," I promised, driving five miles over the speed limit the entire time.

"Are we in a parade, or are we going to my manhunt?" Frankie groused as we turned onto Main Street and positively bolted past the Cookie Corner, Remember When Antiques, and the Yarn Barn.

"Spring Street is a one-way," I said. It ran parallel to Main, a block over. "This is the fastest route."

"You and your rules," Frankie huffed.

"Exactly." I could only imagine what folks would say about my speeding. The avocado-green land yacht wasn't exactly subtle.

We turned left at the corner of Fourth and Main, and I slowed on the narrower street as we passed brick and stone storefronts that had graced downtown Sugarland since the early

1900s. I loved this part of town, not only for its tradition but also for its permanence.

Although now, with Frankie in tow, I also wondered about its past.

"This is a pretty public place for a manhunt," I said, stopping for a senior couple holding hands as they crossed toward Suzie Brown's Biscuit Heaven at the corner of Fourth and Spring Streets.

"It's right there," the gangster said, pointing to a boarded-up BBQ place several storefronts down from the intersection.

"The former Jurassic Pork?" I asked.

Before that, it had been a bagel shop, a yarn store, and a coffee shop.

"No business survives long in that spot," I said, making a left toward the abandoned BBQ joint.

"And you wonder why," Frankie said as I pulled in and parked behind a ghostly black sedan. "Stick with me and I'll show you."

Chapter Seven

The closed BBQ restaurant stood in the shadow between stoplights, as if downtown Sugarland had forgotten it existed at all. Red, yellow, and green painted picnic benches lay stacked and abandoned behind rows of unlit tiki torches, smoke stained at the top. A cheery picket fence separated the outdoor seating area from the deserted sidewalk.

"I remember when this place first opened," I told Frankie, killing the engine. A pair of dead gangsters hustled past the boarded-up restaurant windows and ducked into the alley toward the back of Jurassic Pork. "People used to be lined up halfway down the block to get a table."

Now, the place was shuttered tight with a 1920s wiseguy holed up inside.

How times changed.

Still, this was our chance to locate Frankie's brother. Lou had been lying low ever since Frankie learned Lou was the person who'd shot and killed him.

"I set up a sting in case he runs," Frankie said, scanning the street.

I hated to bring it up, but Lou was a ghost. "What if he disappears?"

Frankie chuffed. "I've got guys stationed at all the gang hideouts. I got a team at Lou's old house, one at his death spot, another at his old thinking spot."

"Dare I ask?"

"It's a very nice bathroom," Frankie insisted. "Anyway, he's got to show up somewhere."

Not necessarily. "What if he goes into the ether?" Frankie might be able to wait him out, but I couldn't.

Frankie gave me a sour look. "Stop complicating things."

"Pesky logic," I murmured under my breath.

He touched two fingers to the brim of his white Panama hat, then flicked them toward the street, giving a signal to…somebody.

The three wiseguys I'd met in my kitchen that morning melted out of the shadows near a closed-for-the-night dog grooming salon. They crossed the street several car lengths in front of us, carrying tommy guns. The guy with the scar down his cheek gave a tip of the hat to Frankie.

We watched the trio walk straight through the darkened front window of the DMV across the street from the restaurant. It had closed for the day at five.

"Those don't seem like the guys I met this morning," I said, marveling at their change in demeanor.

"We're on the job," Frankie said, crossing his ankle over his knee and double-checking the gun in his ankle holster.

"I still can't believe this is happening in downtown Sugarland."

"This used to be disputed territory," Frankie said as if it were a thing. "The Irish controlled south of Fourth Street. We worked the north side over to city hall."

"Sure. Why not?" I supposed gangs did divide territory,

although I'd never thought of this part of town as a rough neighborhood.

"It lasted about a day," Frankie said, shoving his pants leg down to hide his sock holster and giving his ankle a wiggle. "Then my friend Suds needed to go see his sister, who is married to one of the Irish bookies. They lived in one of the apartments above the police station on Fifth. And the O'Malleys weren't about to skip out on their cousin Tony's Italian deli. Not after you'd had those meatballs." He shrugged. "So we tossed the rules."

"How very gangster of you," I remarked.

He couldn't help but grin. "We're rivals—Sugarland style."

"Which means everybody pretty much goes where they want and knows each other's personal business," I concluded.

"Exactly," he said as if he'd planned the whole thing. "Now back to this Irish hole-in-the-wall," he said, eyeing the building across the street. "I've got a team in the black sedan ahead of us, three guys on the roof across the street, and Ice Pick Charlie and his associates in the alley out back." He clicked open the chamber of his revolver and checked to make sure it was fully loaded. It was. Frankie shoved it closed and returned it to his shoulder holster. "When it comes to running, Lou likes to go out the back. He doesn't always remember he's dead."

That was a lot of firepower directed at one man. "I'm almost starting to feel sorry for Lou," I mused.

"Yeah, well, don't," Frankie snapped, drawing a black 38 Special from his side holster and checking the bullets in that one.

"I didn't mean it that way," I quickly corrected myself. "I'm always on your side." It was a little unnerving to witness my housemate in full gangster mode. "I'm glad to see your friends are helping out," I added as he dug out a pair of brass knuckles from his pants pocket and slipped them on.

At least Lou was already dead. A kill shot would knock him

out for a while, but it wouldn't damage him permanently. It wouldn't do anything to help the brothers resolve their differences, either.

I just hoped it would turn out all right for both Lou and Frankie.

Although I didn't see how it could.

"You know, maybe Lou will be glad to run into you," I said, cringing at the small serrated dagger Frankie flicked from the base of the brass knuckles. "Your brother might be relieved to finally talk about this."

"Oh, he'll be talking," he said, folding the dagger back in.

"Frank—" I began.

He closed his eyes. "Look, I hope I talk to him, too." He rested an arm on the back of the bench seat as he turned to face me. "I hope Lou's finger slipped on the trigger. I hope he accidentally stalked me, took aim, and shot me dead between the eyes, but I'm not holding onto the fantasy that this is going to come out sunshine, roses, and puppies, okay?"

"I get it." I did. "I hope you get closure."

He nodded, his jaw working. "Why don't you come with me?"

He asked it so directly, so quietly, that for a second, I wasn't sure if I'd heard him right.

I stared at him.

Frankie had never willingly involved me in gang business before. In fact, he'd actively avoided it. He said I was soft. He claimed I didn't have the guts for it.

He was probably right.

"You've never wanted me to come with you before. Why now?" I asked.

"Why not?" he countered, looking at me for an answer. I glanced past him to the abandoned restaurant across the street and managed to find my voice. "Well, for one thing, it's breaking and entering."

He gritted his jaw. "Like you've never done that while ghost hunting."

Maybe once or twice. "It was for the greater good."

"So is this," he said. He wasn't backing down. Which meant this was important to him.

While I wanted to help, he had to understand. "This isn't only highly illegal, it's not exactly an abandoned part of town, either." Just a very unbusy end of the street.

Frankie stared me down.

"Even if I do make it inside, we'll be hunting down a gangster with a gun." Those guys tended to shoot first and ask questions later. Frankie alone had enough firepower on him to charge Sam Hill. While a gunshot to the head, or any other vital area, would merely knock Frankie out, it would kill me. Ghostly bullets tore through human flesh the same as real ones when I was tuned in to the other side.

He of all people should understand my eagerness to remain gunshot-free and in one piece.

He gave an overly casual shrug. "This'll be an easy job."

I'd hung out with him long enough to know that was a stretch. "How can you say it's going to be an easy job when you're armed to the teeth?" I wouldn't be surprised if he clinked when he walked. "Besides, it's never an easy job."

"Good point," he agreed. "But I didn't bring my machine gun," he informed me as if it were a point in his favor. "Look, all I want out of the guy is the why—why'd he pull the trigger on me?"

"That's it?" I asked. It was never so simple with Frankie.

Frankie shrugged. "Well, if I don't like the answer, I'll probably shoot him."

"Of course."

Frankie glanced out the window. "There's the signal. Everybody's in place." He turned to me. "You coming or not?"

I'd promised my support when it came to working through

his issues with his brother, but I'd really hoped it would be a matter of self-help books and emotional exploration rather than an armed raid in downtown Sugarland.

It was now or never.

My stomach fluttered. I'd agreed to drive him to the manhunt, not be *in* the manhunt. Frankie wasn't particularly calm or predictable on a good day, much less when he got around his old gang.

Not to mention the fact that this afternoon had been particularly trying. I'd witnessed my grandma's good friend fall to her death, I'd fled a crazy organist with a knife, and I didn't even want to start thinking about what would have happened if the gravedigger had gotten hold of me. Truly, it would be nice to just sit in the car with Frankie's power off.

Whatever went on between Frankie's gang and Lou, I wouldn't have to see any of it. I wouldn't have to hear any of it. My friend Maisie had been teaching me how to knit, and so far, I had half a sock. If I kept at it, I'd have even more. I'd have my sane existence back, at least until Frankie and the gang finished raising Cain on the other side.

My gangster buddy crossed his arms over his chest. "You owe me after this afternoon. I didn't ask to go to a haunted cemetery, and worse, you almost made me late."

"I didn't know the cemetery was haunted—"

"When is a cemetery ever not haunted?"

"And it's not as if I had such a great time at the event, either."

He sighed. "You can go places I can't. The dead don't always pay attention to the living. You'll give us an advantage." When I made no move to get out of the car, he grimaced like he'd tasted something vile. "Fine. I'll ask as a favor. This is important to me. I'd like your help. You're good at talking to people and getting them to talk to you back."

I chewed my lip. There were plenty of times he'd helped me. Reluctantly, of course, but then again, I wasn't necessarily doing cartwheels about taking part in a manhunt, so I'd call it even. "Okay," I said, before I changed my mind. "I'll help you."

"Fantastic." He grinned and floated out of the car. "Let's go."

Heaven help me.

It was one thing to hunt ghosts and solve murders, it was quite another to run with the South Town Boys.

"Coming." I grabbed my bag with his urn and slid out of the car.

I had no weapons to prep. It wasn't like I kept any in the land yacht.

Mortal weapons couldn't stop a ghost anyway.

Frankie looked me up and down as I walked around the front of the car to join him. Perhaps he, too, was having second thoughts about a girl in a magnolia dress and kitten heels tracking down a fugitive.

"You bring a disguise?" he asked.

I touched a hand to the baby's breath in my hair. I'd planned on waiting it out in the car. "I brought my knitting."

"Yeah, that'll help." Frankie smoothed on a mustache, a pencil thin number that made him look like Errol Flynn gone bad.

"That's going to disappear," I told him. He could only permanently keep the things he'd died with.

"It should last long enough," he said, crossing the street ahead of me. "I just need to get inside without being recognized."

This should be fun.

I rushed to catch up.

Frankie passed straight through the bright yellow fence while I found the gate near the front entrance. I hurried down the pathway lined with dead plants. A pair of windows with smiling pigs painted on the glass flanked a red door.

"I'll bet this is locked," I said, testing the handle, noting the faded "Closed for Business" sign.

Perhaps I wouldn't be joining him after all.

"Not a problem. The window's open," Frankie said, walking straight through the plywood nailed to the outside.

"Truly?" This wasn't how I'd intended to spend my Saturday night.

His head popped out of the plywood-covered window. "I'm good at noticing things like this."

"I'll bet." I yanked at the bottom of the window to the right of the door and realized he was correct—it lifted from the red-painted frame and slid right up. "I can't believe you talked me into this." What would Ellis say?

Frankie stared me down. "Keep standing there and I guarantee you somebody's gonna walk by and recognize you," he said, not helping my blood pressure at all.

"Right," I said, glancing down the deserted street. "Just this once," I added before lifting a foot over the threshold and cramming my body into the tight opening.

"Attagirl," he said, waiting for me inside. "Remember, it's not breaking and entering if you don't use the door."

"Is that from the gangster bible?" I asked, wrinkling my nose at the stale air, planting one white-heeled shoe onto the dirty concrete floor.

"Yeah, right after, 'Thou shalt not shoot unless shot at first,'" Frankie said sanctimoniously before breaking into a wide grin. "Nah, I'm kidding. There's no rule against shooting."

"Of course not," I said, taking in the shadowy remains of the once-vibrant restaurant as I reached into my bag for my flashlight.

My ghost-hunting habit had left me prepared.

I flipped on my light, skimming the gutted room. The BBQ joint owners had sold off everything that wasn't nailed down. That left a corrugated steel serving counter and a painted chalkboard on the wall advertising a Memphis-style ribs, baked beans, greens, and cornbread special.

Yet as my eyes adjusted to the dim light, I began to see the silvery outline of the ghostly side. A pair of round tables stood at the center of the room, loaded with what appeared to be funereal floral arrangements. Large wreaths and sprays stood propped on stands.

Potted houseplants lined the walls, and right in front of the steel counter of the BBQ restaurant stood a ghostly wood countertop featuring buckets of single blooms along with an old-fashioned cash register.

I never knew this had been a flower shop.

Why not? It had been everything else.

"The O'Malleys were this building's original tenants," Frankie said as if that meant they could haunt the place forever. Well, actually, I supposed they could.

A portly ghost stood behind the counter, chewing on a cigar, his bow tie visible above his white apron. "Welcome to Mildred's Flower Heaven," he said in monotone, his Northern accent thick around his stogie, "where every day is a blooming miracle."

"All right," I said, wondering what kind of manhunt we were on. I didn't expect to find Lou hiding out among the flowers.

Gangsters were all about image, and this...was not the kind of place I imagined I'd find a gangster.

I stepped farther into the shop. The ghostly scent of cut blooms had begun to overcome the stale, dusty air of the real-world former restaurant. Still, I kept my guard up as I checked out a row of potted palms in the corner, half-expecting to find a gangster or a hidden witness.

"I need you with me, Verity," Frankie said, all business as he approached the counter.

"Right," I said, making my way over to Frankie. This was his show.

The flower man looked me up and down like he knew I was dating the fuzz. I pretended not to notice as I admired the ghostly display of heirloom seeds on the counter in front of us. The vintage packets reminded me of the old seed packets my grandmother had saved and reused for years when she harvested her seeds for replanting.

"I wish I could buy some of these," I said, my fingers brushing close to the seeds, careful not to touch.

"Is she serious?" the florist asked.

Frankie ignored the question, and me. "We're here to see the mayor," he stated.

The man's frown disappeared. "He's in the back," he said, nodding that way.

This was getting weirder and weirder.

With supreme effort, I kept my thoughts to myself as I followed Frankie around the counter, toward the rear of the store.

We passed another table of fancy flower arrangements. Behind it, a man with a shoulder holster strapped over his shirt and tie stood arranging a bouquet of calla lilies and hypericum berry.

"Would you like to see our pink peonies?" he asked, glaring at us.

Like we were criminals or something.

"They are lovely this time of year," he added.

Frankie stopped dead in his tracks, and an unspoken message passed between the two. "I'd rather wear a daisy in my lapel," Frankie stated.

The man nodded, tossed his flowers onto the counter, and led us deeper into the building. I didn't detect anyone else in the back, but I couldn't shake the feeling we were being watched. The guy we followed was packing heat. His friend at the counter most likely had a gun as well. The rival gang controlled this establishment. That left us outnumbered already, at least on the inside.

I didn't like it.

I was dying to ask Frankie where Lou could be. But seeing his stiff back and purposeful walk, I didn't dare.

The frowning peony guy stopped in front of a stainless-steel walk-in cooler. Frankie gave a nearly imperceptible nod, and as the guy began to open the door, I decided I definitely did *not* want to see what waited inside.

Chapter Eight

P eony Guy pulled the pin out of the lock and swung open the steel door of the industrial refrigerator. I tried to appear relaxed.

Act casual, I repeated in my head like a mantra as I braced myself for a blast of cold air, along with whatever surprise waited inside. I might not be a hardened mobster like Frankie, but I knew enough to realize it wouldn't be ribbons and daisies. I hoped it might be Frankie's brother waiting for us. Frankie had a flair for the dramatic. Perhaps Lou did, too.

They could talk, we could make things right, and maybe Frankie wouldn't need the squad of wiseguys waiting outside for something—anything—to go wrong.

Frankie stood passively, but I let out a gasp when I looked inside the fridge.

It stood empty.

There was no Lou, no flowers, no…anything. Bare walls and empty shelves greeted us, which was ten kinds of weird.

Even stranger, I'd expected a blast of cold air on the mortal realm or at least in the spirit world.

I focused hard to see past the ghostly illusion. Where on the ghostly side, I saw the stark gray lines of the steel box, I was heartened to see the real-life refrigeration unit stood far away, at the rear of a mostly empty, gutted kitchen.

Ahead of us, an industrial sink jutted from the wall, next to a darkened doorway.

Frankie gave a sharp nod to our host before stepping inside the empty steel box on the ghostly plane.

I didn't know what game this was, but I found myself reluctant to follow.

First off, it seemed quite clear the peony guy didn't plan to join us. And I certainly didn't trust him not to lock us inside. Second, Frankie might be able to drift out through the stainless-steel side, but I couldn't, not unless he turned off my power. And if he got shot and put out of commission, I'd be stuck.

Our host frowned as I retreated a step, then another.

"You going or not?" our host asked, his expression clouding over.

"Maybe." As long as I could escape.

Theoretically, I'd have to pass through the side of the unit on the ghostly plane. It would be icy cold and painful, but doable.

The flower guy eased a hand to the gun in his holster. This was getting better and better.

"Verity," Frankie hissed, craning his neck out at me, "come on."

"Sure," I said as if I hadn't been stalling for all I was worth. I worried for my safety, but that included not getting in the middle of a shoot-out.

I directed a friendly smile toward the flower-shop guy, whom I also noticed had still not set foot inside the unit. "Would you like to join us?"

"Is she for real?" he asked.

"Yes, and she's with me," Frankie said, ushering me inside.

"I think he was about to pull a gun on us," I whispered to my housemate. And before Frankie could even pretend to care (newsflash: he probably didn't), our host slammed the door closed behind us.

"Ohmygosh!" My heart snagged in my throat. "I knew it." I knew we were in trouble.

Cold fear gripped me as the peg lock slid into place.

"Will you stop being so jumpy?" Frankie snapped. "It's fine!"

"Is it?" I turned to the ghost glowing gray in the dark. "Is it? Because I'm not used to being locked up." We were trapped. With an armed guard outside. "I should have listened to my instincts instead of following *you*, who takes too many risks, carries too many weapons, and knows too many people who would lock us in a refrigerator!"

Frankie reared back. "Are you done?" he asked, clicking on a single-bulb light dangling from the ceiling. He appeared more annoyed than worried, which ticked me off all over again. "Look. It's only an empty refrigerator."

Exactly. It offered no easy escape. "Even if I walk right through the wall and shock myself from here to next month, Peony Guy could be waiting out there to shoot me." Worse, I didn't know what a zap like that could do to me. Touching small objects on the ghostly plane could be jarring enough. The wall might be big enough to electrocute me. *Think.* I had to think. "Maybe I could touch the wall," I whispered to him. "Maybe I can make this whole fridge disappear. That might freak the ghosts out enough not to kill me."

"Really?" Frankie lowered his chin to stare at me. "Because I'm ready to kill you right now." He turned and started walking deeper into the refrigeration unit.

Lovely.

"You'd better not disappear on me." Even if he didn't, I didn't appreciate him walking away. I spread my hands out, gathering my courage. Ghostly objects didn't stand a chance when I touched them. They always disappeared after a few minutes, not returning until sometime later. Only I'd never tried to make anything this big disappear.

"Halt! Don't you dare." Frankie turned and pointed a finger at me. "You do one thing to mess this up and I'll never forgive you."

Mess this up? In case he hadn't noticed, "We are trapped."

"*I* am trapped," he insisted. "You are merely locked in a refrigeration unit. And I don't want to explain to Connor O'Malley why you made a key part of his business vanish, even if it comes back at some point later on."

"I—" I would have said something brilliant if I could have thought of a word to say when Frankie opened up a door at the other end of the refrigeration unit. Beyond it stood a lit stairwell.

"You gonna keep staring?" he asked. "Because I was under the impression you were eager to leave."

The jerk.

I walked past him into the stairwell, sparing him a chilly glance. "You could have mentioned how this worked before we got here." It wasn't like my fridge at home had a back door.

"You're usually a little more put together," he grumbled, closing the door behind us.

Frankie might have a point for once. I liked to be in charge of our adventures. I wanted to have as much information as possible so I could anticipate any complications. That way, we could do our best to stay out of trouble. But Frankie and the South Town Boys? They actually enjoyed it when life went off the rails. "This is my first gangster job," I reminded him, hoping I wouldn't regret helping.

If I was honest with myself, I already did.

We stood on a small enclosed hallway landing, with stairs leading up and down. It smelled of old brick and mildew and glowed ghostly gray.

It was haunted.

At least that meant I didn't need my flashlight…

"This way," Frankie said, leading us down toward the basement.

"Why does it always have to be the basement?" I mused, navigating down the narrow steps, wishing I could have changed out of my heels.

Frankie shrugged. "It's the best place for a blind tiger."

I stopped. "You didn't say anything about animals."

"What?" he squinted up at me.

"Is it a live tiger or a ghost tiger?" I asked.

He barked out a laugh, and for a second he almost relaxed as he leaned his shoulders against the wall. "A blind tiger is a speakeasy."

"Ah," I said, wishing I could take back the last ten minutes of my life. So that was why the wiseguys had a flower shop up front. They were using it as a cover for their illegal operations.

"Were the guys in the flower shop part of your gang?" I asked, wondering why the South Town Boys would have pulled a gun on one of their own.

"Nah." Frankie waved me off. "We're not the only show in town, just the biggest. This place here, the Volstead Riot, is run by the Clifton's Rats. It opened on January 17, 1920," he said with a flourish. "Since then, it's been a party every night."

"And some people say small towns are boring." Sugarland never ceased to surprise me. No wonder so many of the dead around here refused to pass on.

"Enough," he said, adjusting his hat. "Let's go find Lou."

I steeled myself. "I'm ready."

The stairwell ended at a wooden door. Frankie rapped three times, and when a small opening slid open at eye level, he whispered a word.

It must have been a good one because the door swung open, and jazz music, laughter, and raucous party noises poured out.

They were playing "Anything Goes."

I braced a hand over my chest. "I love that song."

It reminded me of Indiana Jones.

Then it hit me. We were going into a real speakeasy, not like in a movie, and not like the one I'd visited before where we had to investigate a murder and the ghosts were angry.

This was a real party.

"Try to act cool," Frankie cautioned.

"Okay." I grinned.

"Never mind," he muttered. "Now remember, not everybody in here is friendly."

"As if I'd forget." I never let my guard down completely. Frankie had taken me to plenty of places that had been fun at first but had turned dangerous fast.

Frankie let me enter first, and I felt like I'd stepped back in time.

The ladies wore feathers and rhinestone-studded head-pieces; the men sported crisp white shirts and ties. I fit right in with my magnolia print dress. I touched a hand to the sprig of flowers in my hair. The place was packed with people talking and flirting and weaving in and out of the crowd. A wood bar ran up the right side of the room, with bottles and mixers lining the back.

A corset check stood next to the coat check, which struck me as ten shades of strange. But before I thought to ask, my attention was captured by the band on a wood stage opposite the bar, a four-piece number with a leggy singer backed up by bass, drums, and a pianist playing for tips.

The good citizens of Sugarland danced up front, on the sides, and among the tables packing the middle—men without hats and ladies swinging pearls.

"I never knew *this* happened in my little town," I said, easing into the melee, ducking past a man so he wouldn't touch me. I mean, there had been an exhibit on prohibition at the library once, and there were a couple of faded photographs, and a pencil drawing or two, but nothing like this. "I wish I could take a picture." Only the camera couldn't see what I could.

Nobody did, save for the dead.

"I'm getting a drink," Frankie said, heading straight for the bar.

"I'm with you." I followed, raising my arms to avoid touching anyone. "Do you see Lou?" I asked, searching the party. When he didn't answer, I asked him again.

Frankie held up a finger for the bartender. "Cutty and water," he said, turning around as the young man in a white apron and a black bow tie went to fetch it. He looked like a youthful Nathan Fillion.

"Play it cool," my gangster said, scanning the crowd.

"I thought I was," I told him, shimmying sideways to avoid a drunk flapper. The overlarge ostrich feather on her headband whisked past my cheek and gave me a ghostly chill. I'd have to stay out of the heavier crowds, or I was going to get creamed. "The trick is, I'm not sure what your brother looks like."

"I'll spot him if he's here," Frankie said, tossing a wad of bills on the bar and grabbing his drink. "Your job is to blend in and be ready in case I need live backup."

"Live backup for what?" I still wasn't sure how my living and breathing would help him.

"Trust me, I'll let you know," he said, distracted by someone in the crowd.

Great. Because I loved surprises.

I scanned to see what had captured Frankie's attention when I caught the eye of a woman in a flowing light gray gown, one shoulder bare. She noticed me the same time I did her. I couldn't miss her headpiece, either, which looked like the crown on the Statue of Liberty.

"I love your hat," I mouthed to her.

She started coming straight for us.

Whoops. I hoped I'd done the right thing by being friendly.

Frankie slammed his drink on the bar. "Wait here," he said, striding forward to meet her.

From Frankie's intense stare, she might very well be an ex-girlfriend. She seemed the type of girl who would date a gangster.

She looked to be about my age, her blond hair arranged in tight curls close to her head and her lips stained dark. I watched as Frankie walked straight past her and was soon swallowed up in the crowd.

Oh my. So she was coming for me. The woman continued her advance and pursed her lips as she leaned against the bar next to me.

She had a worldly look about her and a challenging gleam in her eye. "Are you going to vote tomorrow?" she demanded, tilting her head.

She might very well have mistaken me for someone else. I stared at her earrings, which resembled a cascade of stars. "I didn't know there was voting tomorrow," I managed, lest she start quizzing me further.

"You've got to vote," she said, drawing so close I felt her chill. "We can vote now. It's our right."

I could certainly get on board with that. "I've never skipped once. Neither has my mother or my grandmother." I'd been taught right.

She smiled at that. "My grandmother was afraid the first time. She worried it wasn't ladylike. Tomorrow, she'll be first in line."

Good for her. "Can you believe it took till 1920?"

She cocked her head and stared at me.

Whoops. I supposed that wasn't overly long ago for her.

She leaned in so close I could smell the gin on her. "Am I drunk, or are you alive?"

"I'm alive," I said. "And you very possibly could be drunk."

A giggle bubbled out of her. "Oh, my word. Only in Sugarland." She spared a glance and a wink at the bartender, who slid her a French 75 in a tall, stemmed glass. "So…how? Why?" she asked. "Although I admit you blend in well."

"It looked like a fun party," I said.

She lifted her glass in a quick toast before taking a healthy sip.

"You want to dance?" she asked. "I noticed your fella wandered off." She pointed toward the front of the floor. "My friends are up there. Plus"—she pointed to the piano player at the front—"that's Jelly Roll Morton, traveling through up to Memphis. We've only got him one night."

It took everything I had not to grab her arm. "I've heard of him. He was my grandpa's favorite." I searched the crowd, and sure enough, there he was. The man himself, with slicked-back hair and magic fingers, pounded the keys. I turned to her. "You're telling me I can dance to the real Jelly Roll Morton."

"Not if you keep standing there." She laughed.

"Okay, but I can't touch anybody out there," I confessed. "I *am* alive."

"I know." She waved a hand. "That's why I felt sorry for you."

I wasn't above a pity dance at that point.

"Stick close to me and my friends," she said, following my glance toward where Frankie had disappeared. "He'll see where you went."

True. If Frankie could find Lou in this crowd, he could spot me on a dance floor. I'd be up front, enjoying live music from the man I'd only seen on the History Channel and listened to on my grandpa's old records.

Frankie owed me this. After all the times he'd disappeared during my ghost-hunting jobs, the least he could do was let me have this once-in-a-lifetime experience.

"Let's go," I said.

She grinned and grabbed her drink. "I'm Ruth," she called

ANGIE FOX

back and started deftly parting the crowd for me. It was nice. She was way more considerate than Frankie.

"I'm Verity," I hollered over the music, dodging a four-top of laughing couples, with an extra lady sitting on the table.

Then Jelly Roll launched into "My Home is in a Southern Town."

We reached her group of girls, and they waved their greetings as they cocked their hips and swung their arms and danced. I joined the small circle of ladies and let the music lead me. It felt perfect and free. Jelly Roll banged on the piano and I stomped the floor along with it and it was like flying.

I wanted to come here every night.

I wanted Ruth as my friend.

I wanted Frankie to stay away when I saw him winding through the crowd straight for me.

His pencil-thin mustache had disappeared, exactly as I'd warned, and his brow furrowed.

"That's Jelly Roll Morton!" I hollered to him. It felt good to be hip, even if I was 1920s hip.

"I don't care if it's Mickey Mouse," he said, drawing up next to me. "Lou isn't in the crowd. We gotta act fast," he added, keeping an eye out. "Word is starting to spread I'm here." The girls I was with waved at him. He half-heartedly returned the gesture and turned his back. "Technically I'm not allowed in here."

"The guy upstairs let you in."

"I had a disguise."

Truly? I raised an eyebrow. That was the worst disguise I'd ever seen.

"That, and I slipped him a Benjamin," Frankie said. "He'll get to keep it because it was one of his I lifted off him while we were walking back."

Always the charmer.

He glanced over his shoulder, toward a closed door near the

90

stage. "There's a private card game in the back. You got two grand?"

"Not quite." If he'd brought me along as his moneybags live girl, he'd made a big mistake.

Frankie cursed under his breath. "I'm not going to spend it," he said as if I were holding out on him. "I gotta show a wad of cash to get to the back room, past the bouncer packing heat."

"I brought a few fives for the church raffle," I said, "but that doesn't even impress me, much less a bunch of dead gamblers."

Frankie rubbed his jaw. "Okay," he said, turning it over in his mind. "We have to be slick. This isn't our turf, and I don't want to start a mob war."

"That's the smartest thing you've said all day." The last time he took me to a party, I'd accidentally knocked the skull off a dead gangster skeleton, and that guy was still after me.

"I got a plan," Frankie said, easing toward the room.

That didn't sound so good. "Your plans have a way of backfiring."

He didn't bother denying it. If anything, he started gliding faster. "Follow my lead," he insisted. "If we team up, we can pull this off."

Chapter Nine

R ight when I thought we were headed for the hidden
gambling room, Frankie shifted directions and made
a beeline for the bar.

I did my best to keep up, careful not to touch anyone or
anything. He got way ahead of me, and I watched in horror as
he slipped around the end of the drink-prep area nearest the
wall and beckoned me to follow.

It was inconceivable, irresponsible. Unless Lou himself was
bartending back there, Frankie had no business stirring up
trouble.

"This is not the time to call attention to yourself," I hissed.
Not when his disguise had worn off and he was afraid of being
recognized. "And this is definitely not the time to drink."

Frankie ducked his head past the cash register and blinked at
me innocently from the other side. "You need to be on my side
of the bar for this to work," he said as if he were the practical
one. At the same time, he waved the bartender over. So much
for not being spotted. "Trust me. I've done this before."

"Done what?" I demanded.

"Hurry up," he hissed. "You said you'd help."

"Fine!" If he got me in trouble, I was going to leave his urn at home for a week. A month. I'd cover it in kitten and puppy stickers.

My stomach clenched as I skirted around the side of the bar and back behind it, where I plainly should not be. It rubbed against every fiber of my nature.

Frankie studied me like a bug. "You shimmied in through the window upstairs, yet you're worried about sneaking behind the bar."

"That was different." Somehow. I'd figure it out later.

"Sometimes, it's best to breathe through the bad emotions," Frankie said, quoting from the self-help book I'd read to him from outside his shed. "Let yourself feel."

"Can it." I felt like I was back in grade school, sweating bullets in front of the class, expected to do a math problem I had no hope of solving. "I told you I'd do this and I am." I'd agreed to back up Frankie. I was his secret weapon. "Now, what's the plan?"

Nathan Fillion's slightly younger ghostly twin appeared mildly annoyed, but not surprised as he grabbed a cocktail shaker and closed the distance between us. "What do you two want?" he demanded, his features clouding. He was bigger than he looked. I could hardly see around him.

Frankie drew his revolver and held it low. "I want the money in your drawer."

Sweet baby Jesus. "This is a stickup," I gasped.

The bartender eased his shaker onto the bar and held his hands up slightly. "I don't want any trouble, sweetheart," he said to me.

To me? I wasn't holding him up.

Although I had just told him I was.

Frankie hit a button on the side of the metal cash machine, and the drawer flew open.

"I see you brought a professional," the bartender gritted out.

"Do you see me holding a gun? I'm not the one robbing you," I pointed out, insulted he'd even think it. It was Frankie who grabbed the stack of bills.

"I'm not robbing you, either," Frankie said, shoving the cash into his coat pocket. "I'm borrowing this. Like when I pawned that armored bank truck in '35. I don't need the O'Malleys hating me any more than they do now."

The bartender cursed under his breath. "I knew it. Frankie the German. They told me to watch out for you."

"Good job, you saw me," Frankie said, slamming the drawer closed. "Now you keep facing toward the wall," he ordered, and I realized the way the bartender stood, he blocked the room's view of the gun.

Maybe Frankie was kind of smart after all.

His ruse had worked in the short-term, but I could think of no way to get out of here without being seen, chased, and shot like Swiss cheese.

And it wouldn't take long for the patrons at the bar to pop their noses up from the party and start looking for another drink.

"Now for phase two," Frankie said as if he'd had this all planned out when I was almost certain he didn't. "You take this," he said, handing me the ice-cold ghostly revolver.

I almost dropped it.

I probably should have.

"Point it at him," Frankie growled, his temper short.

That was the absolute worst idea in the world. Only I couldn't think of one better that would still get us out of here.

"What are you doing?" I hissed at Frankie, keeping the gun on the bartender even though I knew I should drop it and run.

I'd never make it out on my own.

The bartender eyed me as if he were thinking the same thing.

"I'm going to go crash a card game," Frankie said as if it were the most obvious thing in the world. "I will bring this right back," he added to the bartender, patting the cash in his pocket. Then he left us—he left me!—and ducked back into the party and toward the back room.

"He's gone," I said. I couldn't quite believe it.

"Yet you are still robbing me," the bartender pointed out. I could almost see him thinking about going for my gun.

"I'm not," I said, struggling to maintain my icy grip. This was pure self-preservation, not greed. I was stuck. Trapped. And if I showed any weakness, the bartender would grab me or shoot me, and it would be all over.

Worse, ghostly objects disappeared when I touched them, much less held them for too long. My fingers had already gone numb from the chill of the revolver. It was like gripping a block of ice. Not to mention the fact I was taking part in an armed robbery when I didn't even like to speed, jaywalk, or fail to compost Lucy's banana peels.

"Um…" the bartender managed.

"Okay, I am robbing you," I said, keeping the gun steady.

Anything to keep living and breathing for as long as I could.

Any moment now, the crowd at the bar would realize what was happening, and I had no idea what to do next.

I most definitely did not sign up for this.

The bartender sized me up. He probably had his own gun hidden in his pocket and would kill me the second he realized I'd never in a million years pull the trigger on him.

And the barrel of my gun was halfway gone now.

"I'm so sorry," I whispered to the bartender.

"Then drop the gun," he told me, his voice hard, his hand moving slowly toward the back of his pants.

"Don't even think about it," I said, leveling the revolver at his head, still hesitant to shoot him but very much against getting shot myself.

Maybe I should shoot him. It would only knock him out

since he was already dead. I heard it stung like the dickens. Still, it was better than what he'd do to me.

"This'll be over in a second," I promised him, repositioning my finger on the trigger. It was more a promise to myself, because when it came down to it, it horrified me to think of shooting a person, even a dead person. "Frankie needs to hurry the heck up and find his brother in that secret card room."

"Is that what he's after?" A glimmer of amusement touched his lips. "Lou's not in there. Lou's got a safe room up above the shop." He cocked his chin up toward the ceiling. "It's the only apartment up there. You can't miss it."

"Really?" I asked, lowering the gun a fraction before I realized and corrected it. "Thanks for telling me." That was sweet.

"You're holding a gun on me," he pointed out. "What choice have I got?"

"Right," I said. "I'm sorry. Is there anything I can do to help you?" When he started to speak, I added, "Besides putting the gun down?"

He looked at me like I'd asked him to dance a jig and call me Mary.

"Sweetheart"—he shook his head slightly—"you need to ditch that gangster and go back to Sunday school."

I barked out a laugh. "I'm not with him." Well, I kind of was. "I'm alive," I clarified. "Look, do you have any unfinished business on the mortal plane? I have a knack for helping the dead with their problems."

When I wasn't holding them at gunpoint.

He paused for a moment before a bemused expression bloomed over his features. "No regrets, doll."

"Even now?" I asked. "Because working nights at a mob bar doesn't seem like a good life choice."

He raised a brow. "Says the woman holding a gun on me." He looked me up and down. "Although you are a sweet little thing, aren't you? If you like the bad-boy type, I'm available."

Was he actually hitting on me? My finger tightened on the trigger. "I'm not dead," I reminded him.

"Not yet," he replied as people at the bar started looking and pointing. "Go out with me and I'll tell them it's all a joke."

I had a boyfriend, one who would be very unhappy to see where I'd ended up tonight. And I didn't want to give my ghostly bartender friend any hope that I'd be dead soon—or any incentive to make it happen.

But as a man in a polka-dot bow tie two seats back drew a revolver out of his suit pocket, I changed my mind. My heart sped up as he pointed it at me.

"You can take me out if I live through this," I promised.

But the truth was if I got out of this, I'd be gone so fast I'd blow his hair back.

He treated me to a saucy grin and cocked his chin over his shoulder. "Put the gun away, Milo. I don't need any help with my girl trouble."

Milo laughed and slammed his gun down on the bar. "Jeez, Brennan. Maybe treat her nice next time. Or don't get caught."

The guy next to him craned his neck to see. "You and your love life. I'm missing my drink here."

"Next round's on me," Brennan said to them before smirking at me like he'd won the prize. "I'm gonna take you out for pie."

I wasn't even sure what that meant. And now the entire barrel of my gun had disappeared into thin air.

"Neat trick," Brennan said, lowering his hands and advancing on me.

I caught Frankie out of the corner of my eye, darting through the crowd. "Hurry up!" I urged as he whipped around the bar, tie askew.

"Lou's not in the card room," he said, grabbing the gun from me. He cursed under his breath when he saw what was left of it. He pocketed the half-vanished revolver and drew a spare out of his jacket.

"Now give the man his cash back," I ordered Frankie.

He gave me a quick side glance. "I think I lost it," he hedged.

Once a gangster, always a gangster. "Do it," I insisted. "He told me where Lou is."

Quicker than lightning, Frankie raised the butt of the gun and clocked the bartender over the head. I fought the urge to catch poor Brennan as he fell, out cold.

"That's my chaperon," I said to the gaping bar patrons.

Two of the ladies cheered while a man at the very end of the bar pointed toward Frankie and shouted something.

"I think he recognizes you."

"Let's go," Frankie said, leading the retreat.

"Put the cash back," I said, not budging.

Frankie gritted his teeth but didn't argue. We had no time, as more and more of the party crowd began looking our way.

He yanked the cash out of his pocket, jammed it in the bartender's apron, and ushered us both the heck out of Dodge. "Where to?"

"Third floor," I said. "Lou's got a safe room above the shop."

"This way." Frankie led me toward a pair of black swinging doors. I hadn't even seen them until we got close. They opened into a galley-style industrial kitchen, with no staff and no food that I could see. Cases of booze lined the walls.

"Been here often?" I asked as Frankie barged into a small broom closet, opened a door at the back, and led us straight into the lobby.

The lady at the corset check room waved. "Hiya, doll." As if she saw this every night.

Maybe she did.

We dodged a trio of incoming patrons and escaped out to the stairwell.

"You think they'll follow us?" I asked as the door slammed shut behind us.

"Hopefully they just want me out of there," Frankie said, moving fast, with me hustling to keep up.

"What did you do to get banned in the first place?" I asked as we took the stairs two at a time.

"The owner made a pass at my girlfriend in '32," Frankie said, rounding the landing on the second floor. "So I broke into his establishment and left him a present."

"I shudder to think," I told him. My toe caught on a stair and I stumbled, but I hauled myself up and kept running.

"A live pig. Figured he'd want to hang out with his own kind." Frankie snickered as we raced to the third floor. "How was I supposed to know the old boar would tear the place apart?"

"Because it's an animal," I said, breathing hard as we made it to the third-floor landing.

"So am I," Frankie said, having finished our dash up the stairs with not a hair out of place. "This it?" he asked, eyeing a wood door with 3A painted in white letters. On the mortal side, it said "Office."

"I don't see anything else," I said. This had to be it. "Brennan said Lou has the third floor."

"All right, then," he said, eyeing me. Frankie appeared a little hesitant as he squared his shoulders, drew his gun, and kicked the door open.

Chapter Ten

With a swift, efficient kick from Frankie, the ghostly door cracked and swung open.

"Come on," Frankie drew his gun and rushed inside, straight through the still-closed, very solid wooden door on the earthly plane.

"Wait." I tried the handle.

Locked.

I heard the muffled sound of Frankie swearing.

"What do you see?" I called, rattling the handle again as if that would make any difference.

"Get in here," he demanded.

"I'm working on it," I said as if wishing would force it open.

"Kick it in," Frankie ordered.

"In kitten heels?" The only thing worse would be trying that type of ninja move in bare feet, and honestly, I didn't have the strength. Or the skill. I mean, I'd kicked in a door once before in a rotted mill, but that thing was halfway to collapse before I'd gotten there. Most days, I had trouble opening jars in my kitchen.

But I was decent at thinking on my feet. A flash of inspira-

ANGIE FOX

tion hit, and I dropped down to check under the plain brown rubber door mat. If the restaurant owners had moved out, they might have left a...my fingers closed around it. "A key!"

I slipped it into the lock and rushed inside to find Frankie standing in the living room. The room lay empty in the real world. On his side, in glowing ghostly gray, I saw how it had appeared in the past.

A metal pole lamp with beaded fringe stood next to a wooden floor-model radio. A pair of beat-up wingback chairs flanked a round coffee table. A magazine lay open on the arm of the chair closest to the window.

The room smelled of violet and vanilla.

Through an open door near the radio, I saw a deserted back bedroom. A small kitchen with a checkered floor jutted off to the right.

"I've been here before," Frankie said, walking around, studying the place. "Lou used this room to hide out from Lucindo the Rat when he blew into town."

I studied the magazine closer. A woman in a black silk kaftan graced an ad for Humming Bird Hosiery while on the opposite page, an article explored the eating habits of various celebrities. It seemed some things never changed.

"Can we focus on what we came to do?" Frankie asked, walking over to a drink left on the side table. He picked up the crystal spirits glass and sniffed it. "Water," he said with a wrinkle of his nose.

Maybe Lou had led a double life: hardened gangster in public, ladies-magazine-reading teetotaler in private.

It could happen. I'd certainly seen stranger things.

I caught a movement out of the corner of my eye. A shimmering gray figure watched us through the cracked-open bedroom door.

From the curl of the hair and the smoky eye shadow, it appeared to be a woman.

I gave her a small reassuring smile to let her know we meant no harm.

"Frank," I said quietly.

"Don't call me Frank," he ordered.

"Look," I pressed.

He'd barely turned his head when, with the swish of a polka-dot dress, the ghostly door began to ease closed.

Frankie raced over there in a heartbeat and blocked it with his foot. "Hey, doll," he said, going easier than I'd expected, given his mood. "We're just looking for Lou."

"Stay away from him," she ordered, voice quivering.

"You got something to hide?" he asked.

"Stay away from us both!" she cried, and before he could get another word out, what I could see of the polka-dot dress evaporated. Her hold on the door slackened, and Frankie nudged it open the rest of the way with his foot.

"She's gone," he said, more than a little frustrated.

"You scared her."

"I am pretty tough," he said, taking it as a compliment.

He held his gun ahead of him as we ventured into a sparse bedroom furnished with little more than a bed on a plain metal frame.

"Who was she?" I asked, moving to the skirted table by the bed. It seemed she'd known Lou, but in what capacity I couldn't say.

"I've never seen her before in my life," Frankie said, checking under the bed.

"You sure about that?" I asked, scanning the room. "If this is Lou's hideout, she could be his girlfriend."

Frankie barked out a laugh. "Lou didn't have a girl. He wasn't the type to commit."

"Care to explain this?" I asked, directing him to a framed photograph on the nightstand. The decorative glass held a photograph of a dark-haired, smiling woman in a dress speckled with daisies, and a long-faced, hook-nosed man who bore a passing resemblance to my friend.

Frankie nearly dropped his gun. "Holy hell. That's Lou."

"I think she's the one I saw behind the door." I'd only managed a glimpse, but the hair was the same, the smoky eyes as well.

"I don't believe it," Frankie said, stunned.

I checked out the tiny tiled bathroom while Frankie stared at the photograph as if he could make it make sense by sheer force of will.

The closet-sized space held a plain tub with a slight rust stain flowing from the base of the faucet to the drain. A cake of rose-shaped soap rested in a dish perched on a porcelain pedestal sink. On the small glass shelf above it, I watched as a ghostly silver-backed hairbrush began to fade away.

Quickly, I opened the medicine cabinet over the sink and caught one last glimpse of a neatly rolled toothpaste tube, an antique loose powder with the fuzzy puff on top, and a toothbrush as they disappeared.

"Why is there only one toothbrush?" I asked.

The room darkened as the silvery light from the ghost faded.

"I think this was her room, not his," Frankie said as I dug into my bag for my flashlight and clicked it on.

"So the girl is the dominant ghost?" I asked, joining him in the now-empty bedroom.

All traces of the ghostly furniture had disappeared, even the photo.

"The closet had dresses and a lady's shoes," Frankie said. "No guy's clothes."

"A daisy flowered dress?" I asked.

"Yeah." He nodded. "I don't get it." Frankie planted his hands on his hips, studying the empty room as if he could will the ghost's vision back into existence again. "This is supposed to be Lou's spot."

"Do you think she's controlling him?" I asked, moving to the living room. It, too, had lost all traces of its ghostly past. The room stood stark and empty, four walls and a hardwood floor.

"Lou would never allow it," Frankie said. "He's bossier than I am."

"Perish the thought," I said, training my flashlight over the empty spot of the wall where the radio had stood. "Maybe it was less romantic and more blackmail." Although I wasn't sure how... *Take me to your safe house or else?*

Frankie considered it, not convinced. "Lou owned his dark side. He didn't leave any room for blackmail."

"Okay, well, if she was staying up here, then she's connected to him." The bartender had said this was his hideout, and I didn't think he'd lie to me at gunpoint. "If it's not love or blackmail, then what? Does any of this make sense to you?" I asked Frankie, who had gone strangely silent.

He stood looking at the floor. "None of this has made sense since I found out my own brother killed me."

And we were back to square one.

He brushed past me. "Let's get out of here."

We opted to make our way out via the rear fire escape, seeing as Frankie had lost his disguise and the club owners didn't like Frankie even when he wasn't robbing the bartender downstairs.

"I'm proud of how you handled your first stickup," Frankie said, hovering next to me while I took the metal stairs.

"It wasn't a stickup," I said through clenched teeth. It was more like trickery, which was only slightly better in my view. "I wasn't going to take anything."

"Nobody gets it right the first time." He shrugged. "But the important thing is you kept your cool."

Next time, give me a choice in the matter. "You could have warned me."

"If I did, you wouldn't have done it," Frankie reasoned.

Oh, for the days when I didn't have a ghost by my side and an urn in my purse.

We reached the bottom, and I jumped the last few feet, landing hard. Kitten heels were not made for this. "You realize you got me into big trouble," I said, smoothing my skirt. "Either Brennan tells on us and the O'Malley family will be after me for the rest of eternity, or I owe that bartender a date."

"Hold up," Frankie said, winding in front of me, nearly causing me to trip as I avoided running into him. "You and Brennan," he said, pointing at the building. "Brennan and you? I thought you were the loyal type." Frankie took off his hat and stared at me. "I might not like you dating the fuzz, but Ellis is a good guy despite his job, and he doesn't deserve you skirting around on him."

Seriously. I looked him in the eyes, right below the bullet hole in his forehead. "I'm not going to cheat on Ellis with a dead prohibition-era bartender."

His shoulders relaxed a fraction. "Good, because Brennan is a player."

I couldn't believe Frankie was actually watching out for me. And for Ellis. When had this started?

"I made a deal to get us out of there alive," I told him. Simple as that.

"Speak for yourself," he huffed before turning and gliding toward the alley without me.

"In one piece," I corrected. The gangster was far too sensitive about being called dead. I mean, wasn't it obvious?

I held back while he called off Ice Pick Charlie and the guys guarding the back door of the club. They faded away, promising to pass the word to the guys on the roof across the street.

Frankie and I made our way up the side alley in the dark alone.

"You've changed," Frankie said, shoving his hands into his pockets.

Not this again. "I'm doing fine," I insisted. I'd helped him tonight. I'd done my best for Jorie this afternoon. What else did he or anyone else want from me?

"I'm not saying it's bad," he said, passing straight through a line of trash cans. "I mean, it took nothing to get you to sneak into the gin joint tonight. And I liked how you handled a gun."

"I resisted. A little." I ran a hand down my face. Now Frankie was proud of me.

"But did you have to hit on the bartender?" he pleaded.

This was really bugging him. I searched for the right words. Kicked a rock. Considered how to put it. "I misled the bartender." For a good cause. "You of all people should know things aren't black and white." We emerged onto the shadowy street. "Perhaps I am learning to bend the rules a little, but I'm doing it with the best of intentions."

Frankie considered my explanation, then broke into a grin. "You know, that's what I always say. You do what you gotta do." He shook his head. "Still, I'd never promise a date to anybody but Molly." He started across the road toward the car.

"Yeah, I have a feeling that's going to come back and bite me," I said, following.

"It always does," he agreed.

Lord above. Since when did I have anything in common with Frankie? Maybe Ellis was right. Maybe I was looking at the world a little differently than I had before.

Although, it had worked out so far.

Frankie stopped short of the passenger-side door of my car. "Can I give you some advice?"

"That depends on the subject," I said, leaning against the car.

Frankie drew a smoke out of his suit pocket and held it in the corner of his mouth. "I remember my first holdup," he said, striking a match.

He was not going to Obi Wan me into any more criminal activity. "Unlike you, my first holdup will be my last."

ANGIE FOX

He lit up and tossed the match. "It was an armored car out of Memphis, and the driver was on the take."

"So the exact same thing as tonight," I added, with more than a touch of sarcasm.

He took a long, slow drag. "I was so nervous I dang near forgot half the money, and I didn't even take the guard's gun." He chuckled. "I might as well have baked him brownies and asked about his kids. But I proved I could do it, and I was a different person when I got home that night than I was when I left in the morning." He eyed me and took another drag. "Do you get what I'm saying?"

"No." I really didn't.

Smoke streamed out his nose. "When you choose to do something different," he said, gesturing with his smoke, "when you step outside of what you've done before, take another path from who you say you are—it changes you. You might not be the one to realize it, but it does." He raised a brow and took another drag. "My brother recognized it the second he saw me after that robbery."

"And he was proud," I concluded.

Frankie coughed and waved the smoke away from his face. "He was furious," he said, recovering. "Lou dang near tore my head off."

That didn't make any sense at all. "Lou's a gangster." He should have been proud. It wasn't as if he could tell by looking that Frankie had let the guard off easy.

Frankie shrugged. "Lou's my big brother. He wanted a better life for me," he said, taking a drag. "He always said he got into the mob to keep me out of it."

Part of me couldn't imagine Frankie before he embraced a life of crime, the Frankie who was not a gangster. "But you're such a natural."

"I know," he said, with a little too much enthusiasm. "Lou

saw it as a way to survive." He pointed his smoke at me. "I saw it as a way to *live*."

It never occurred to me that there might have been another path for Frankie. But it seemed like there had been other choices, ones his brother had wanted him to take. "So did Lou ever get over it?" I asked. "I mean, it's not like he could judge if he joined the South Town gang before you."

"I never asked," he said, without an ounce of regret.

"Of course not." Frankie wasn't big on communication.

His eyes went cold. "He shot me before I got the chance."

"I'm aware."

Frankie tossed his cigarette. "Come on, I need a drink." He passed through the car door and took a seat, leaning his head through the window. "There's an underground party I know."

"Absolutely not," I said, digging out my keys as I walked around the front. For one thing, my feet were killing me. I opened the driver's door and looked down at him. "I don't trust you not to stuff liquor bottles down my dress and try to sneak me out the back."

Frankie rolled his eyes. "That would never work because touching you would make the booze disappear."

I sat down on the edge of the driver's seat and nudged off my heels one at a time. Pure bliss. "I've had enough action for one day," I said, to the tune of his long sigh. I glanced over at him. "In case you forgot, I've been busy with murder, armed robbery, and a manhunt"—I tossed my heels into the back seat—"when all I wanted was a nice afternoon out followed by an evening of knitting in my car."

"This is your problem," Frankie stated as I pulled onto Main Street. "You need to learn how to live it up."

"And you need to settle down." I'd kept my promise and then some by helping him track down his brother's whereabouts tonight. At considerable personal risk. I'd earned the rest of the evening off.

"There's a gin joint above the old sugar warehouse," Frankie suggested as we made a left onto Third Street.

"Those are loft apartments now, and I don't think those people want us traipsing through."

He considered that while I drove through a cute neighborhood of 1940s bungalows. Ellis lived only a few blocks away, I realized with a pang. I wouldn't mind stopping by his place if I were sure I'd be welcome. After our fight this afternoon, I just didn't know.

"How about the card game at the library?" Frankie suggested.

I waved to an older couple sitting in lawn chairs under a porch light, drinking wine.

"The last time we crashed the card game at the library, I almost got shot," I reminded him.

"Actually, it was the time before," he corrected.

Either way. "The library is closed at this hour. I can't get in."

Frankie leaned his head back against the seat rest. "It's like you only want to think of the problems and not the solutions."

I glanced at him. "And you like creating problems, period."

He eyed me, his head still back. "Daisy Marple's crypt at Holy Oak Cemetery is always hopping."

It went on like that until we pulled down the long drive to my house.

Frankie stared out at the young peach trees I'd planted the spring before. "Nothing ever happens at your house."

Should I remind him of the time he opened a high-stakes casino on my back porch?

"Hold that thought," I said, pulling around to the back. Ellis's police cruiser sat parked in front of my rosebushes.

I wished nothing interesting happened at my house. But since Frankie got stuck there, interesting was better than some of the alternatives. At the moment, Ellis stood on my back porch, knocking.

"Maybe he's coming to apologize for our fight this after-noon," I said, hastily shoving my car into park and killing the engine.

"You do look like you went a few rounds," Frankie said, taking in my appearance.

Heavens. I must look a fright after dancing and robbing and running up stairs and down fire escapes. I ran my fingers through my hair, realizing both barrettes were gone, along with the baby's breath.

"I'm out of here," Frankie said, disappearing as I debated rooting through the back seat for my shoes.

Seeing Ellis shouldn't make me nervous, but it did. Despite our troubles, I hoped he'd be glad to see me because he loved me.

I slipped barefoot out of the car, with a ready smile that died on my lips almost as quickly as it had appeared.

"Where have you been?" Ellis asked, tromping down my porch stairs, his tone a bit too accusing for my taste.

I crinkled my toes into the dirt. There was no sense lying about it. "I just got back from a manhunt with Frankie," I declared, daring him to challenge me on it.

His brows knit and his pace slowed as he crossed the yard. "What do you mean a manhunt with Frankie?" he asked, looking me up and down before he stopped in front of me. This was not the greeting of a happy boyfriend. "Where did you go?"

I notched my chin up. "You could be happier to see me."

"You're a mess." His jaw clenched. "Did you do anything illegal?"

I brushed past him and headed for the house. "I'd rather not say." Breaking and entering was outside the law, but I wasn't sure about the robbery part because it wasn't in our world. So did Ellis even have jurisdiction?

"Get back here," he said, on my heels.

I would not allow him to order me around at my own home.

"Why did you come over in the first place?" I asked, mounting the back stairs. "Was it just to argue, or are you even a little glad to see me?"

We disagreed on a few very important points, but that didn't mean he had to greet me like an angry police officer. He was my boyfriend. He'd driven across town to see me. He'd be wise to begin with a sweet hello and a kiss before giving me the third degree.

Especially after the day I'd had.

I hadn't taken two strides when he said, "I found this at the murder scene."

In the glow of the yellow porch light, I saw him hold up a clear plastic evidence bag with Jorie's big manila folder inside, the one she'd brought with her this afternoon.

"You found it," I said, ten kinds of relieved as I made a grab for it. It had contained the photograph. I'd worried I'd never see it again.

He held it back from me. "Why is your name on the folder?"

So he hadn't come here because he missed me. My heart sank a little.

Nevertheless, I explained all about Jorie and the sentimental items she'd tried to give me. "Now can I see what's in it?"

"It's empty," he said, handing me the sealed bag.

I turned it over in my hands, disappointed. "I'd hoped the picture would still be inside." Jorie had placed it there minutes before she died. I'd give anything for that shot of my grandmother and Jorie outside the Three Angels Church on her wedding day, especially now that both of them were gone. "I don't understand it."

"Duranja didn't say much about it in his report," Ellis said, clearly unhappy about that. "He did go into detail about the letter you took."

"That was a terrible mistake," I admitted, willing him to understand. "I got carried away."

"Ghost hunting?" he asked pointedly.

I ignored his tone. "I had reason to think a certain ghost may have witnessed her fall. He's a gravedigger, and he haunts the tower."

Now I had his attention.

"And?" he asked.

"The gravedigger went after me and I had to run," I admitted. "If he saw anything, he's not talking. Yet," I added, with a touch of optimism.

He sighed and dragged a hand through his hair as if he were trying to hold onto his temper. "It was a mistake that wouldn't have happened if you were prepared for the dangers of ghost hunting, which you can't be because it's impossible to predict what's going to happen next."

He had me there.

He dropped his hand. "You were explicitly told to stay with the rest of the witnesses."

"It was a quick fact-finding jaunt up the tower," I insisted.

"I didn't ask for your help."

That was cold.

"So now I need your permission to do my job?" I asked. Honestly. "My grandma's friend died, and I was in a position to see what might have happened. I'd be ashamed if I didn't step up in that position."

He gritted his jaw so hard a muscle in his neck jumped. "You chose to strike off on your own during an active death investigation."

He made it sound bad. "I didn't mean any harm."

"You used to talk to me first. Once upon a time, you would have held back and at least thought about it."

"Once upon a time, you'd have wanted me to go." I glanced past him, out to the darkened backyard.

The more I'd braved otherworldly situations, the more I

realized I could help people in a way nobody else could. I could see nothing bad about that.

Except when I got into trouble.

I chanced a glance back at Ellis. The soft porch light played across his handsome features, and I paused a moment to enjoy it.

"Why don't we head inside the house for a nice glass of lemonade?" I asked, taking the Southern approach.

Tough conversations always went down better with a cold drink.

But Ellis was the stubborn sort. He remained rooted to the porch. "I don't want any lemonade. I want you to listen to me."

As if I had a choice.

"You're getting too bold," he stated flatly, "and you're not always staying on the right side of the law like you used to."

Boy, that was hard to argue after the night I'd had. "I'm doing my best," I insisted, walking toward the porch swing by the stairs. I needed space.

"And yet Duranja caught you breaking into the Adair estate a few months ago."

I turned. "How could I resist a Gatsby-era house party? The ghosts invited me in." At his thunderous expression, I added, "Then I got permission from the live owner, so it was all fine."

He ran a hand down his face. "You took evidence."

"Not that time," I clarified.

"Today," he countered.

Right. "I do feel awful about that," I said, closing the distance between us once more. "I was flustered. And I don't see how a personal letter is major evidence anyway."

He pinched the bridge of his nose. "It has been in the past."

"I'll try to do better."

That earned a small look of understanding from Ellis. "In this case, you got lucky. We read it, and it appears to be just a chatty old letter."

Oh, good. "Can I have it back, then?"

"No." He started to speak and then stopped. "Look, I know you feel a certain responsibility for your grandma's friend, and I get that, I do. But you need to cool it. Not every incident has a ghostly witness, and not every accident is a crime."

He was one to talk. "I remember a time when you were right there with me, investigating every angle, no matter how unlikely."

"Yes," he said immediately, "when we were investigating clear cases of foul play that led to murder."

"The ledge is waist high. It would be hard to fall."

"But still possible," Ellis stated. "From what I've seen, this one looks cut and dried." He held up a hand when I began to protest. "Not every death is nefarious, but we are looking into it."

"Then tell me what happened to the photograph," I said, crossing my arms over my chest.

"It could have been dropped, like the letter," he said quite reasonably.

"But you didn't find it on the lawn with the envelope."

A muscle in his jaw twitched. "No."

It bothered him. I could see it. Well, it nagged at me too.

When it came down to it, I didn't think I could let it rest until we'd recovered that photograph.

I had a feeling that would be a problem for him.

The clickety-click of animal nails on glass interrupted my rumination. "Look," I said, pointing to the window off the parlor. A furry skunk pressed her nose to the glass. "Lucy is dying to see you."

He tried to resist. He even kept his frown for a few seconds while watching her snurffle and dance on her back legs.

But he was too weak to resist her charms.

"Hello, pretty girl," he said, directing the smallest slip of a smile at her. That was all right. I wasn't jealous.

I winked at the skunk—we were a team, after all—as Ellis followed me inside, keeping an eye on me the entire time.

"I'm glad to see you, pumpkin," he murmured, kneeling down to greet the skunk, who rushed him as soon as he cleared the threshold. "And you need to remember to lock your doors," he added to me, letting Lucy do a back bend over his thigh so he could rub her belly.

Leave it to my girl. She had a way with Officer Wydell, and he was soon scratching her under her chin as she kicked out her back leg and grunted happily at the attention.

Oh, to have the charm of a Lucy, I mused, pouring two glasses of lemonade with ice.

"I have a feeling you're still going to try to investigate without me," Ellis said, lavishing attention on my skunk.

"I'll keep my eyes open," I hedged, knowing it was better to ask forgiveness than permission.

Ellis's attention shot up to me. "We've already searched the grounds."

I placed a glass of lemonade on the kitchen island for him.

He didn't take it.

"Maybe there is another copy of the photograph somewhere," I mused. Then I could at least have a better understanding of what had gone missing.

He eyed me. "How come you can't go back to graphic design?" he asked, standing. "I'm sure my mother's not trying to turn every client against you anymore."

"It's not that simple," I said, taking a sip of lemonade.

Ellis touched my arm. "Hey, if my mom did try to hurt your business in any way, I'd be on her and so would Beau."

"It's not that," I said, walking away, abandoning him and the lemonade. "I wanted that before. Badly. I like being creative and I like working with people. Every day was different from the day before." I closed my eyes tight. "But now, I have something better."

"How?" he thundered. "How is this better? You're chasing down spirits I can't even see. You're getting into situations where nobody alive can help."

I turned to face him. "Tonight, I went to a speakeasy that was as real to me as my house and my kitchen." Boy, did Ellis look angry. But I kept going. "I danced to my grandpa's favorite jazz band. Live. And that's not all. I've seen things. I've been a part of history. How do you expect me to live a life on the mortal plane knowing all this is happening on the other side and I'm not a part of it anymore?"

For once, he was speechless. "You just...do." He looked at me intently. "It's called real life."

The ghosts I interacted with every day were part of real life, too.

"You haven't seen it." Now that I had, I couldn't ignore it. "I've made friends—good friends—on the other side that I never would have met because they're not living and breathing anymore." And, yes, I didn't know what I'd encounter when I walked into certain situations, but that was part of life even in the mortal realm. And then there was Frankie. "If I stop venturing out on the ghostly side, how can I help Frankie with his issues? Are you saying I can't do anything with Frankie anymore?"

"Frankie will be fine with or without you," Ellis said as if it were a fact.

Hardly. "We're working on getting him free, but he needs my help. He has a chance"—however slim—"to mend things with his brother. I think that might be a stepping-stone for him. He needs to stop being defined by his death and his ashes in the yard. He needs to grow emotionally, and if he does that, I really think we can free him."

"Or you could be chasing another ghost up a tower," Ellis countered.

He didn't need to get snippy. "Listen to yourself. I just opened up to you, and all you did was try to blow a hole in it."

He pinched the bridge of his nose. "I can't deal with this right now."

"Nobody asked you to. You came to see me," I reminded him.

He nodded, jaw tight. "Maybe that was a mistake."

It hurt to hear that. It hurt badly. "I will talk to you about ghost hunting. I will work through the issues you have with ghost hunting, but I refuse to be sorry for it."

"Then I suppose we have nothing more to say to each other," Ellis said, watching me, eerily calm.

"I suppose we don't," I said, and let him walk away. I let him slam the door, and I let him launch himself into his patrol car. My stomach hit my shoes, but I let him drive away.

A warm ball of fluff brushed my leg.

"Lucy." I reached down for my skunk. I folded her into my arms, and she snuggled deep. Ellis might not understand what I needed right now, but Lucy did.

I walked her over to the couch and sat down. I buried my face into the back of her warm, soft neck and felt her sigh against my arm. Lucy was always glad to see me, no matter what. She cared.

It would have to be enough.

Chapter Eleven

I expected Ellis to call and apologize. He wasn't one to stand on principle when he said or did something wrong. But my phone didn't ring.

At about eleven o'clock, I fired off a text to my best friend, Lauralee. She'd always been a good sounding board—she'd been my rock when my engagement had fallen apart.

She texted back right away.

She was up late with a sick kiddo. Her second born, Hiram, had the flu, and she was in bed, snuggled with him. I didn't get into my troubles but asked her to call when she had the chance.

Needless to say, I didn't sleep well that night. And by the next morning, the fight with Ellis still weighed on my mind.

"It's not like I can change who I am," I said, stirring up yogurt and blueberries for Lucy and myself. I added a sprinkle of Vita-Skunk supplement to hers. "I mean, he knew this about me when he asked me out in the first place."

We'd fought off a particularly terrorizing poltergeist, and we'd been buried alive and shot at before he'd even taken me out for pasta and a glass of wine.

Lucy snorted and spun in circles that should have made her

dizzy. I took it as enthusiastic agreement, even though it was more likely her appreciation for the pecans I sprinkled over her breakfast.

"I'm careful. You know I am," I said, and to my skunk's delight I placed her bowl down for her. I did need to be more careful about law breaking. And I would. I never set out to break any rules. Sometimes it just...happened.

Ellis had been on jobs with me. He'd seen what it was like. I had to adjust to each situation. "I always try to do the right thing," I reminded Lucy, who munched away, "and if he can't see that, well..."

The niggling pit in my stomach worried Ellis would walk out for good.

I mean, wasn't I worth a little trust, and perhaps an occasional flare-up with the police department?

I'd never lied to him, never pretended to be anything other than who I was.

The screen door flapped behind me as I walked out onto the porch with my breakfast, hoping a change of scene would lighten my mood. The morning air was crisp, and the pond in my yard placid and serene. Still, I couldn't enjoy it. I mean, I'd wanted to clear the air with Ellis for a while, ever since I'd over-heard him at the haunted asylum. I'd put it off because I hadn't known how to solve it.

And he'd put it off until the organist with the knife had made it impossible to ignore.

But I didn't like fighting, and I really didn't like the way we'd left things last night.

I ate my breakfast with a hip dug against the back porch rail, watching a broken branch of an apple tree graze the pond.

Lucky for Ellis, I wasn't the type to fly off the handle or commit relationship hara-kiri over a seemingly impossible fight. Although if I was honest with myself, I didn't feel oblig-ated to compromise much, either. My talent for exploring the other side had become a huge part of my life, and as long as Frankie let me, I'd keep at it.

We'd figure it out. Somehow. All I knew was my mother didn't raise a quitter. Not when I had so much to lose.

The kitchen phone rang, and I nearly hurt myself dashing inside to pick it up. At the very least, it might be Lauralee. With any luck, it would be Ellis. Perhaps he'd just needed to think it through before realizing what a terrible mistake he'd made yesterday picking those fights. We'd talk. He'd apologize. I'd invite him over.

I answered the phone and found Fiera on the line.

"Do you still want to go?" she asked.

It took me a moment to figure out what she was talking about. I also didn't want to speak too fast and betray my disappointment at the sound of her voice.

She cleared her throat. "Verity? You said yesterday you wanted to run over to MayBelle's place."

"That's right." Fiera never let a detail drop. I'd be very interested to hear if MayBelle could shed any light on the events leading up to Jorie's fall.

"MayBelle will be there if we make it before lunch," Fiera assured me. "After that, it's anybody's guess. MayBelle likes to sleep late, make a big brunch, and then she's off like a pistol shot."

Truly? "We're talking about visiting MayBelle at the retirement apartments, right?"

"Not everyone does retirement the same way," Fiera admonished.

Of course not. No one could accuse me of being an early bird, either. I checked my watch. It was already eleven o'clock. "I can be there in ten minutes."

"Sold," Fiera said. "See you soon."

∿

Park Manor was a former luxury hotel just north of the town square. Built in 1908, it graced the edge of one of the fancy old neighborhoods and, at five stories, was one of the tallest buildings in Sugarland.

But times had changed. We didn't get as many out-of-town visitors these days, and in the past year, our new mayor had converted the old hotel into rent-controlled senior housing.

It made me proud all over again to live in Sugarland.

I parked in the street across from the white stone entrance, glad for once to have left Frankie's urn at home. He was most likely resting up after our adventure last night, or busy plotting new trouble.

Either way, I didn't want to know.

Fiera waited for me on a pink couch in the lobby, under a painted glass ceiling, her attention captured by the ornamental plaster work gracing the doorway to the elevator bay. "I'm moving here when I retire," she vowed.

"Good plan." One flaw. "Are you the type to ever retire?" She was in her mid-seventies and showed no sign of pausing, much less slowing down.

She grinned at me with a sparkle in her eye. "Okay, I'll just live here and walk to do my tours at the library."

"That's a great idea," I said as we headed toward the elevators. "The Coffee Cartel just opened up along the way."

"Holey Moley donuts is a block over," she added.

Not to mention the diner going in across from the square on Main Street. "This is the perfect spot to live if you don't mind being in the city."

She laughed at that, which was strange because I didn't get what was so funny.

Fiera sobered as the polished walnut doors of the elevator eased closed. "It feels like I'm on my way to visit Jorie." She blinked hard. "At least she can be with Ray now."

I smiled, thinking of how she'd landscaped his grave with dwarf rosebushes. "She really loved him."

"To brave that creepy church once a week?" Fiera sniffed and swiped at her eyes. "That was true love."

The tiny crystals on the chandelier above us tinkled as the elevator lurched on its way up. "Okay, I agree it's creepy, but I thought it was because I'm tuned into the ghost side," I said. "What about it made you uncomfortable?"

Fiera's brows rose. "Do I want to know what's on the ghost side?"

"No," I told her. I'd keep the stabby organist and glowering gravedigger to myself.

"I do like to sleep at night," she smirked as the doors opened onto the fourth floor. She stepped out and then waited for me. "It's an uncomfortable place. Pastor Mike blames the newer churches for siphoning off members, but I think it's more like people just don't like the way it feels there."

"I could see that." I'd felt it even before I was tuned in. "Did anything bad happen at the church?"

Fiera considered the question for a moment. "If it did, I think I would have heard."

"Me as well." The Sugarland grapevine never missed a thing.

Fiera glanced down the hallway as we huddled by the eleva-tor. "I will tell you that I've watched Pastor Mike's mood go downhill since he took over for his father as pastor." She pursed her lips. "And his dad seemed to get happier the minute he retired from that place."

"Interesting," I said as Fiera led me down a bright yellow-painted hallway with vintage plaster accents. Art glass sconces lined the walls.

The residents had decorated their doors with photo collages and flowered wreaths. I saw one veteran had hung a pair of small flags crossed over his door—Marine Corps and the Stars and Stripes.

"Two more down," Fiera said, nudging me along. She stopped and knocked at a door covered in zebra wrapping paper. "I called her on the way over, but she didn't pick up."

"Do you think we missed her?" I asked, disappointed. We should have set up a time to see her.

"Oh, she's always home in the morning," Fiera insisted. An elaborate pink-framed dry-erase board hung below the peep-hole. Fiera grabbed the pen. "She either forgot to turn her ringer back on after she woke up, or she's sleeping in," she said, penning a quick note to MayBelle. "Don't worry. We'll track her down. She's a diva anyway, but she's worse if you wake her."

"I suppose we can grab a coffee around the corner. Or..." I turned to the door across the hall.

A white poster board hung on the door. Residents had written welcome messages to Jorie over the entirety of it.

This was her place.

It warmed my heart to see Sugarland hospitality in action.

Wonderful to have you here. If you play bridge, join us in Room 314 on Tuesdays at 1:00 p.m.

Welcome! Welcome! I baked cookies for you. It's worth the elevator trip. And, no, I can't leave them at your door because Bart will eat half of them. –Gloria in 201

Bart promises to eat only three. Love, Bart

I don't know what I'm going to harass you about now that you've moved here at last—and across from chez MayBelle! Heaven help you. I'll think of something. –MayBelle

. . .

I tried the door and found it unlocked.

Of course it was. This was Sugarland.

"Instead of coffee, do you think we can stop in to Jorie's apartment for a few minutes? I'd like to see if she had any other old wedding pictures like the one she brought me." Especially if the police had been unable to locate the photo she'd tried to give me at the church.

I hated to go in uninvited, but with Fiera along, it should be all right. They'd been neighbors and friends.

"That's a good idea," Fiera said, grabbing MayBelle's pen again and adding a note that we'd be across the hall. "MayBelle can join us when she can. She'll either get my phone message or see this when she's going out."

"I just hope the photos aren't still at Jorie's old house," I said as I opened the door.

"All of Jorie's things are out of the house," Fiera said, following me in. "It sold a month ago. She found your picture while unpacking boxes at her new apartment."

We walked down a short hallway to a cozy living room. A pair of tufted chairs flanked a table in front of a wide picture window framed by yellow-flowered curtains.

A comfortable-looking couch topped with a cozy green and yellow afghan graced the wall to the right. Across from the couch, a television took up a tasteful portion of the wall over a green-painted apothecary cabinet. I placed my bag on the coffee table by the couch and admired the framed photos of Jorie's family in San Diego. They looked so tan and happy by the beach. It pained me to think how much they must be hurting from her death.

"Jorie kept her photographs in here," Fiera said, opening up the doors to the apothecary chest. What had at first appeared to be dozens of little green drawers was in reality two large doors that opened to reveal a pair of long storage shelves.

Decorative boxes in a yellow and gray chevron pattern lined

ANGIE FOX

the shelves like a page out of a catalog. It was all rather cute. "Jorie's only been here a few weeks, but her place is better decorated than mine," I mused.

"All of this came from her house," Fiera said, making me feel slightly better. I'd lost everything and had to start over. Jorie had developed her taste over time. "But yes, she did have a knack for making things look nice." Fiera settled onto the floor in front of the cabinet. "The photos are in here," she said, sliding a box out.

It was empty.

"Well, in this one, then," she said, sliding out another as I settled on the plush carpet next to her. But the second box lay empty as well.

A small furrow appeared between Fiera's brows. "This is weird."

Together, we started pulling boxes.

Empty, empty. My stomach sank with each featherlight empty box.

"These had pictures in them," Fiera vowed. "I saw them quite recently."

"Here's a full one," I announced, welcoming the heft as I pulled out a box full of photographs.

Thank goodness.

"She could have sent a bunch to her family," I reasoned.

"She'd talked about doing that, but said she hadn't had the time yet," Fiera said, taking the first photos from the top of the box. "In fact, she asked me to help. Only we hadn't gotten around to it yet."

Fiera handed me a stack of photos. These were of Jorie's children growing up. I recognized her daughter Suzanne. She was a few years behind my mom in school.

"She always meant to put these in albums," Fiera said as we gently sifted through old school pictures, family picnics, birthday parties, and camping trips. Some of the prints had faded with time, the back of each neatly printed with the date in Jorie's scrolling hand.

"I'll put these aside for Suzanne," Fiera said when we'd finished.

"I almost feel bad for snooping." These were intimate family moments.

"Jorie wouldn't mind," Fiera said, sighing as she pulled out another empty box.

"Let's hope not," I said, disappointed when the rest of the boxes yielded only one more collection—this one filled with more recent photos of Jorie and her friends on various outings. I recognized Fiera and MayBelle, but my grandma wasn't with them. These must have all been taken after she'd died.

"I can't believe there are no wedding photos," I said, returning the boxes. "Does she have a wedding album somewhere?"

"She has to," Fiera said, not sounding optimistic at all.

We looked everywhere—in the bedroom dresser and under the bed, in every closet.

Jorie did have a framed photo of her and Ray standing in front of the Three Angels altar, with their daughter and a very young-looking Pastor Bob, but it had been taken well after their wedding day and didn't bear any resemblance to the photo she'd tried to give me.

I even tried the kitchen, which would be the last place I'd expect to find a keepsake wedding album.

"Jorie's daughter is coming in from San Diego the day after tomorrow to make arrangements," Fiera said as I stood empty-handed in the Spanish tiled kitchen. "She may know what happened to all of those pictures."

"I just can't believe this is it," I said. It didn't make sense. If Jorie had an envelope for me, if she had kept pressed flowers and a letter from my grandmother and a wedding picture, there had to be more. At least more wedding photos. "Are you sure there's nothing left in her old house?"

"She closed on it last week," Fiera said. "It's now occupied by Betty from the high school and her three kids."

"All I know is there have to be more pictures." The one she tried to give me was so random—bridesmaids outside the church. "She had to have saved others."

"I don't know what to tell you," Fiera said as we heard a knock at the door.

"Are you in here?" a woman's throaty voice called.

"MayBelle!" Fiera acknowledged, and we were soon greeted by a woman wearing a maxi dress and a long beaded necklace. A pair of cat-eye glasses perched on the top of her sleek black-haired bob. "Verity!" she announced as if I were on a game show.

MayBelle wrapped me into a hard hug that smelled like bergamot, saffron, and cigarettes. Just as quickly, she let me go. "Enough of that. How are you, dear?"

She raised a dark, heavily lined brow and regarded me like she expected an honest answer, which she probably did. From what I remembered of MayBelle Clemens, she wasn't the type to sugarcoat life.

She was a preacher's daughter. Born into a preaching family was more like it, one of the nine children of the original head of the Three Angels Church, the venerated Pastor Clemens. He'd had eight boys and MayBelle. Her brother Bob was the current retired Pastor Clemens. His son, Pastor Mike, ran things now.

You'd think with all the holy men in the family, MayBelle would be a proper lady. But she'd gone the opposite way. Rumor had it she'd even pierced her belly button. I personally think she enjoyed shocking people.

It didn't make her a favorite around our small Southern town, but at least with MayBelle a person knew where they stood.

"I'm upset about what happened to Jorie," I told her, putting it plain.

"It's criminal," she agreed, her strong features clouding. "I never would have left the fundraiser if I'd known she was in trouble." She said it as if she could have single-handedly defeated the killer.

Then again, maybe she could have.

"Why did you have to go?" I asked, curious.

"Poker game," MayBelle said.

"For real?" I asked.

"You said your joints were bothering you," Fiera countered.

MayBelle shrugged a bony shoulder. "Everything aches at this age. And if it gets me out of small talking with Virginia Wydell and her crowd, I'll take it."

Fiera rolled her eyes. "Figures you'd skip out."

MayBelle grinned. "I did my duty at the Three Angels. I gave my check. I said hi to Mike and a few of my friends. And I still made it to Lucky Joe's by one o'clock."

"Who's Lucky Joe?" I wondered.

"My bookie," she said.

Sure. Now I understood better why my grandmother had liked MayBelle in small doses. "While you were at the church, Jorie showed you the photograph and the letter she'd planned to give me—" I began.

"That's why I wanted to find you," MayBelle interrupted. "Jorie gave me a photograph as well." She grinned at my surprise. "Want to see it?"

"Yes," I said as she beckoned me to follow.

"Why didn't you tell me?" I asked Fiera.

"She didn't tell *me*," Fiera said, hurrying behind me.

"I was trying to get out of there," MayBelle stated as if that explained everything. "Now Fiera says your picture is missing. I wonder why."

"That's the million-dollar question." The answer could lead

me to Jorie's killer. "Do you remember who else saw the photo Jorie had for me?"

"I have no idea," she said, leading me across the hall. "But face it—it could have been anybody."

She was right.

And she didn't lock her door, either. She opened it right up and hustled us into an apartment I could only describe as classic Marilyn Monroe meets Southern charm. Colorful pots of glossy hibiscus accented a motley assortment of antique furniture. Her couch was rattan with white cushions. A gold chandelier hung above it all, dripping with party beads.

I stopped cold to stare. It all came together in an unexpected sort of way. It wasn't gaudy. It was simply a lot to take in.

Kind of like MayBelle.

"I'm eighty-three. I can live how I want," she said dryly.

"Yes," I said. Yes, she could. I almost tripped over the woven Indian rug laid over the already plush carpet.

"Here it is," she said, taking a gold-framed photo from an assortment on the coffee table.

MayBelle's photo bore a certain resemblance to the one Jorie had planned to give me. Only this one showed the full trio—my grandmother, Jorie, and MayBelle—on Jorie's wedding day, standing on the church steps, holding flowers, smiling as if they didn't have a care in the world.

"This is lovely." I sighed.

And I had no idea how it could mean anything to anyone other than us.

"Your grandma was a great lady. Kind, with a heart of gold and a streak of fire," MayBelle said, looking at the photo with me. She touched her throat where my grandma's necklace had hung all those years ago, and where it now graced my neck. "I see a lot of your grandma in you."

I looked up into her eyes, crinkled from smiling. "Thank you." It meant a lot for her to say that.

"I hear the good you've been doing," she added. "The Sugar-land grapevine isn't all bad."

"Even if it is all-knowing," I said, returning my attention to the photo. "We hit a dead end at Jorie's place. We came looking for wedding pictures, but most of Jorie's picture boxes were empty."

"Well, Fiera took three boxes last night," MayBelle said, glancing past me to where her friend stood looking at her phone.

"Oh." Fiera's cheeks reddened and she almost dropped her phone. "That was for the library," she said quickly. "There was nothing overly personal in there."

I would have thought she'd be too broken up to visit Jorie's apartment just hours after she died.

"Why didn't you mention it?" I asked. Just a few minutes earlier she'd stood there and wondered with me exactly where all the pictures could have gone.

"It's not as if Jorie gave them to you," MayBelle pointed out as if oblivious to the way Fiera had begun to fidget. "At least you returned those gray chevron boxes."

"It was nothing," Fiera insisted, stuffing her phone into her pocket. "Maybe a few letters now that I think about it. But nothing her family would have wanted." She'd turned pink at the ears. "Nothing that has anything to do with you, Verity," she was eager to add.

"Still, you were surprised to find less at Jorie's apartment than you expected," I said. "Were the other boxes full last night?"

"I don't know. I didn't look," she said, genuinely distressed. "It really was no big deal."

"All right," I said noncommittally. She'd better not be lying to me. My sister worked at the library, and I'd be double-checking her story.

MayBelle crossed her arms over her chest. "I think I know where the other things might have gone." The preacher's daughter had gone from friendly to lethal on a dime. I started to see why MayBelle liked poker. She had the temperament for it. "After Fiera left with her boxes last night, my dear nephew dropped by Jorie's apartment."

"Pastor Mike?" Fiera gasped.

"I watched him go in and I watched him go out," MayBelle said, fishing around in her pocket. "Jorie kept a bunch of pictures in an Amazon box under her bed. He snagged that and loaded up a box of his own. Took two trips."

Fiera appeared ready to faint. "Why didn't you stop him?"

"Why didn't I stop you?" she countered, fishing around in her other pocket and drawing out a small cigarette case. "He'd just try again, and I have to sleep sometime." She flipped the case open and selected a smoke. "Frankly, I wanted to see what he'd take."

"Do you have to do that now?" Fiera asked as if she couldn't endure one more thing.

"It's why I have a balcony," MayBelle said, drawing a silver lighter out of the pocket on the other side. "Now what else are you not telling your partner in crime, here?" she asked, drawing aside a pair of gauzy white curtains to reveal a set of French doors.

"There is no crime. I'm just trying to help Verity recover what she lost," Fiera said. I didn't miss the tension in her voice.

"Um-hum," MayBelle said, stepping outside.

I was no fan of cigarettes. In fact, I was glad Frankie's smoke was ghostly. But the balcony could have been burning down at that point, and I'd have still wanted to go out there.

"Got room for one more?" I asked, parting the billowing curtains.

MayBelle was brutal on the cross-examination and seemed to be holding all the cards. She could be bluffing, but I didn't think so. I wanted to learn her angle and why she'd thrown her friend and her nephew under the bus.

She eyed me as she took a drag, and I'm not sure if it surprised her when I closed the door behind me.

I liked Fiera, but she'd just proven she wasn't always going to tell me the truth. And I wondered what Fiera had taken that was worth lying about.

The small balcony stood high enough to catch quite a breeze, but luckily the wind blew away from me as MayBelle took another long drag.

I leaned against the rail. "Tell me more about the photographs in those Amazon boxes."

She cocked her head slightly as if she liked the question. Smoke curled out of her nose. "They were some of Jorie's oldest, most cherished pictures. My nephew had no business taking them." She glanced at the French doors. "And I was just trying to get Fiera's goat in there. I did ask Mike what in Hades he was doing." She took another drag. "He said Jorie had left them to my brother Bob."

The second Pastor Clemens.

I nodded, trying not to cough on the smoke. I'd be paying a visit to both Pastor Mike and Pastor Bob. "Do you know where Pastor Bob is living these days?"

She flicked the ash of her cigarette over the balcony and sent it tumbling down. "My brother lives three doors down from me." She cocked her cigarette and seemed greatly amused at my surprise. "This is a great building."

"I love the painted glass ceiling downstairs," I confessed. "And this balcony." You could see the entire town square.

"I thought I'd see more of my brother when he moved in. But Bob likes to read all day. Not my style."

"There are a lot of great restaurants around here," I suggested.

She twisted her lips ruefully. "Mike visits Bob every night." She took another drag. "They either go out to dinner, or Mike brings it up. Or so I hear. They never invite me."

"Well, maybe it's boy bonding time," I tried to reason.

She tried to smile and failed. "You are a sweet one. So was Jorie." Her expression hardened. "Want to go on down the hall and talk to my brother? See what his son stole?"

"I don't think we should say it to him that way," I began.

"That's why I'll get you in there, and you can ask the questions," she said, a little too calculating for my taste. "People actually like you."

"I like you," I told her. Sure, she was as subtle as a cattle prod, but she wanted what was best for her friend, and I had to admire that.

"Oh, darling. You warm my heart," she said, stubbing out her cigarette on the balcony rail. "Now come on. You came all this way for answers. Let's go get you some."

Chapter Twelve

❦

"**O**ut you go," MayBelle said to Fiera, ushering her toward the front door ahead of us. "I'm stealing Verity."

"What were you two talking about out on the balcony?" Fiera glanced over her shoulder, unhappy, but moving. "You know I don't like smoke."

She directed that last accusation at me as if I'd been lighting up alongside her friend.

"Verity and I are going to pay a visit to my brother Bob. And I'm sorry, but you know he can only handle one or two people at a time."

Fiera softened at the mention of Pastor Bob. "How is he?" she asked once we were all out in the hall. MayBelle fished a key out of her pocket.

"Bob's doing better every day," MayBelle said. "He'll never have full movement on his left side after the stroke, and his arthritis isn't doing him any favors, but he's hanging in there."

"I'm glad to hear it," Fiera said.

MayBelle locked her apartment door and then tested the handle. Very unusual for Sugarland.

She truly was a rebel.

Or perhaps she was worried someone might try to make off with her photograph of Jorie's wedding.

"Thanks for showing me Jorie's apartment," I told Fiera as we said our goodbyes. She might have kept some secrets from me, but at least she'd gotten me up here.

And in a position to investigate.

Once we had Fiera heading toward the elevators, MayBelle led me down the hall farther from the elevator to a door with a lovely painted clay cross hanging under the peephole. To my surprise, she knocked softly on the door.

"Bob rests a lot during the day," she said, the corner of her mouth turning up. "These days, he can hardly open a book without napping."

She pushed the door open and led us down a short hall lined with family portraits into a cozy living room. Bob sat in a recliner by the window with a thick hardcover book on his lap. He held up a finger as if he couldn't quite tear himself away until he finished.

Pastor Bob looked older than when I'd seen him last, his mostly bald head mottled with sunspots, his arms thinner, and his face more lined.

Bookcases lined the wall to the right, broken only by a wooden writing desk. Bob clearly didn't entertain a lot. The man didn't even own a couch.

He shoved his black-framed glasses from where they'd slipped down his nose as he drew a thick green ribbon over his place and gently closed the book.

"Why, Verity Long," he drawled like a proud grandfather, "is that you?"

"Don't get up," I said as he struggled to stand. I sank onto the kitchen chair next to him and folded his hand in mine. "It's wonderful to see you."

He'd been one of my grandmother's favorite pastors.

He squeezed my hand gently. His skin felt chilly, but his grip was warm. "Did you know I conducted the wedding ceremony for your mamma and daddy?" he asked as if I were still a child.

"I see you every time I open their wedding album," I said, smiling.

He pinkened with pride. "How is your mother?" he asked knowingly. Nobody in Sugarland understood why she'd left town to travel the country in an RV with my stepfather when everything you could ever want was right here.

"She's wintering in Galveston, Texas," I said. "So far. They're talking about heading to California."

"At least she's married again," he said as if that were the goal in life. His gaze went to the table next to us, crowded with wedding pictures and family portraits in tasteful frames. One stood out from the rest—a colorfully framed photo of a younger MayBelle climbing Machu Picchu.

"I figured he needed one of me in there somewhere," MayBelle said dryly, noticing where my attention had gone. She'd dragged another chair in from the kitchen and set it in front of the bookcase, next to mine.

"You could still get married," Bob reminded her, subtle as a sledgehammer.

"If I did that, it wouldn't be long before Verity had to solve another murder," MayBelle countered, taking a seat.

Still, I noticed MayBelle treated him gentler than she did most people.

Bob shook his head and folded his hands in his lap. "You need to trade in that red convertible. It gives men the wrong message."

"You don't know what kind of message I want to send," she said, waggling her brows. Teasing. Or heck, she could be telling the truth. It was hard to tell with her. Before I figured it out, she changed the subject. "Bob, you know Jorie Davis died at the church yesterday."

The lines around his mouth deepened. "I'm arthritic, not forgetful." Then, remembering his place, he added, "Such a terrible loss."

MayBelle planted her elbows on top of her thighs and leaned in closer. "Here's the thing—I saw Mike go in and take a few boxes of Jorie's keepsakes last night. Do you know anything about it?"

Pastor Bob moved the book of reflections off his lap and propped it next to his chair. "Why don't you ask Mike?" he asked, getting defensive.

MayBelle shot him a rueful look. "Because I'm not sure he'll tell me, and I know you never lie."

Bob glanced at me, then back to his sister. "There's nothing to lie about," he finally said. "After the accident, Mike called Jorie's daughter and offered his support. She was in need spiritually, you understand." He folded his hands in his lap. "He asked if he could possibly do anything for her, and she said she needed him to secure a few mementos. She hasn't been back to Sugarland in a long while and didn't know who else to ask."

I felt terrible hearing that. "I should have called."

"You still can," he reminded me. "Of course, Mike was more than willing to hold a few things for her. It seems Jorie never locked her doors."

"It seems that way," I agreed.

MayBelle huffed at me like I was giving her nephew an easy out.

Well, she did say I was the nicer one.

I'd have to stop by the church and see if Pastor Mike told the same story. While I had him, I'd ask if any of those mementos included Jorie's wedding photos.

"Mike also brought over something for me," Bob said, pointing to a large frame leaning against the opposite wall near a thriving schefflera plant. "Go get it, MayBelle."

"Let me," I said, popping up before either of them could tell me not to. I hefted the fairly awkward and surprisingly heavy frame, noting Jorie's handwriting on a piece of masking tape affixed to the back. It read *Pastor Bob.*

At least this one item from Jorie's house had ended up in the right place.

"She always wanted me to have that picture of the angel altar installation," he said as I turned the frame to admire the photo. It had been taken in artful black and white, or maybe it was just old. The photo captured the shadows and the light of the carving, like an Ansel Adams portrait.

"It's beautiful," I said, unable to take my eyes off it.

Hand-printed script at the bottom read *1939 Three Angels of the Tabernacle Blessed Reform Church of Sugarland.*

"Before that, the church was simply called the Reform Church of Sugarland," Bob said, gazing fondly at the photo.

I hadn't realized I'd read the inscription out loud.

"Mike is going to hang it over my bed for me. My father commissioned that installation when I was a boy." I could hear the pride in his voice. "He said it was so angels would watch over me when I took over as pastor."

"When was that?" I asked, placing the piece in his outstretched hands.

He admired the altar. "The workers started it in 1938," he said, handing over the frame to MayBelle as his elbows sagged with the weight. "He brought in three well-known artists all the way from Munich, Germany. It took them almost a year to carve the full altar. They also carved a lectern as a gift to my father when they saw all the charitable work he did for the people of Sugarland."

"Run for the hills. He's in sermon mode," MayBelle joked.

"Get the blue album off the bookshelf," he said to his sister.

She did and he opened it onto his lap. "Scoot up," he told me. "Now you have to realize how hard life was back then. The depression had worn the town down. Lots of people were worried where their next meal might come from or how they'd pay the bills. My dad set up a fund to pay for mortgages, groceries..." He turned pages until he found the spread he was looking for. "Here," he said, a crooked finger pointing to a black-and-white photo of an enormous hall filled with tables. "My dad borrowed a spot of land from the mayor just west of the town square. He hired local men to build a town kitchen, and paid all the wages himself. That kitchen fed hundreds of families, no matter what their background or religion. My dad made sure we took care of our neighbors in Sugarland."

"How wonderful." It was town legend, in fact. It made me so proud to be a part of this place. "My grandma told me her mother worked in one of the kitchens."

"People needed jobs back then," Bob said. "Our legendary town reporter Howard Dupre supported his sick father and his two brothers by delivering meals and Bibles for shut-ins after school. And when dad saw Howard had a knack for taking pictures and telling stories, he bought him his first camera and tasked him with reporting on the church's benevolent works for posterity."

"I've met his son." Ovis Dupre was the most dogged reporter in Sugarland and a legend in his own right.

"Ovis is a generous donor to our church," Pastor Bob said. "He helps us get press coverage for our charitable works and lends a hand with pictures, just like his father did."

I had to smile. Ovis had too many questions early on about my ghost hunting, but he was a good person.

"I'm so glad we had men like your father to see us through the tough times," I told Pastor Bob.

I had a feeling it was part of the reason why the Sugarland Heritage Society worked so hard to support the Three Angels Church and keep it open for future generations. It was a living part of our history, the Clemens men included.

"Regarding the church itself," I began, wishing for an easier way to ask my next question. "Has there ever been trouble on the grounds itself?"

"I beg your pardon?" Bob asked, clearly not getting it.

"Any tragic incidents?" I pressed.

"I hardly think so." Pastor Bob appeared surprised at the question. "Unless you count the shrinking congregation." He shook his head slowly. "You should have seen it in the old days. In fact…" He turned to MayBelle. "Would you fetch me the green albums from the bottom row of the bookshelf?"

We spent the next several hours looking at the way things used to be, when the congregation had been large and vibrant.

A soft knock sounded at the door. "You awake, Dad?"

"My favorite son," Bob announced, giddy with talk of his family's history.

Pastor Mike walked in carrying a toolbox in one hand and a bag of takeout in the other, clearly surprised to see me and MayBelle.

"Looks like a party," he said, stopping to deposit his things in the kitchen. The scent of garlic, basil, and oregano made me realize I'd skipped lunch.

"Italian?" I asked.

"It *is* Thursday," Bob said as if that settled it.

"We were just looking at some of the neat things your grandfather did for Sugarland," I told the younger pastor.

"And Verity knows you took the boxes of photos from Jorie's apartment," MayBelle said, forgoing all tact.

Pastor Mike paused.

"Jorie wanted to give me a picture from her wedding because it had my grandmother in it," I quickly explained, keeping it deliberately vague. I'd see how much he knew of the incident later. "I've been trying to track it down."

"Of course," Pastor Mike said, recovering quickly, touching a hand to his chin. "You're more than welcome to come by the church tomorrow and see what I have from Jorie's. The boxes I

ANGIE FOX

have are promised to her daughter in San Diego, but if you find a picture you'd like, I'm sure we could have a copy made."

"Thank you," I said. Hopefully, there would be one similar.

"Fiera also took several boxes from Jorie's," MayBelle said bluntly.

Pastor Mike blanched. "I wasn't aware," he said, rubbing a few fingers along his chin, clearly uncomfortable. "I'll be sure to let her daughter know."

"Well, that's all I've got to say. We're out of here," MayBelle said, standing.

"Wait. I haven't shown Verity the pictures of Grace Park," Bob said, flipping pages in the album. "My father bought the land from a widowed farm wife who needed the money, and he hired people who needed jobs to build and landscape a lovely park for the whole town to enjoy."

"In the middle of farmland," MayBelle added. "It's great, Bob, but we have to go."

"I enjoyed visiting with you," I told him as he reached out a hand.

He gave me a squeeze. "You're such a lovely young lady. You're welcome anytime."

"I'll be praying for you," he added as I said a quick goodbye to his son Mike before MayBelle practically dragged me out the door.

"What was that about?" I whispered after she'd closed the door firmly behind us.

She didn't say a word. She just strode down the hall toward her place and beckoned me to follow. I had to rush to keep up with her. "He's lying," she stated as if it were a stone-cold fact.

"About what? You said he had pictures. He says he has pictures. This is good. It all adds up." We were learning things.

She dug the key out of her pocket and inserted it into the lock. "Trust me, Mike is lying about something," she said, glancing down the hall toward her brother's apartment.

"How do you know? We barely saw him."

She shoved the door open. "The same reason I love playing poker with him," she said, leading me inside. "He's had the same tell since he was a kid."

I leaned against the door at my back, trying to think. "But wait. Both things he said were truthful. He had pictures, and he brought dinner." He hadn't said anything else.

"He rubbed his chin the whole time. There's something he isn't telling us."

"Perhaps he knew about Fiera's pilfering and lied about that," I suggested, trying to think.

"But what would that solve?" MayBelle asked, frowning. "I wonder if he's really doing a favor for Jorie's daughter."

It would be easy enough to prove or disprove. I'd just ask her at the funeral. "I doubt he'd have told Pastor Bob if he were hiding anything."

It could be Pastor Mike was pretending to be glad to see me and his sister crashing the start of a boys' dinner.

MayBelle's face fell, and I wondered if she'd come to the same conclusion.

"I appreciate you taking me down there," I told her. "And letting me know what you saw. You've helped me a lot."

"I'm helping Jorie," she corrected as I went to retrieve my own keys. "Call me if you need me," she said as I left her and Park Manor.

Before I drove home, I walked over to the library to see my sister, Melody. She worked full time now at the historic building with a rusting iron Civil War cannonball still embedded in the white limestone near the foundation.

On the way, I checked my cell phone and saw Lauralee had called only twenty minutes before. I quickly dialed her back.

"Verity," she answered, out of breath, her words coming in a rush, "I'm so sorry I couldn't call back last night. I only heard about Jorie this morning. How are you doing?"

"I could ask the same about you." She sounded like she was running on coffee and adrenaline.

"I'm just tossing in a load of sheets while Hiram has a Popsicle. We were up all night, so I hope he sleeps some today."

"Poor thing." Hiram was her second oldest and the mamma's boy. "I won't bother you," I told her. "I was just upset about a fight I had with Ellis."

"I heard about that too," she said reluctantly. "Tell me about it," she urged. "I've got time."

That was a fib, but I appreciated it all the same.

I waved to a truck that had stopped to let me cross the street to the town square and hurried to fill Lauralee in. My stomach churned when I told her what Ellis had said last night about me changing too much for him. It figured that would happen right about the time I started to feel like I was getting the hang of it all.

"Why does he want me to quit ghost hunting?" I asked, entering the town square. "I'm good at this," I added, crossing the broad expanse of green grass, veering south toward the library. "I like what I do; plus it's important. People evolve. I'm evolving in a positive way."

"You are," she agreed. "But you need to invite Ellis along for the ride. If you're in a relationship, that means talking to the guy," she said pragmatically. "You can't just spring things on him."

"What happened to you blindly being on my side?" I joked.

"I'm always on your side," she vowed. "But it sounds like you shocked him a few times, and knowing Ellis, that's not going to go over well. You need to talk about it."

I let that sink in while Hiram asked for another Popsicle. I heard her murmuring to him and digging for a grape-flavored one.

Had I shocked Ellis? Perhaps.

Yes.

But I'd expected him to understand.

"Verity," she said when I hadn't spoken, "you can't just do what you want and apologize later."

Why not? "It works for Frankie."

"Didn't he get shot in the head?" she asked innocently.

"Well, when you put it that way..." I stopped outside the library, not quite ready to end the call. Lauralee's perspective had been refreshing, yet difficult to hear. And I didn't relish what I might have to do next. "Talking to Ellis about this is going to be hard for me," I admitted. Usually, I'd be the first person to stress the importance of communication, but that was when I felt confident my ideas would be well received. "Ellis is one of the most important people in my life. What if our talk goes badly?"

She paused.

Oh no. Lauralee thought it was about to go off the rails, too. "What? Tell me."

"Relax," she coaxed. "I was only wishing I could give you a hug."

I ran a hand through my hair, feeling fidgety. "Can't you just tell me I'm right and we can be done with this?"

She chuckled and I heard her son snuggling up to her in the background. "You are wise and wonderful, and he's lucky to have you," she said to me. "But if you're always looking to be right, you're going to have to make him wrong."

Dang. "I hadn't thought of it like that."

"Why don't you try to find a way through this together? Trust me, it's better than being right."

I let her get back to Hiram. She had a point. I would have to talk to Ellis, never mind that it was hard. I'd try to involve him even if I'd rather do things my own way.

I sighed, thankful to have a friend like Lauralee, someone who knew me so well and was always there for me. Had it been this way for Jorie and my grandmother? Maybe someday in the

ANGIE FOX

far-off future, Lauralee would be giving a dried wedding flower to my daughter.

That thought made me smile as I approached the red limestone columns flanking the entrance to the library. The door itself resembled something out of a medieval castle. I pushed it open and was rewarded with the heady scent of old books.

I continued into the main room, past the displays of spring craft books and Southern mysteries. I wound my way through the expansive reading room off the lobby and spotted my sister at the desk. She wore her blond hair up in the kind of loose, twisty French braid that I'd only seen in magazines and on her. She'd tucked a pink flower pen behind her ear and managed to appear both studious and charming at the same time.

She ducked around the desk and met me halfway, treating me to a sisterly embrace while giving a short tug on my hair, the same as she did when we were growing up.

"I knew it. I knew you were going to be by today," she said, pulling back.

"You heard about my fight with Ellis?" I asked.

"Yes." Her blue eyes clouded. "And there's more. I swear to heaven your ghost has been calling me all day."

"Frankie?" But that was impossible. "He can't talk to you."

"I think he figured out how to call," she said, beckoning me toward one of the research rooms lining the back wall. The library had four in total, all with thick wooden doors and old-fashioned windows overlooking the courtyard below. "My phone's been ringing all day, and when I answer, I get crazy static."

That was a new one, even for Frankie.

"I think he's looking for you."

I did leave without telling him where I was going, but it wasn't as if I owed him an explanation. We weren't due to set off on another manhunt this morning.

I'd deal with him later.

146

"Look, I was at the church when Jorie died yesterday," I told her, watching her expression fall.

"I heard about that as well." Because the Sugarland grapevine was more like a bullhorn. "What a terrible accident."

"I'm not sure it was an accident. There's something strange at that church—on the ghostly side," I said as I followed her into the nearest research room. "I think it's bleeding into the experience of live people who are on the property. And the ghosts don't seem too happy, either. Will you see if you can find any tragedy or traumatic event that happened at or near the church?"

"I'm on it," she said without a moment's hesitation. "Although, you'd think the kind of terrible event you're describing would be common knowledge."

"Agreed." But if anyone could find it, Melody could. "You should know that isn't the only thing that seems strange about Jorie's death."

I told her everything that had happened, including Fiera's insistence that she'd acquired Jorie's treasured memories for the library.

Melody frowned. "Why would we want Jorie's pictures?"

"Historic display?" I asked.

She thought about that. "We're putting together a Sugarland celebrations exhibit for Memorial Day. I'll ask what Fiera brought in and if you can see it."

"I need to see it," I insisted.

Melody smiled. "Well, then we'll ask first so we'll know if you need to sneak."

That was my sister. She understood you had to bend the rules sometimes.

I let her get back to work and headed home. I had an inexplicable craving for Italian food, so I stopped by La Cozza Infuriata on Main Street for a plate of spaghetti and garlic bread to go. I made small talk with the owner's son until my order came up, then headed home, eager for a delicious and well-deserved break. But as I steered up my front drive, I instead found a ghost standing stiff-backed in the driveway. Frankie was waiting for me.

And he was ticked.

Chapter Thirteen

✦✦✦

"You left," Frankie accused, sticking his head through my window before I had a chance to roll it down. "You said you'd help me hunt down my no-good brother, and you took off instead."

"Hop in," I told him, not exactly thrilled to be having a come-to-Jesus with a cranky gangster in the middle of my driveway.

He shimmered into being in my passenger seat, arms crossed, giving me the scat eye like he expected an answer.

"I was investigating Jorie's death," I said, pulling the car around the side of the house. Rocks crunched under my tires as my car trundled over the uneven drive.

"What about *my* death?" Frankie countered. "I've been dead longer than Jorie."

It wasn't a contest.

"What happened today?" Something had him all worked up. "Did you learn something new?"

"No," he admitted. "But I have an idea."

"Heaven help us."

"I have a lead on Lou. We need to sneak over to the movie theater."

"All right." I stopped the car in front of the rosebushes out back. "The closest movie plex is the AMC off the highway."

"I'm not talking about your version of a movie theater," he said as if I'd lost my marbles. "I'm talking about mine. And this," he added, spreading his hands and looking at my lovely backyard, "this is not the way to get there."

"Is the movie theater burning down?"

"No," he answered sullenly.

"Then we'll go in a bit," I promised. "As soon as possible," I added at his frown. "I need to eat and tend to Lucy first." The skunk would be expecting her dinner too and, at the very least, a quick jaunt around the backyard.

"Lucy's been squirrely all day," he grumbled, trailing me up the back steps.

"Have you been pacing in my house?" When Frankie got agitated, he'd been known to wear a path in front of his urn and the parlor fireplace. Poor Lucy liked to sleep on the couch right across from it, but it would be impossible for her to relax if my ghost had been carrying on.

"It's my house too," Frankie said, rubbing a hand over his neck, pretending he didn't feel guilty about bothering Lucy.

I loved that he cared, although he'd be mortified if I pointed it out.

"Won't take but a minute," I promised, opening the door to an overjoyed skunk. "Lucy!" I crouched to greet her.

She took one look at Frankie, and that was it. She turned tail and dashed away down the side hall.

I sighed.

"It's not my fault she doesn't like me," Frankie said defensively.

I glanced up at the ghost. "That's true. You've been nothing but sweet to her." In the seconds before she would flee.

While the gruff gangster held a soft spot for animals, this particular skunk wanted nothing to do with him. "Why don't you rest in your shed, and I'll come get you when I'm ready?" Ellis had built him a perfectly wonderful place of his own next to the pond.

"Oh, no," Frankie said as if I were up to something nefarious in my kitchen. "I'm keeping an eye on you until we leave."

"Suit yourself." I grabbed some carrots from the fridge, along with some fresh green beans I'd snapped yesterday and some cooked brown rice that would go nicely.

Frankie blanched as I added it all to the pan. "This isn't Thanksgiving, you know. I'd like to get out of here before breakfast."

Please. If anything, it had started to resemble Chinese take-out. "I'll only be a minute," I said, sautéing the vegetables in a bit of olive oil. Skunks liked to eat a variety of foods, and the virgin olive oil would give Lucy a beautiful, shiny coat. I'd add the rice in after. "I can easily take care of you both."

"Now you're comparing me to a skunk," he gruffed, reaching into his suit pocket for his revolver and checking the bullets.

"Never." Lucy was far better behaved. "You prepare that. I'll prepare this," I said, adding some rotisserie chicken thigh I had left over from a couple nights earlier. Lucy preferred dark meat.

"My pre-manhunt routine is not the same as you cooking a skunk dinner."

It wasn't all that different, either.

"So who are we hunting down at the theater?" I asked, noticing Lucy as she poked her head into the kitchen to see what I had cooking.

"We're intercepting Wally Big Ears," Frankie said, replacing the revolver in his side holster and going for the gun in the back of his pants.

"I hope that's not his real name." My stomach grumbled at the savory smell of sautéed vegetables.

"Might as well be." Frankie shrugged. "The guy knows things."

"Well," I said, giving Lucy's dinner a stir, "I'm looking forward to meeting him." Meanwhile, Lucy took a few more steps into the kitchen, waving her tail back and forth like a barometer of her emotions. Dinner was exciting for skunks, even if she had to share the room with Frankie to get it.

"I'm glad you said that," Frankie said, nudging his suit jacket aside and planting his hands on his hips. "Because you're the one who needs to get Big Ears to talk."

I almost dropped my spoon. "Why me?"

Frankie's shoulders stiffened. "Due to an unfortunate incident where I happened to shoot him in the crotch, he doesn't like me much."

"Frankie!" I admonished.

"He was already dead at the time," he muttered, as if that made a difference.

"You need to work on your people skills," I said, spooning Lucy's dinner into her bowl.

"Yeah, I'm ranking that right up there with my dream to be a prima ballerina."

"I'm not sure I know where to begin questioning a gangster," I said, carrying Lucy's dinner to where she stood dancing in place at the edge of the kitchen. "Free delivery," I told her, letting her keep her distance from the ghost.

"It'll be easy," Frankie assured me. "You just need to find out what Wally Big Ears knows about Lou's whereabouts. And you have to remember that my entire mental state rides on you making it work."

"Sure." No pressure there.

"That's the spirit," Frankie said. "Now, do you have a bullet-proof vest?"

"No." I gaped at him. "Is there something you're not telling me?"

"Nah!" Frankie waved me off a little too vigorously for my

taste. "It'll be great." He shrugged. "It just occurred to me last night at the speakeasy how fragile you living can be."

I popped the lid on my carry-out spaghetti. "I take it to mean you didn't think about my fragile human self the time you ticked off that dead hit man, or the time we snuck into that creepy ghostly animal exhibit? I mean, that snake was huge."

"Steve." Frankie nodded.

"What?"

"The snake's name was Steve," he said.

"Whatever."

"Now who doesn't care about animals?"

"Have you been listening to anything I've said?" I asked, dipping my garlic bread in red sauce. Truly, the ghost was infuriating.

"Look, you're going to be fine," he concluded. "I shouldn't have said anything. Now keep eating or we're going to be standing around the kitchen all night yacking."

He didn't have to tell me twice. The pasta hit the spot. After I ate, I refreshed my lipstick, put my hair in a ponytail, and was ready to go.

"Any day now," Frankie said as I let Lucy out into the yard. She scrambled past the ghost and made a beeline for her favorite apple tree by the pond.

"I'm ready," I said as my house phone rang. "Just a second."

"Argh!" The gangster threw his hands up while I rushed to the avocado green wall phone.

"Ellis! I'm glad you caught me," I said, ignoring Frankie's wide-eyed stare. He could wait. Wally Big Ears wasn't going anywhere in the next two minutes. Meanwhile, my stomach knotted as I considered how to put Lauralee's advice to work.

"Heading out?" Ellis asked.

"Hmm…" I said, trying to figure out how to put it. "I'm doing a favor for Frankie." That sounded safe enough. Ellis knew how demanding Frankie could be.

"Where are you going tonight, Verity?" Ellis pressed.

I took a breath and answered him truthfully. "A haunted theater."

"The AMC multiplex?" he asked, surprised.

"No. I'm not sure where this one is." For all I knew, it could be an abandoned property.

"You'd better not be breaking in anywhere," my boyfriend warned. "I'm on duty tonight."

Dang. I wound the phone cord around my arm. "That was last night," I said before I lost my courage. "But everything worked out," I added quickly while he swore under his breath.

Then I told him everything about the speakeasy and the holdup and how well it had all gone.

"Verity," he said. There was no mistaking that tone.

"I'm trying to be honest." Although, I did leave out the part about promising a date to the bartender.

"You're losing your mind," Ellis declared.

This was not at all the love and support I'd hoped to get out of this conversation. "Maybe I'm changing," I informed him, pacing the kitchen, unwinding the cord as I went. "If that's what you want me to say, I'll say it. But I like who I'm becoming. And I like you, so I hope you'll be able to like the person I'm becoming, too. Lauralee says I need to invite you along for the ride."

"Straight off a cliff?" he barked. "No thanks."

"Are you even listening to me?" I demanded, stopping short of the kitchen island. I took a deep breath. *Calm down.* "I'm supporting my friends," I said, keeping my tone sweet, yet unyielding, "the same as I did before I was a ghost hunter. Only now, some of my friends happen to be dead."

Frankie waved at me from the door. "I'd be more supported if you'd get off the phone."

But I was on a roll. "Maybe if you joined us for another ghost hunt, you'd see that."

"You're really doubling down on this," Ellis said as if I'd told him I was off to join the circus.

"I'm simply asking you to try to understand." Was that so hard? "Be the man who knows everything about me and loves me anyway."

I held my breath, waiting for his response.

"You're starting to take risks like Frankie," he said guardedly.

Hardly.

I glanced at the ghost, who was busy polishing his brass knuckles with his suit jacket.

"It's a slippery slope," Ellis added.

"Indeed," I said woodenly.

I didn't know what else to say to get through to him. I didn't have a lot of practice baring my soul, but I'd tried my best.

"A year ago, you never would have held up a bartender," Ellis said, still stuck on that.

"I'm being open with you, and you're using that to twist everything around," I said, working to keep a hold on my temper.

"I'd better not have to arrest you tonight."

"You wouldn't," I assured him, and myself, feeling my pulse pick up.

"I would," he warned.

"What a terrible thing to say," I choked.

"I'm only being honest," he said, turning my words around on me.

"No boyfriend of mine would arrest me," I said, refusing to give credit to his threat.

"No girlfriend of mine would act like a criminal," he stated. "Think about what you're doing," he urged, leaving me speechless as he hung up.

"I can't believe that just happened," I said, staring at the phone.

Frankie winced and held his hands out. "He's a guy," he said, by way of explanation.

"What does that have to do with anything?" I asked, unwilling to let go of the phone.

"Guys say stupid things," Frankie reasoned. "I do it all the time. Just ask Molly."

Yes, well, Ellis wasn't one to make idle threats. I really could lose him over this.

"Are you ready to go now?" Frankie pressed.

"I am," I said, still shaken. Regardless of what Ellis had said, Frankie and I still had a job to do. My housemate's entire after-life could depend on finding his brother and reconciling his death. I wasn't about to sacrifice that just because Ellis didn't understand.

"Verity?" Frankie prodded.

The phone began beeping, and I realized I still hadn't hung up on my end.

"I'm okay," I said, replacing the phone in its cradle. "Let's go."

I could do nothing more about Ellis tonight. Except pray that I didn't run into him.

Chapter Fourteen

"So are we going to have to break in anywhere tonight?" I asked, steering the land yacht away from the house.

All things being equal, I'd rather not be arrested by my boyfriend.

Frankie sat with his arms folded over his chest, brooding. It wasn't my fault it had taken thirty minutes to dig Lucy out from under the porch before we left.

I didn't want her wandering outside after dark.

"How am I supposed to know when the theater building is open?" the ghost snipped. "Or what's there now?"

Oh, please. "Perhaps you could—I don't know—pay attention? You've been hanging around Sugarland for about a century."

"Doesn't mean I've been to the movies lately," Frankie countered, slinking down in his seat.

"Well, it might be nice to take Molly sometime," I suggested.

"I do fine with Molly," he retorted.

Probably because he didn't show her that attitude. I changed the subject. "What do I need to know about Wally Big Ears?"

That perked him up. "Technically, Wally is affiliated with the

Irish mob," Frankie said as if it were a major liability. "However, he's not beholden to them anymore."

I'd had no idea mob life could be so complicated. "Why's that?"

Frankie shrugged. "He seems to be leveraging his information well."

"Interesting guy," I mused.

We trundled past a series of tidy bungalows that lined the road on what had once been my family's land. A parked car flipped on its headlights and pulled out behind us.

"Head downtown," Frankie ordered. He leaned back, making himself comfortable. "You see, Wally deals in information. It gives him the freedom to do what he wants. And it allows him to make a very comfortable living."

Wait. "Are we going to have to bribe him?" I asked, glancing at my ghost. Frankie and I never discussed his financial situation, but I definitely didn't want a repeat of last night's holdup.

Perhaps Ellis was right—to a degree. This could be getting out of hand.

"No bribes," Frankie said, waving me off. "I don't have enough money. And even if I did, you're the one talking for me. It's not like I could hand you a suitcase of cash to do my business."

"Wally wouldn't be happy if it disappeared," I agreed.

"Instead, you're going to charm him," Frankie concluded. "You know, like you do with all the ghosts."

"Like I do with you," I scoffed. Amazing how he just expected me to turn it on.

"I'm immune," he said. "Frankly, I don't get your appeal at all."

"This is a heck of a pep talk," I said, turning left onto the road leading to the highway. The car behind me followed.

His brights flashed in my rearview mirror. Most of my

neighbors were more courteous. And they usually didn't follow so close.

I didn't find it terribly concerning, not really. Okay, maybe it set off a few bells. But still, it was perfectly logical for a driver to want to take the highway.

"Why are you getting squirrely?" Frankie asked, eyes narrowing.

"There's a car on our tail. It's probably nothing."

"Speed up," he ordered.

"I—" I hesitated.

"Try it," he coaxed. "I'm curious."

He was the gangster. A true expert in being followed and getting away.

I hit the gas and switched lanes.

The car behind me lurched into my new lane and sped up to catch me.

"Holy smokes." I gripped the wheel tighter.

Frankie grinned. "Oh, he wants to play."

"No. I don't care if he wants to play. I don't want to play. Not even a little," I said, trying to discern what kind of car it was. I could only make out headlights and a big dark shadow. The lights sat too wide to be Ellis's police cruiser. I knew that for a fact. Ellis had pulled me over more times than I could count.

Frankie braced a hand on the bench seat and twisted to look behind us. "Gun it," he ordered.

"I don't like to speed," I warned, hitting the gas.

Our tail easily closed the gap between us. He was definitely following us.

Ellis's Jeep sat too high. These lights were low. Maybe a sports car? I didn't know who it could be. I mean, I'd been making progress on Jorie's case, but I still had a lot to learn. I couldn't have caught anybody's attention yet.

Or had I discovered the key to the mystery and I just didn't know it?

Think.

If Fiera wanted to get me, she'd show up under the guise of friendship and I'd let her right into my kitchen. Same with MayBelle.

I really had to rethink my open-door policy.

Pastor Bob couldn't walk well, so it was hard to imagine him speeding around in a low-profile car. Although the man who had almost killed me last year boasted a similar alibi.

Pastor Mike was having me over tomorrow, so he could have simply waited for me to come to him.

It didn't make sense.

"That's not a ghost car back there," I said, voice shaking.

"That's a real one," Frankie agreed, with way too much relish. "Pull off here."

I did. I didn't even question it. Frankie had been in more car chases than I could count, and he was a seasoned killer to boot. He knew how they thought. How they stalked their prey. "Why are we pulling off the highway?" I asked, taking the exit that led onto a darkened road.

"This is the way to the theater," Frankie said as if it were obvious.

"What?" I choked. He was right. We were headed directly toward town. "Why on earth would we want to lead them to the very place we're going?"

"Town is crowded. We'll do fine," Frankie insisted. "Plus, there's no way I'm letting you stall again."

Oh, for Pete's sake. "For your information, downtown clears out after dinner."

"Huh," he said, surprised. "The dead are out all the time."

"You're putting me in danger," I insisted as the road opened up onto the beginnings of Main Street.

"You missed a stop sign," Frankie said as we whizzed past.

"So now you care about the law," I said, wincing. My stomach dropped when the car behind me blew past the sign as well. "I need to drive straight to the police station," I vowed. "I need to park outside and call Ellis."

"Oh, yeah, because that's the way to convince him ghost hunting is a swell idea," Frankie shot back.

"Well, it's better than getting hurt." I'd told the truth when I said I didn't take unnecessary chances. I wasn't going to stand on principle or my pride.

We were coming up on the library and town square. I must have taken more time than I'd realized with Lucy because it was all dark. Closed.

Not good.

I was just about to make the turn onto Fifth Street and toward the police station, manhunt be damned, when the car behind me pulled out into the oncoming lane next to me.

"He's going to be hit!" I exclaimed.

"There's no traffic," Frankie countered.

"Still." My hands sweat and my heart hammered as a big black Mercedes drew parallel to me. I braced myself. If he had a gun, I would hit the brake and honk my horn and then drive over the grass toward the town square and the library. I gulped, gathered the nerve to look over, and saw Ellis's brother Beau, my ex-fiancé, waving at me.

I hit the brakes in shock.

Frankie flew straight through the window, which was fine. He'd be fine.

I was fine.

What the hell was Beau thinking?

The red brake lights on the Mercedes flashed, and then I watched, stunned, as Beau put it in reverse and backed up next to me.

He rolled down his window, grinning. "You're a hard one to catch."

"You—" I cranked down my window frantically. "You scared me to death!"

His broad smile went flat and his good humor vanished. "Ellis said you were in trouble."

Unbelievable. "Ellis sent you to watch over me?" His pesky, entitled, clueless brother who would only delay my investigation and drive me crazy.

Ellis really did have it out for me.

Beau ran a hand through his tousled blond locks. "I'm here to help," he said cheerfully.

Yes, he'd be about as helpful as a porcupine in a balloon factory. I'd never expected Ellis to stoop so low. "Go home," I ordered. "This doesn't have anything to do with you."

"Yes, it does. I need to keep you on the straight and narrow," he said, like a deranged Dudley Do-Right.

"Nope. No way. Absolutely not." I planted my forehead on my steering wheel. "What do I have to say to get you to leave?"

A car honked behind me.

"Traffic," Beau announced.

"I cannot stress enough how much I do not want you here," I said, giving a "sorry" wave to the irate couple behind me. They must think I was a crazy person. Loony Verity out "ghostbusting" again—doesn't even realize she's having a conversation smack-dab in the middle of the street.

It wasn't like anyone could mistake the girl in the 1978 avocado green Cadillac.

"We'd make a great team," Beau called as I pulled out.

No. And shame on Ellis for suggesting it. It was clinically insane for my boyfriend to send my ex-fiancé to babysit me while I talked to a mobster in the haunted theater.

It was also invasive, disrespectful, and a real dick move.

"I'm okay, by the way," Frankie said. I wasn't sure when he'd reappeared in my passenger seat, but he'd made it back.

"Sorry, Frank."

"Don't call me Frank," he said.

I watched as Beau began to follow me again. Dang the man. "I'm just distracted."

"Less talking, more driving," Frankie said. "You are not going to blow my shot at Wally Big Ears over trouble with your love life."

"Well, we can't go to the theater now with Beau on our tail," I said, gripping the wheel.

"I don't care if we lead a marching band in there," Frankie said. "Wally don't haunt the movies full time. We can get him tonight. This is our shot, and we're going."

"What is the grand and elusive Wally Big Ears going to think when we walk in there with Beau?" My ex didn't understand subtle. In fact, he was the kind of guy who'd been born on third base and thought he'd hit a triple. Beau said what he thought, went where he wanted. He skated through life on his charm and his looks, and he could get us into real trouble.

"You can keep him in line," Frankie stated as if he'd never met the man.

Beau was not a force to be contained. We'd once struck a wobbly truce during a particularly harrowing moment on a haunted train. He'd agreed to stop pursuing me, and I'd agreed to put up with him for Ellis's sake.

But tonight? At best, he'd be in the way. At worst—and I expected the worst—he could trigger a deadly confrontation.

"Here," Frankie said, directing me to the Sugarland Players Community Theater right off Main Street. "This is the place."

"For real?" I asked. That was one bit of good news. The Sugarland Players held Sunday evening performances, so the building would be open. I wouldn't have to break in anywhere tonight.

"You know, I saw *Godspell* here," I said, my mood improving as I took in the scrolling stonework over tan brick and the marquee jutting from the old building. "It was a fine show. A little confusing with forty apostles, but the director at the time must have realized that the bigger the cast, the more friends and relatives who'll buy a ticket."

"Your town is weird," Frankie said as I parked in front and cut the engine.

"It's your town, too," I reminded him, pleased to spot a ticket taker at the booth.

I was less happy to see so much available parking outside. The marquee advertised an 8:00 p.m. performance of *Sugar Town*, an original musical. That sounded lovely, although it would be well underway by now, and we were practically the only ones there.

"Poor actors." I'd heard they had a new director. He must not understand the "friends and family" rule.

"Poor me," Frankie said, making a quick check of his leg knife. "I think I went gray getting you here."

"You're always gray," I reminded him.

Beau pulled in behind us, right up to the edge of my bumper, and my good humor disappeared.

"I'm going to end this right now," I said, shoving open the door.

"Not until you talk to Wally," Frankie called after me. I heard him curse as I slammed the door behind me.

Beau leaned against his car, smiling.

"Tell Ellis I don't need you to babysit me," I said. "The theater's open. I'm not doing anything illegal."

Beau pretended he hadn't heard me. "Remember our third date?" he asked brightly.

I turned and began walking toward the theater.

Beau rushed to join me. "We saw *A Chorus Line*," he said to the empty air next to me as if he could pick a spot and expect Frankie to be there.

Half the time even I didn't know where Frankie was.

"You haven't lived until you've seen Mrs. Proctor's entire dance studio on stage at once." Beau laughed.

I turned to him. "They were adorable and talented, and they drew a crowd," I said, not happy with his insinuation that the kids couldn't hack it.

"Mrs. Morris's hearing aid kept whistling near the speaker," he continued, "and then it fell out during her one dance number, sending all those kids scrambling for it on stage."

Mrs. Morris had made a fine lead dancer. She did better than I could. It wasn't her fault the kids were overly enthusiastic. "Now that you know I'm here and I'm safe, you can leave," I told him.

Beau at least had the grace to appear chagrined. "Look." He raised a hand. "I promise I won't get in the way. I can be an extra set of hands. Let me do this for you."

I didn't understand why he thought I needed an extra set of hands. We weren't building a barn.

I took a deep breath.

He grabbed a program from a stack at the ticket window and began to flip through it. "Besides, you know I love to patronize the arts."

"I'll shoot him myself if it'll get you moving," Frankie said, waiting for us at the entrance.

If only it were that simple.

"I'm coming," I assured the ghost. Although I'd need a ticket first.

"Two, please," Beau said, beating me to it.

"Maybe just graze him," I said to Frankie.

Either way, it was official; my ex was now my babysitter.

Chapter Fifteen

The ticket taker sold Beau two tickets, ripped them in half, and gave us a schedule of upcoming events. "Enjoy the show."

"We will," Beau said, handing me a program.

I wondered if I could smother him with it.

Beau opened the physical door and I walked in ahead of him.

Gilded frames built into the wall housed show posters from past performances. Gold paint chipped off at the corners, exposing grayed wood cracked with age. On each side of the lobby, a staircase with a gold railing wound up to the second floor.

"I'll bet this was a beauty back in the day," I murmured, detecting the faint smell of dust and popcorn.

"Yeah," Frankie said, gliding ahead of us. "I remember when this theater opened for Christmas of 1926. They had ushers with gold buttons on their jackets and spiffy hats. Christmas trees in the lobby. The place glittered like a palace."

That sounded lovely. "Want to tune me in?"

I took in the red carpet, the gold ceilings. And this was the earthly side of things. No doubt it was even fancier on the other side.

Frankie hesitated.

"What's wrong?" I asked, on immediate alert. Frankie jiggled his left leg, and I realized his foot had gone missing. "You're losing power?" That was impossible. "You haven't given me any yet."

"This thing with Lou is really getting to me," he said, stiffening. "I don't have juice to spare."

"We'll take it easy," I promised him. "Only turn me on when you need to."

"I can't believe I'm on a ghost-hunting adventure," Beau declared.

"You and me both, buddy." He was making it hard for me to forget he was there.

The lobby stood empty. There was no usher, just a "take one" table with local coupons and flyers advertising future shows. Frankie stood in front of it, fuming. "Am I going to have to separate you two?"

"Please." Too bad Frankie was big on ideas and bad on the follow-through.

"This place might not be as safe as you think," Beau said, his hand passing through Frankie to take a flyer.

"Watch it!" Frankie said, taking a quick step back through the table.

"My landscaper does maintenance for this building, and he said to beware of the ghost who haunts the old projector room," Beau said, tossing the flyer back on the table and glancing toward the stairs to the second floor.

"Morty Levinson," Frankie said, brushing himself off, clearly squicked out by Beau's touch. "He built this place. Ran the projector for years. Swell guy. Kept his hands to himself."

Beau looked both ways as if Morty was going to come rushing down one of the staircases. "This past winter, a big light fell down onto the stage and almost killed an actor. You see, they angered the ghost," he whispered, drawing nearer than I preferred. "It was right after they unlocked the old projection room."

I'd heard that story, too. "Lauralee said it was an accident caused by a faulty rope, not a ghost."

You couldn't blame everything on the deceased residents of Sugarland.

"It was totally a ghost," Beau said as if he'd been there. Which he hadn't, according to Lauralee. "They should never have messed with that lock. That room hadn't been touched since the 1930s, and the spirits liked it that way. Now the scary old ghost is angry and dangerous," he added, with more relish than fear.

"First off, he might not be scary or old." One could never assume. "And another thing—"

"I know one ghost who's getting angry and dangerous," Frankie said, cutting me off. "Our contact is in the main theater. Focus."

I couldn't believe Frankie of all people had to tell me to focus. But he was right. Beau had me off my game.

"Let me see what we've got." Frankie stood next to an easel featuring photos of the cast and crew of *Sugar Town* and stuck his head through the door to the theater.

I stood by the board, surprised to see only one cast photo displayed: the portly image of Lowell Sanders, the self-proclaimed Sugarland choir director. He also waited tables at the diner, and now it seemed he was directing, producing, and starring in *Sugar Town*, a one-man show. He'd also written it.

"The guy's got talent." I'd give him that.

"Ellis needs to take you to New York," Beau snorted.

"Why?" I asked, genuinely puzzled.

Frankie popped his head back out of the door. "You ready?"

Before I could say anything, I felt his power wash over me

like a thousand tiny needles. His energy prickled across my skin and sank in deep to the bone.

Before my eyes, the theater lobby transformed. The doorway gleamed with fresh metallic paint, the chandelier sent off sparkles, and everything old—from the carpets to the stairway banisters—was new again.

"Stick close," Frankie ordered. "Follow my lead."

"Gotcha," I said, waiting for him to pass through before I opened the door.

The ghostly movie theater glowed in shades of gray.

Rows of empty velvet seats faced an actual wood stage framed with brocade curtains held back with thick tasseled ties. On the ghostly side, a movie screen took up the entire back wall of the stage. Painted stars glittered from the ceiling.

The ghostly screen flickered in black and white. A trio of cowboys on horses galloped across the badlands, waving their guns in the air. The one in the lead shot into the air.

Bang!

Bang!

Bang!

Past the ghostly vision, I saw that the modern theater had lost the luxurious curtains along with the movie screen. The stars on the ceiling had been painted over. The seats appeared worn—and still empty.

Lowell Sanders stood under the spotlight, dressed as a steampunk version of our first mayor, Colonel Ramsey Larimore. I knew this because he said it plain:

Larimore is my name and Sugarland is my game

I never wanted fame, I only want rain.

He did a jig that appeared sort of like a modern rap dance. It would have come off better if he'd had rhythm.

Our crops need rain! I feel the pain...

He raised his hands to the cloud dangling from a hook above him, imploring.

Rain!

He dropped to his knees.

Poor man. He was trying hard. There were only two people in the theater, both in the first row. An older couple. Probably Lowell's parents.

"Ah, yes." Beau nudged me. "There's nothing quite like community theater."

"Hush up," I murmured. "He's trying his best."

An icy chill enveloped my left side, and I turned to see the flickering image of an usher in a pillbox hat. "Shhh…"

"Right." I nodded. "Sorry."

"Is that a ghost?" Beau hissed, drawing closer. "I feel a chill." He touched my arm. "It's just like when we were on the train."

I shook off his touch. "You never helped me ghost hunt on the train."

"I'm making it up to you," he vowed.

I didn't know where his sudden fervor had come from, but I didn't like it.

"Hey, Bobbsey Twins." Frankie swept toward us down an empty row of seats, his Panama hat cocked low over his forehead, his jaw clenched. "He's up there," the gangster said, glancing up toward the back of the theater.

"There's no one here, Frankie." The theater appeared completely empty save for the couple clapping politely up front.

"In the balcony," Frankie added.

Then I saw him, a dark shadow of a man underneath the flickering beam of a ghostly projector.

He hunkered in the very last row at the top, and he didn't glow like ghosts normally did. I squinted to try to see better. "Are you sure he's dead?" It could have been anybody.

Frankie gave a sharp nod. "That's Wally. He always sits back there," he said, leading us to a set of stairs off the main aisle.

The figure never moved.

"I suppose it is very private," I whispered.

"Exactly," Frankie said as we began the climb up the steep steps. "The back row is neutral ground. It's the best place to buy and sell secrets." He paused near a sconce casting a triangle of yellow light. It shimmered straight through him. "Wally provides a vital service, a point of contact. He's above the petty gang business."

"Until he sells you information." It was a wonder somebody hadn't bumped him off to keep him quiet. Then again, maybe they had.

We came to a wider, curved step before a sharp turn had us climbing higher. I heard Beau stumble behind me. With any luck, he'd realize he didn't belong here and give up.

For me, Frankie's gray glow lit the way. "For the right price, Wally can give you information nobody else has got."

Like the current location of Frankie's on-the-run brother. "Are you sure he knows where Lou is?"

"If anybody does, it's him," my gangster said with chilling certainty. "We used up my lead last night."

We'd make it work this time. "Okay. What are we going to give Wally for the information?"

Frankie glanced back at me. "That's up to you."

"What?" He'd said I had to negotiate. He didn't tell me I had to pay as well.

"Shhh…" Frankie hissed. Somehow it had sounded more compelling coming from the usher. "You're always so proud of how ghosts bond with you and confide in you. Well, now's the time to get Wally talking."

Great.

Frankie wanted me to get free information from the guy who sold secrets. How did one even go about asking a mob information broker for the goods on a gangster who shot his brother and now didn't want to be found?

Frankie halted at the top, and I almost went straight through the back of him.

"This is as far as I go." His gaze flicked past the arched doorway leading to the balcony. "Good luck."

"You don't have any other advice for me?" I asked.

The gangster shrugged. "I told you, 'good luck.' Also, hurry up. My leg is starting to disappear."

He was right—Frankie's left leg had gone transparent up to the knee. He hadn't lost power like this in a long time, and we were burning it fast if he'd begun losing body parts this quickly.

"I'll try to hurry," I promised. "In the meantime, think happy thoughts."

I can do this, I reminded myself as I climbed to the top. *Maybe.*

Beau staggered out onto the balcony. "Who put a curtain here?"

The shadowy figure never moved.

I put on my best smile and edged down the row toward the figure in the dark.

Beau followed. He caught up to me about halfway down.

Oh, no. I stopped. "Go. Find a seat somewhere and let me work. Now." I didn't have time to argue with him.

Beau stood his ground like a wall of stubborn. "Just because you don't love me anymore doesn't mean I won't be here for you."

I was going to kill him. Or Ellis.

Maybe both.

Wally Big Ears sat staring forward, an outline in the dark. Even as I drew near, I still found it tough to make out his features.

He wore a hat with the brim pulled low over his forehead, like another gangster I knew. He appeared lean and broad shouldered, but that was all I could determine. I couldn't even tell if he had big ears or not.

"Hey, Wally," I said, drawing as close as I dared. I mean, how did one open conversation with a mobster in the balcony of a darkened theater? Especially with a live play going on and an ex-fiancé listening in. There was no rule book for this one.

"My name is Verity," I said quietly, making every effort to be friendly as I took the seat next to him. "Do you like cowboy movies? I've never seen this one."

The flickering screen illuminated the hollows under his high cheekbones. He didn't answer.

Beau took the seat on the other side of me and did not even attempt to hide the fact that he was eavesdropping.

"He's watching a cowboy movie?" Beau sighed. On the stage below, our one-man community theater star had put on a ladies' bonnet and was rapping about women's lib. "I'd sure take a cowboy movie over this."

"Hush." I elbowed Beau in the ribs. Ex-boyfriends should be seen and not heard.

"I'm from here in Sugarland," I murmured to the ghost. "Are you?"

Wally's jaw tightened, but he didn't answer. He didn't even look at me.

"I just realized I'm the girl talking during the movie," I whispered, trying to laugh it off.

"She's always been terrible about that," Beau interjected.

I ignored him. This was not a team sport.

"You know, I suppose it's your job to talk during the movie," I said to the ghost. "Where do you go when you're not being the information guru?" He had to say something. Anything.

He turned to look at me, and I felt my hard-won smile waver as I stared into the coldest, deadest set of gray eyes I'd ever seen.

"I don't talk to friends of Frankie the German," he said, his voice low and deadly.

"Oh." That took me by surprise. Hmm... "Well, I wouldn't say I'm 'friends' with Frankie the German," I hedged.

Although, I couldn't say that I wasn't.

"Who's Frankie the German?" Beau whispered.

"Nobody," I said quickly, dismissing him, racking my brain for a way I could explain Frankie's and my complicated relationship.

Wally stared at Beau, then at me. "He's never heard of Frankie the German?"

"That's Beau and he's alive," I said, by way of explanation. "I mean, I am as well. But he can't see ghosts. He has nothing to do with any of this, and I have no idea why he is here."

"I'm a lawyer turned folk artist," Beau said to the general spot where Wally sat.

"He's also my ex-boyfriend," I explained. "Do you mind?" I added to Beau.

I had to get on with the ghost hunting. This was my specialty.

"So he's a lawyer," Wally said, looking past me to Beau, warming. And suddenly, I could see more of his face. He had a Roman nose and he needed a shave. "Say, how much time would a guy get for using a cop car to transport a trunk full of bottles over the Tennessee line?"

Truly?

This guy had access to all kinds of secret information, and this was the kind of thing he worried about?

But I had to keep him talking, so I repeated the question for Beau and watched him break out in a grin. "The guy would get nothing if I was his lawyer." He laughed.

Wally joined in with a big guffaw. "That's what I'm talking about," he said, smacking the armrest.

How had Beau gotten him talking at all?

It didn't matter. I took the opening and ran with it. "What we're really here to ask is if you know the whereabouts of Lou Winkelmann of the South Town gang. It's important," I added.

Wally looked past me to my ex. "You dated this doll?"

"Beau and I were engaged," I said, admittedly a little defensive.

"She had lower standards a few years ago." Beau grinned, and I swear the two of them would have fist bumped if I hadn't been in the way.

How was Beau doing better than me when he couldn't hear half the conversation?

"Your ex seems like a swell guy. I wish I could be talking with him," Wally remarked.

I would have fallen over in my chair if it hadn't been bolted down. He liked Beau. Not me. Beau.

Well, fine. As long as we accomplished what we'd set out to do, those two could ride off into the sunset together for all I cared. I leaned closer to Beau. "Tell him you need to know the whereabouts of Lou Winkelmann of the South Town gang," I hissed. Maybe if Beau asked, Wally would tell us.

Beau leaned back in his seat, elbows out, resting his head in his hands with a satisfied smirk. "I'm just glad to meet a ghost who's willing to make conversation."

Sweet puppies. Was he trying to torture me?

From the wink he gave me, I'd have to say yes.

Wally thunked his elbow on the wall behind us.

"Oh!" Beau said, his attention drawn to the movie screen as a cowboy fell off his horse and was dragged by a foot in the stirrup.

"You can see that?" I gaped.

"It just started playing out of nowhere," Beau said, shocked and ten kinds of excited. "How did it do that?" he asked, gripping the armrests on his chair.

"Morty owed me a favor," Wally said.

The audience members up front started to clap. Lowell stood gaping at the movie that had suddenly begun playing on the screen behind him. He removed his steampunk stovepipe hat and took a bow.

He stayed down there until the clapping had subsided, and

when he straightened, his eyes darted wildly. "Why, let me tell you about the wild west of Sugarland," he improvised.

"See?" I said to Beau. "Talent."

"Nice," Beau exclaimed as another cowboy started doing lasso tricks.

"That's Rex Bell," Wally said with appreciation. "If you've gotta watch one movie for the rest of eternity, this would be it."

"He's dynamite," Beau said, fixated on the screen. The scene jumped as Rex leaped off a rock and back into the saddle. "I can't believe I'm seeing this in the theater."

"I can't either," I said out loud.

What had happened to questioning Wally? I wasn't sure how we'd gotten so far off track.

"Back then, actors did their own stunts," Beau added, as if I cared.

He was seriously into this.

"I saw Rex Bell ride standing through a river," Wally gushed. "It was in *The Winds on the Plains*. Great movie."

I didn't get it. I honestly didn't. How could men sit around and have a conversation without even speaking to one another?

It was bizarre.

"I really like Tim McCoy," Beau said, leaning an arm over the back of my seat.

"Yes," Wally said as if it were obvious everyone should love Tim McCoy.

Beau settled into a man-spread. "They used to show Tim McCoy movies on television when I was a kid. It was one of the only things my dad would watch with me."

And then it hit me. Beau had accomplished what I could not, just by sitting next to me with a grin on his face, watching a movie. Wally had visibly relaxed to the point that the shadow had lifted from his face. I could see him clearly now—the individual hairs on his unshaven jaw, his guarded eyes, his side-cocked grin as he watched Rex Bell walk into a saloon only to be held at gunpoint by a pretty barmaid.

"She's a feisty one," Beau joked. "Totally my type," he added, and he and Wally shared an honest-to-goodness belly laugh.

Unbelievable. Beau could talk to ghosts and he didn't even have to hear what they were saying back.

Oh, who was I kidding? Beau had always had that way about him—the ability to get along with anyone. It was one of the things that had gotten my attention when we'd first met. I'd always said Beau could make friends with a doorknob, and it seemed he'd now proven it beyond a shadow of a doubt. And it was nice to see the elusive ghost having a good time.

If Wally Big Ears had to spend every evening in the back row of the movie theater for eternity, he deserved to spend a little time with someone who "got" him.

The play on the stage ended. Lowell took his bow and did an encore—a look at future Sugarland. I'm not sure where he got the idea that we would all be wearing space helmets, but I'd give him points for forward thinking. Even if Lowell did seem a bit upset to have to compete with Tim McCoy chasing down a runaway train behind him. And right before it almost went off a cliff, too.

The couple in the audience gave a standing ovation, which seemed to pacify the temperamental actor. And when nobody kicked us out—per chance they assumed we'd left?—the boys watched the entire rest of the movie together, talking, but not. It reminded me of guys watching sports, come to think of it.

Beau even sang along to "My Texas Rose" as the cowboys gathered around the campfire at the end of the movie. And darned if Wally the gangster didn't sing right along with him.

"My trail, my home. My Texas Rose," they crooned in unison, both off-key. And when the credits rolled, I wasn't sure what to do with either one of them.

"God, I haven't had this much fun in fifty years," Wally mused.

"Can we start the movie again from the beginning?" Beau asked.

"No," I said before Wally got any ideas. For one thing, the theater would close soon on the mortal plane. Contrary to what Ellis might believe, I didn't relish being anywhere I didn't belong. For another, "We need to find Lou Winkelmann. If Wally won't tell us where he is, then it'll take twenty times longer to track him down. Of course, *after* we find Lou, you're welcome to spend as much time in the theater as you want," I added, sweetening the pot.

"Aw, man," Beau groused.

"She's not subtle," Wally said.

"I'm serious," I told the gangster.

"I realize that," he said slowly, looking at me with fresh eyes. "At least you're more charming than Frankie."

"That's not hard," I said, generating no argument from the gangster.

He glanced past me to Beau. "Is it that bad to want a spot of company to watch a movie with once every few decades?"

It was actually quite sweet, but I couldn't let my emotions get in the way. "I gave you something you wanted. Now you're going to give me the information I came for. Do we have a deal?"

"I want another movie. Next Sunday night," the gangster said, laying it on the table.

"Next Sunday good for you to hang out here again?" I asked Beau.

"Heck yeah," Beau said with relish.

Wally gave a stiff nod. "Then we've got a deal."

Who knew my annoying would-be bodyguard would be such a hot commodity?

Wally tented his fingers. "Okay, here's the story. Lou's in a bind, has been since he died. The poor guy's got a secret he's kept even from his gang."

Yikes. That didn't sound good.

Wally raised a brow at my surprise. Like he wasn't used to seeing that look from people. Although to be fair, perhaps mobsters had better poker faces than I did.

"So what's Lou's secret?" I asked.

"A murder?" Beau suggested.

Wally leaned back in his chair and glanced past me to Beau. "Lou's been spending a fair chunk of his afterlife tracking down a particular woman of interest. He's been obsessed with her since he died."

"Did she have anything to do with Lou's death?" I asked. Perhaps she had something to do with Frankie's as well.

Wally shrugged. "I don't know much about her, only that those two were thick. Word has it he kept her holed up above a flower shop when they were alive."

"Mildred's Flower Heaven." I gasped.

"That's the one," he said, impressed.

Frankie and I had been there last night.

"So where's Lou going to be tomorrow night?" I asked. He'd never answered my original question, and I doubted very much it was an unintentional oversight.

Wally sighed. "Listen. Sometimes it's best to keep the past in the past. You nosing around like this, trying to expose the whole thing… It might trigger a mob war."

"Let us worry about that." And believe me, I'd worry.

He didn't appear convinced. "It's your funeral," he finally said. "Lou will be at Carson's Supper Club downtown tomorrow after dark."

"I know where that is," Frankie declared, shimmering into view in the seat on the other side of Wally. He'd lost his entire left leg. We were on borrowed time.

"Damn it. I'm not dealing with you," Wally growled then

pointed to Beau. "Remember. Sunday night movie. Next week. Make sure he gets here, or I'll send someone to remind you," he added to me before he faded into a shadow and disappeared.

"He just had to be threatening right when I was starting to like him," I mused.

"Just like a gangster." Frankie grinned. "Now we know where to go. Good job!" he said, rubbing his hands together.

"It was Beau who made it happen," I said honestly. He'd gotten Wally to open up. He'd given me the leverage I needed to ask questions. "But what did he mean about starting a mob war?" I asked.

"Yes," Beau answered for Frankie. "Ellis won't be happy about you being in some ghostly mob war."

"I don't know what any of it means," Frankie said. "But I'll bet my brother does."

"We'll ask him when we see him," I agreed, glancing at Beau, hoping I wouldn't regret what we'd just learned.

Chapter Sixteen

I said an honest-to-goodness thank you to Beau as we left the theater.

"Never in a million years would I have pegged you as a ghost hunter," I admitted, stepping out into the alley as he opened the door for me.

"Hey, I'm just along for security," he joked, allowing me to pass. "But, seriously, I'm glad I could help. I owe you that and a lot more."

He gave me a quick, brief hug and I let him. "I have to go," I told him, suddenly uncomfortable.

I didn't want him getting too personal on me.

When you got right down to it, Beau Wydell possessed a lot of good qualities or I wouldn't have dated him all those years ago. I liked that he was a friendly guy, ready to believe the best of everyone. I appreciated that he was as comfortable talking to the small-time chicken farmer in line with him at the bank as he was the big shots at the Wydell family law firm. And I praised Jesus, Mary, Joseph, and the apostles that Beau seemed to have at last accepted that his brother and I were together. But Beau and I had been chummy enough tonight. It was time to not talk until the next family gathering.

He let me go with a frown and a wave. "Are you going to be okay?"

"I guarantee it," I said, slipping into my car, which was parked ahead of his. "I'll be sure to thank your brother as well."

"You do that," he called after me, his smile wooden.

Frankie sat brooding in my passenger seat.

"Who popped your balloon?" I asked, starting up the car. He'd been excited a few minutes ago when we learned where Lou would be tomorrow night. "It's all coming together."

"Look at me," he said, pointing down to his leg. It had disappeared up to his hip. "I'm a mess."

I felt a prickling jolt as he drew his power out of me.

"Your leg will come back," I assured him. "And we definitely put your energy to good use tonight."

Despite Beau—or perhaps because of him—it couldn't have gone better.

"Yeah, but I've got to thinking," he said, drawing a hand through his hair.

"Well, don't start doing that," I joked, pulling out. Frankie liked to leap before he looked.

"I'm serious," he said, leaning stiffly back against his seat. "According to Wally Big Ears, Lou's been chasing this girl for his entire afterlife. He's obsessed with her. But he never said a word to me about it."

"Maybe Wally is wrong," I suggested, turning at the intersection.

"It'd be the first time," Frankie said, absently cracking his knuckles. "The kicker is, he's my brother and I don't know either way. Lou and I..." He swirled his hands around. "We hardly talk now that we're dead. For a long time before that, even. Lou could have joined the circus for all I know. He comes around the old gang once in a blue moon. I can go years without seeing him at all. And when we do say two words to each other, it's either small talk or we fight."

"Were you okay with this before you learned Lou was the one who killed you?" He'd never spoken much about his brother.

"I mean, it is what it is." He sighed. "There's nothing I can do about it."

I didn't want to lecture or remind Frankie that he was half of this relationship. I knew firsthand how hard it was to change the status quo in certain relationships and how impossible it could be to try to change another person.

But still. "Did you start losing touch gradually?" I asked. "Sometimes, things like this sneak up on you before you know it." I made another right turn, heading back to Main Street. "It's hard to know how to break through and talk again."

"Exactly." Frankie flopped against the seat. "I mean, how do you start with a person you hardly know anymore?"

"Some people don't say anything at all. Time goes by and they never get the chance."

"And then some of us die and still don't talk," Frankie mused as I turned right onto Main and headed toward the highway.

"Were you ever close to your brother?" I asked.

Frankie rested his head against the back of the seat and stared straight ahead. "Lou basically raised me after our parents died. I quit school and worked at the feed lot. Lou joined the mob."

"How old were you?" I asked, keeping one eye on the darkened road and one on my gangster.

"I was nine. He was thirteen, almost a man. He started as a runner for Gas Pipe Joey."

"Gas pipe?" I asked.

"That was Joey's favorite weapon. Bad luck for him, he died

holding an umbrella," Frankie snarked. Ghosts could only keep what they'd died with, which I imagined could be limiting in the afterlife. "So now he's running around threatening to whack everyone with an umbrella," Frankie continued. "Don't get me wrong, that thing still smarts. But it doesn't have the same impact, if you know what I mean."

I did.

"Anyways, between Lou in the organization and me bagging feed, we had a rat-trap apartment and two squares a day."

"Wow. That sounds hard," I said, focusing on him as much as I could as I merged onto the highway.

"Those were actually the best days," Frankie said with a smile in his voice. "We had a lot of fun back then."

"No bedtime," I joked, glancing at him.

He smiled a little. "No. Didn't need one. I fell into bed every night, beat. They worked us six days a week back then, dawn to dusk. And Lou was out at all hours." He glanced out the window. "Lou rose up to working the numbers, and when he got bigger, he did some time in enforcement."

"That sounds...pleasant." Perhaps.

Although not really...

"Good enough if you weren't the one who missed a protection payment." Frankie guffawed.

Oh my. I'd always said I wanted to know more about Frankie's former life, but now I wasn't so sure.

"Lou did okay, but he never loved it like I did," Frankie mused.

"So when did you join?" I asked, watching him dig a silver cigarette case out of his jacket pocket.

"July 4, 1928," he said, resting a smoke on his bottom lip and lighting up. "I call it independence day," he added with a smirk, taking a deep drag and blowing out.

I wasn't crazy about him smoking in my car, even if ghostly

smoke didn't do much to the upholstery, but I let him go this time.

How did one put in an application for the mob? "Did Lou sponsor you in or something?"

"Hell no!" He laughed. "Lou hated it. His entire goal had been to work hard and make enough money for me to go back to school. He thought I should be a dentist. Me!" Frankie announced as if Lou had suggested he fly to the moon.

I probably should have agreed, or at least suggested something else respectable, but I wasn't going to lie. "I honestly can't see you as anything but a mobster."

"Me neither," Frankie said, taking another drag. He relaxed a bit, letting his hand drape outside the glass window. "It's like this: Lou would get told by the boss to keep the vagrants out of the moonshine stills. I mean, we had dozens of suppliers with hundreds of stills hidden all over the woods around here."

"In Sugarland?" I gasped.

"It got a lot of people through the depression," he said as if he were providing a public service. "It also made a lot of other people happy."

"A regular Norman Rockwell moment," I deadpanned.

"I don't know who that is." He took a drag. "Anyhow, you had a lot of bums at that time, a lot of folks riding the rails looking for work. They didn't realize that they were stealing liquor from protected suppliers, our people, you see."

"I can't believe all this went on in Sugarland," I said, turning onto the rural road toward home.

"Really?" Frankie drawled.

I supposed we had seen a lot together.

"You know, I did run across some copper coils in the attic a few years ago."

Had my ancestors been distilling moonshine too?

"You sell those coils?" Frankie asked.

"No." I hadn't thought of that. "I recycled them."

"Of course," the gangster groused. "Anyhow, we had a good business going back then, and it became crystal clear to anybody with half a brain that Lou never loved his job," Frankie said, blowing smoke out the window. "He'd get told to teach a thief a lesson, and what did Lou do? He'd just shoot in the air and yell at the guy. Very boring. And not one hundred percent effective." Frankie rested an elbow on the windowsill and looked at me as if he expected me to gasp at Lou's lack of finesse. He rolled his eyes when I didn't appear properly put-out. "What you do is you lock them in your trunk and drive around for a while. That way, the low-down dirty thief is scared, you get rid of a few spiderwebs in the trunk, and the muck who tried to take from you has no idea where the moonshine even is anymore."

"Frankie," I admonished.

"Or if you want to get more creative, maybe you make them drink moonshine until they puke and fall asleep. Then you drop 'em off on the front porch of the president of the local Temperance Society," Frankie reasoned. "I've done that, and it is a lot of fun. But you don't just shoot in the air and call it a night. At that point, you might as well give the guy a glass of warm milk and tuck him into bed."

"Not everyone has your flair for the dramatic." Thank goodness.

The gangster shrugged. "All I'm saying is I figured Lou got tired of the life. He stopped showing up at the parties. He pulled all the boring shifts. He didn't even congratulate me when I set fire to Al Capone's houseboat and didn't get caught."

"That is…" I wasn't going to go there. "Okay, it's tough when you don't have common interests with someone you love. I mean, you and Lou went through a lot together in the early days."

He took a drag, but he didn't protest. "I assumed he was avoiding me because he didn't approve of my lifestyle. I figured

SOUTHERN BRED AND DEAD

he'd come around. Now I find out he shot me." Frankie shook his head and took another drag. "He hated to shoot anyone, and he shot me."

"Well, we'll talk to him tomorrow night and sort it out."

He looked at me doubtfully.

"We'll at least learn the truth."

"That's all I ask," Frankie said, ashing his cigarette out the window. "Maybe that and a single shot to each of his kneecaps."

We'd worry about that later.

I turned down the long driveway to my house. A few raindrops scattered over the windshield, and I hit the wipers.

Looked like we made it home just in time.

"By the way, there's someone following you again," Frankie said.

"What?" I looked into the rearview mirror and saw a pair of headlights. My heart jumped, and then I realized they appeared to be the same headlights that had sent me into a tizzy earlier tonight. I slowed as we neared the house, and a black Mercedes took shape behind me. "Dang it, Beau."

"That's my cue to head for the shed," Frankie said, evaporating from the seat next to me.

Lucky gangster. I needed to learn that trick.

I pulled around to the back of the house and flew out of the car before my annoying ex could finish parking. "It's bad enough you followed me to the theater, but now you're following me home?" I asked, storming up to his car.

It was presumptuous and out of line and exactly like Beau.

A fat raindrop smacked my forehead, and I brushed it away.

"I know this is weird," he said, leaving the windows open as he shut off his engine.

"Ya think?" Honestly. "Seeing as you don't need to 'protect' me from any ghosts here at the house, you need to go."

"I have a confession to make," he said, getting out of the car.

That was the opposite of leaving.

A smattering of rain pegged my arms. "Tonight's not the night," I said, retreating toward my back porch, brushing away the chill of the rain. I had enough going on with the hunt for Frankie's brother, my own boyfriend threatening to arrest me, and Jorie's death. I didn't need Beau misinterpreting our success at the theater as a springboard to a new phase in our polite-yet-distant friendship.

"This is important," he said, oddly determined.

"Then tell me now," I said, taking the stairs. I'd be inside in a minute, and Beau wasn't invited.

"Ellis didn't send me to help you tonight. He said he was worried, and I sent myself."

I stopped at the top of the stairs and stared down at him. "You lied to me."

"Not exactly. You thought he sent me, and I just didn't correct you." He stood kind of helpless at the bottom of the steps. "So when you said you were going to thank him, I wanted to tell you he doesn't know."

"Why, Beau?" I asked. "What part of your conversation with my boyfriend made you think you should invite yourself on my ghost hunt tonight?"

He ground his jaw. "I didn't want to see you screw up and get arrested, you idiot. And I didn't want to see you get hurt."

Oh, please. "I can take care of myself." I'd proven that to him, to Ellis, and to the entire town. Many times over.

The rain started falling harder. I backed up to keep my toes dry. He kept talking.

"I'd like to clear up a few more things as well," he announced from the yard.

"Me too," I said. "Just because we are friendly doesn't mean I want to be friends." Beau and I had worked to bury our animosity after our broken engagement, and we'd done a decent job of it. But he had to understand one important distinction.

"You are not my buddy, and my relationship with your brother is none of your business."

"That's where you're wrong," he ground out. He launched himself up onto my porch, rain dripping from his hair down into his eyes. "You and Ellis are screwing things up, and I'm not going to stand by and watch it happen."

"And you think you're a relationship expert all of a sudden?"

"Absolutely not. I have no idea what I'm doing," he said as I backed up to keep him from dripping on me. "But you need to know Ellis was extremely upset when he called me. Think about it," he pleaded. "When does Ellis ever ask me for advice? Never. But he did tonight. I've never seen him so defeated or you so dumb, so I'm stepping in. For better or worse."

"Are you saying he was sad?" I asked, surprised and a little heartened. "Because my main takeaway from our conversation was the whole 'I'm going to arrest you' part."

"Yeah." Beau shook the wet from his button-down shirt. "Ellis wished he hadn't said that. I told him it was a good move, though."

And I immediately regretted saving him from the rain.

"You can't tell a police officer about your plans for breaking and entering and then expect him to ignore it." He sat heavily on my porch swing, and I listened to the wood crackle under his weight. "Verity," he said softly, seeing my reaction, "my brother is in pain, you're clueless, and I'm trying to fix it."

"By telling me that I'm dumb. Twice." He truly was terrible at this.

But Beau being Beau, he plowed forward anyway. "Ellis has never had anything really good his entire life," Beau said, brushing the rain out of his hair. "He wasn't the first son. That was Harrison. Ellis was never the favorite son. That was me."

"The spoiled rotten one," I corrected.

"Yeah," he said, with a sheepish grin. "Ellis is the guy who pulls the weight. He takes on the hard work, the thankless work.

I can admit that now. Harrison always did what Dad said, so both of them had a super easy time checking out and disappearing. I had no problem beating out Ellis for Mom's favorite so long as I did everything 'right.' All I had to do was join the firm and rack up more stuff, more people admiring me. That was simple. I am, after all, delightful company."

"You can be quite charming," I admitted. Shallow, but charming.

"Right," Beau said as if I finally understood. "Ellis was the odd duck, trying to make everything right for the rest of us, only it never quite worked out. In this day and age, he still watches out for other people. Like, all the time. It's easy to take him for granted, but when I think about it, I don't know what we'd do without him."

I turned at a scratching on the back window and found Lucy feverishly trying to dig her way out to us. "What are you getting at, Beau?"

He shook his head. "I guess what I'm trying to say is that Ellis isn't one to ask a lot for himself. He's too busy protecting, providing. I don't think he even realized he needed you to stay safe—for his sake—until you almost got yourself killed in that haunted asylum."

"That's—" I wanted to argue, but he had a point.

Beau stood. "I don't think Ellis is trying to change you so much as he's scared to death of losing you. He's trying to protect himself for once."

"I don't know what to do with that." I honestly didn't. I mean, I couldn't close the door on my new life, but I didn't want to torture Ellis.

"He's scared to death he's going to lose you either way," Beau said.

"I—" I wasn't sure what to say.

"I don't want Ellis to go through the hell I did," Beau said. "I deserved it. He doesn't. He's just a guy in a tough spot, trying to do the best he can."

"So what do I do?" I asked.

"Give him a break." Beau shrugged. "Show him you're willing to work things out."

"I'm not sure how." Obviously, my approach wasn't cutting it. I'd been expecting him to do all the work. Or at least most of the compromising.

"Figure it out," he said. "He's my big dumb brother, but he's worth it."

"He is." That was about the only thing I knew for sure. "Thanks," I added. "I think I am glad you followed me home."

He smiled at that. "Awkward, I know. I promise I won't make it a habit. I really have moved on."

Lucy began squeaking like a drunk Muppet as she tried to dig a hole through the glass.

Beau transferred his grin to her. "I see Lucy's still as stubborn as ever."

"You want to say hi?" I asked. A skunk meet-and-greet and perhaps a towel were the least I could offer. Beau had given me a lot to think about.

He and Lucy had been close once. He'd helped feed her bottles as a baby, back when our relationship was new and he'd do anything for me or my skunk. He'd invented the special vegetable nut mash she'd inhaled as an adolescent. Skunks didn't understand awkwardness or breakups, so when I opened the back door, she rushed straight past me and into his arms.

"Hey, girl!" he said, crouching to pet her, failing to get in a good scratch as she went bonkers greeting him.

A large thunderclap echoed over the yard, and she dashed inside.

"She's been terrified ever since that tree went down in the yard," he said, following her in.

I couldn't believe he remembered that.

I tossed him a towel from the laundry room while he and

Lucy settled in for skunk snuggles on the kitchen floor. Beau had a way of scratching her ears that made her thump her tail on the floor like a beaver. "She doesn't do that for anyone else," I told him.

"Good," he said, then lost his grin. "I can show you how I do it if you want."

"No." I waved him off. "It can be your thing."

Lucy leaned into him so hard she almost toppled over. Beau caught her with his arm. "That's always been my problem. I have to tell the best joke, give the best belly scratch. Gotta have everyone's undivided attention."

He sure had Lucy's.

"Well, you grew up in such a cold family," I said, leaning against the counter. I could see why he needed people to love him. He knew how to make Lucy love him. And he'd had my love at one point.

"I think that's why I messed up," he said, keeping his attention on the adoring skunk. "I needed everyone to want me and love me and—" He glanced up sheepishly. "I didn't care if it was real."

He wasn't the only one in the world who did that. "We all have our ways of coping."

"I want you to know I'm done playing that game," he said, turning his attention back to the skunk. "I'm going to be better than that. Now that I know what's happening, I can control it. I can decide."

Okay. "Good for you."

"I owe you one," he said as Lucy tried to climb him for kisses. "If I hadn't lost you, I don't think I would have ever looked at myself and realized I could change."

"Thank you," I said, surprised and—I had to admit it— touched. "I'm proud of who you're becoming."

He grinned, letting my skunk lick his cheek while I grabbed her bowl and washed it out from dinner.

"Oh," Beau said, springing to his feet with Lucy in his arms. "Can I make her my special skunky bananas foster?"

It was a lot of work. "I'm not even sure if the pan you used to use is…"

"Here," he said, triumphantly pulling it out from the bottom drawer I never opened.

Lucy about lost her mind.

He set her down and let her run circles around him.

"It is the choice of discerning skunks everywhere," he said, brandishing his pan like a top chef.

"She hasn't had that since you made it for her last." Back before we were engaged, before he'd started taking me for granted.

"It's easy," he said, going for one of the bananas I kept on the kitchen island. "Do you have butter?"

I gathered what he needed from my fridge and cabinets— cinnamon, dry bread crumbs, cream, a bit of vanilla extract— and hoped Lucy wouldn't have a stroke in the meantime. Beau's recipe was custom-made for a skunk's diet, but I'd also tried it and found it delicious.

I refilled Lucy's water and tried to keep her from stepping in it as she danced around, watching Beau cook.

"I'm serious about what I said earlier." He glanced up from browning the butter. "My hopeless brother is suffering as we speak."

"He's got to be up to his ears at work."

"His shift ended ten minutes ago," Beau remarked, peeling bananas.

"You think he's going to call?" I dredged my phone out of my bag.

He hadn't called.

Beau chopped the bananas—*thwack, thwack, thwack!*—a little harder than he needed to. "One of you needs to figure this out." He flipped a piece of banana to Lucy. "You realize how much my brother loves you," he said it as a statement rather than a question.

"I guess. We've just been having trouble lately," I said, fiddling with my phone.

Beau pursed his lips and chopped harder. "He may be bad at expressing his feelings, but he's got plenty, I guarantee it. And he needs you."

"If I call him, he'll ask where I was tonight." Although, I hadn't done anything illegal. "Do you truly think this is a good idea?"

"If I were you, I'd just show up. Of course, I'm the one who is terrible at relationships," Beau reminded me. "Worse than either one of you."

"If I pop by, we have to talk," I said. Or not. It could be that we'd done too much talking lately. Maybe I should simply kiss him and go from there. We could start our evening with a reminder of why we were together in the first place.

"Just don't overthink it," Beau said, sprinkling cinnamon into the pan. The kitchen was starting to smell amazing.

"I should go," I said, realizing I'd have to kick Beau out of my kitchen and ruin Lucy's fun. Poor girl. This was going to be quite a tease.

"Go," Beau said, waving me off. "I'll feed Lucy and give her some attention. I missed this pretty girl," he added, reaching down for an ear scratch.

"I don't know," I hedged. He was getting awfully chummy. But she had been starved for love all day.

"I'll be gone in an hour," he promised, "easily by the time you make it home. Although I hope you have mercy on my brother and stay longer."

"I—"

"I suggest you make him forget why either one of you was mad in the first place."

He had a point. Ellis and I had been through our differences, but we'd always come back out the other side, stronger for it. If anyone could figure this out, we could.

"You've got this," Beau said, with a wave of the spoon.

"I do," I said, grabbing my bag. I hoped.

At least I'd give it my best.

Chapter Seventeen

I plunked Frankie's urn on the counter and hurried out the back door into the rain.

Don't overthink it.

Ellis would be glad if I showed up at his door. Or at least he'd have to talk to me.

Part of me hoped that I would discover a magic key, an easy solution to our problem that would make both Ellis and me happy. We could go back to the way things were—the easy, fun part. I liked that part. I *missed* that part. Ellis going with me on my jaunts to haunted places. Both of us being as amused as we were amazed by what I discovered on the other side.

And who was I to complain about a few stolen kisses along the way?

Maybe we could have that back and then some. Maybe we just had to find a new way that worked for both of us.

I tossed my bag into the passenger seat of the car and slid into the driver's seat, wiping wet strands of hair out of my eyes.

I'd make things right tonight.

Or I'd make things worse.

Either way, we had to face our problems if we were ever going to push through this mess and come out the other side.

I turned the key and took comfort in the familiar catch of the land yacht's eight-cylinder engine. Sturdy and dependable, the way I liked it.

With a glance back at the warm light in the windows of my ancestral home, I steered out into the dark night.

The swish of my wiper blades comforted me with their steady rhythm.

You can do it. You can do it. They seemed to say.

Or maybe I just really wanted it to be true.

I steered past the budding peach orchard. Beau had made it clear that Ellis was suffering. Well, I was too. I mean, here we were, two people who loved each other, stuck butting heads. Neither of us willing to give an inch because that would mean changing who we were.

Ellis couldn't stop being the protective sort, and what he'd seen on our last adventure scared him bad.

I couldn't pretend that I wasn't captivated by the whole new world I'd discovered on the other side.

And as I reached the end of the drive, I fought the sudden urge to turn around and go home. I could hug my skunk, maybe visit the shed and see what Frankie was doing. I knew what to expect from both of them.

Ellis, on the other hand? I hadn't always been very good at figuring out what went on in his head.

I forced myself to make the turn onto the main road.

My two housemates would always be with me, no matter what. Well, at least until I freed Frankie. Even after that, I didn't think I'd be rid of my ghost altogether.

But Ellis? I was scared to death of losing him.

I turned onto the nearly deserted highway, the beams of my brights cutting through the pitch dark. Ellis was fun, he was brave, and he had a talent for saying what was on his mind, whether or not it sounded right.

That one drove his mother crazy. And Ellis wasn't so fond of it himself.

But I loved it.

I liked that Ellis always gave the unvarnished truth, or at least his version of it.

Well, I liked it most of the time, anyway. When it didn't hurt so much.

Ellis didn't try to be anything other than who he was—which was a problem at the moment. I chewed my lip, wishing my grandmother were along to give some advice.

She'd tell me to find a way to respect him and myself.

It was easier said than done, but she'd never pretended life— or love—was easy.

Ellis lived in one of the older neighborhoods west of downtown. Thick, mature trees lined the road. The neat, bungalow-style houses along Magnolia Street had stood since the early 1900s. I loved the neighborhood's wide variety of styles and personal touches as well as the inviting porches. No two were alike.

Ellis lived in a cozy brick story-and-a-half built in the 1940s. The porch light shone like a beacon in the night. I parked in the driveway behind his police cruiser, heartened to see lights on in the front room.

He was home, and he'd be glad to see me.

I reached into my bag and pulled out my lipstick and the hairbrush I always carried. I sat in the dark and freshened up. I liked to look pretty for my boyfriend.

I wasn't hesitant at all to actually knock on that door and face the music.

Maybe a little.

Ellis knew I'd been ghost hunting tonight. I didn't have to hide it, I reminded myself, as I rubbed my lips together and dug in my bag for a mint. One couldn't underestimate the importance of fresh breath, and a bit of mascara never hurt, I decided as my fingers brushed the tube.

I applied the mascara by the light of the visor's vanity mirror.

The trouble with Ellis was he never liked to ask for anything for himself. Instead, he gave too much.

And now, when he finally got around to asking, he wanted the impossible.

I found a powder compact and considered dabbing a bit on my nose.

No. I had to admit at this point that I wasn't freshening up; I was hiding in my car. Which was silly. I had no reason to remain glued to my seat or be nervous at all as his front door opened and he stepped out onto his porch. He watched me, curiously, as I added a layer of lip gloss.

I'd look like a runway model by the time I got done stalling.

At least the rain had stopped.

"Hi," I called, forcing myself out of my car. I slung my bag over my shoulder and fluffed my sodden hair, feeling terribly exposed, which was ten kinds of ridiculous because this was my guy and he loved me, and I had nothing to be worried about.

Still, I felt raw walking up the pathway to his house. He stood on the porch, a broad-shouldered mountain, watching. He didn't do it to make me uncomfortable. He was a soldier, a protector. It showed.

Beau had told me Ellis was scared, but at that moment, he didn't appear to be afraid of anything.

"Verity, I—" he began as I embraced a sudden bolt of energy and bounded up his stairs.

"No talking," I said, and then I kissed him.

And into that kiss, I poured all of my love and my hope and my faith in him. In us. We could make this right. Our unexpected, crazy, adventuresome kind of love was enough.

He wrapped his arms around me and drew me closer.

He kissed me back, long and hard. It was exactly what I'd craved from him from the very start. For always, really. And after a long, lovely while, he smiled in the dark and said, "Damn. I needed that."

"Me too." If I could have frozen the moment, I would have.

He drew a lock of hair behind my ear and looked at me like I was the prettiest girl in the world. "About earlier," he began.

"Nope," I said, nipping him on the bottom lip. "No talking." I wasn't going to let either of us screw this up.

I kissed him again. And again. And only when I felt him surrender did I tilt back and whisper into his ear, "I missed you."

"Am I allowed to say anything?" he asked, his voice hoarse.

"No." I felt his shudder and an intake of breath as I ran a hand down his side and rested it on his belt.

"I do like a girl who knows what she wants," he said, drawing me into the house.

His living room was a mess.

"Sorry," he said, clearing the video game controllers off his black leather couch. When I'd met him, the inside of his place consisted of white walls and minimal black leather furniture. I'd helped him pick a warm gray for the walls and new curtains. He'd paired those with an explosion of video game equipment. "Killing Nazis makes me feel better," he said, by way of explanation. "And so do you," he added. "God, I missed you."

I shoved him down on the couch and kissed him again.

"You know, eventually we need to talk about our problem," he said when I moved to kissing his neck.

"Eventually." He needed to put his persistence to better use. "We also need to focus on the good," I reminded him, reaching under his T-shirt and caressing his rock-hard chest.

"Like the fact that you drive me crazy?" he asked, leaning up to kiss me. "That I love you enough to yell at you in front of church ladies?"

"You owe me big time for that," I said against his lips.

But who was I kidding? We'd never be a conventional couple, and I didn't want to be. I wanted this. Him. One disagreement didn't change who we were or what he meant to me.

He kissed me again and I stopped thinking at all. I wrestled him out of his shirt. He flipped me on my back. We were right about to get to a very good part when—

The doorbell rang.

"Ignore it," Ellis said against the soft skin at the nook of my shoulder, his breath setting off a cascade of sensation all over.

Bing-bong!

"Are you expecting anybody?" I asked, distracted, my fingers running through his short, thick hair.

The door cracked open, and I felt cold and abandoned as Ellis sprang up, ready for action in two seconds flat.

"I'm so, so sorry." Beau peeked his head around the door. "Mortified, actually."

"What the hell?" Ellis's shoulders relaxed now that the threat had passed, but the rest of him stood stiff and held his ground. "This isn't a good time for a visit," he said as I admired his hard, muscled back.

"I can't help it," Beau said, pushing the door open anyway. My skunk snuggled up in his other arm.

"Lucy!" I'd lost one shoe somewhere on or near the couch, so I kicked the other one off and went to fetch her. Beau was supposed to feed her and let her settle in for bed. "What's going on?" I asked, sidestepping Ellis so I could take her.

"I was making her the skunky bananas foster," Beau said, handing her to me, "but she got into the compost while I did the final flambé."

Ah, yes. Keeping her out of the compost was a constant battle. "She does that if you don't watch her like a hawk. Trash smells delicious," I added to Ellis, who stood ramrod straight while Lucy licked my chin.

"I thought it might make her sick," Beau said, "but I didn't know, and you weren't answering your phone. Neither was Ellis. Bree's not at the shelter, and I couldn't call anyone else."

"No, you can't," Ellis agreed.

Pet skunks were technically illegal in Tennessee.

"I couldn't leave her alone if she was in trouble, so I brought her to you," Beau said, his grin faltering. "Hey, brother."

"Hey, yourself," Ellis said, looking him over, taking his measure. "What the hell were you doing at my girlfriend's house?"

"He was worried about me, so he went along on my ghost hunt tonight," I said, stroking Lucy's head, hoping to make it sound like it didn't matter.

Which it didn't.

"I invited myself along," Beau admitted. "Verity didn't want me there."

"So therefore you enabled her and then you hung out at her house," Ellis said, his words reasonable, his tone a little too threatening.

"He actually helped me a lot," I said, running a hand down Ellis's arm. Ellis didn't react.

"I kicked butt," Beau said, trying for charm, although he didn't quite pull it off.

"I had to get information from a gangster who didn't want to talk to me, but Beau saved the day by being a guy's guy and talking cowboy movies," I said, trying to downplay my need for help, but at the same time, sell Beau's accomplishment. Hard. "Isn't that terrific?"

"Yes," Ellis lied.

"You'll be happy to know Lucy looks fine," I said to the guys. While her belly gurgled from her rich meal, she seemed alert and healthy. Maybe some skunks would get sick from compost

—heaven knew I tried to keep Lucy out of mine—but it seemed she'd built up a tolerance.

"I'm glad," Beau said, "and I'm really sorry to interrupt. You two have a good night," he said to Ellis. Then, with a smile aimed directly at me, he added, "You too, Verity."

Ellis closed the door the second Beau cleared the threshold. "What the hell was that?"

"How about we go back to kissing and not talking," I suggested, placing Lucy on the floor.

Ellis gritted his jaw and ran his hands through his hair. "I tell you I worry about keeping you safe when you're ghost hunting, so you take *my brother* with you?" he accused. "I mean, you're using Beau to hunt down mobsters!"

"Not by choice," I pointed out. "He led me to believe you sent him."

Ellis stared at me, but he didn't speak, so I kept going. "It's not going to be a habit," I insisted. "It happened to work out this time."

Ellis cursed under his breath. "You never would have partnered with Beau before."

"Believe me, I resisted it."

He began to speak, huffed, and had to start again. "It just makes me wonder how well I know you."

That wasn't fair. "Your brother said a lot of nice things about you tonight. He followed me on my ghost hunt because he wanted to help fix things between us. I want that, too." I wrapped my hands around his waist and laid my head on his chest.

He cradled my head in his hand. We stood for a moment, simply breathing each other in. "I love you, dammit," he murmured into my hair.

"And I am one hundred percent crazy fool in love with you," I said against his skin.

"We'll figure this out," he promised.

We didn't make it back to the couch that night, but it was all right. We snuggled together in his bed in the dark while Ellis ran his hands through my hair and made it feel like everything would be fine.

At some point, Lucy managed to worm her way between us and start snoring. We stayed that way until we fell asleep.

When I woke in the morning, the sun shone brightly in the sky and Ellis had already gone to work. I scratched my yawning little skunk on the head.

She'd showed no sign of sickness after her venture into eggshell heaven last night. I was glad for her and for myself because I had a busy day ahead.

Lucy sneezed and rolled over to reveal the corner of a piece of scratch paper.

"What's this?" She resisted as I slid it out from under her.

Ellis had written me a note.

Last night was great. Why don't you take a day off? Maybe meet Lauralee for lunch? Lay off on the ghost hunting while I'm at work. We'll talk tonight and figure it out.

One hundred percent crazy fool in love with you,

Ellis

"Hmm..." I stroked Lucy's silky ears. It would be nice, but Lauralee had a sick kiddo, and I had a few things I wanted to check out.

"Ellis isn't going to be happy, but I need to go see Pastor Mike," I told my skunk, who promptly reclaimed the note as a pillow.

I showered and changed and slipped into the white jeans and pink sweater I kept over at Ellis's for the occasions when I neglected to go home.

"I'll drop you on the way," I promised my skunk, grabbing one of Ellis's strawberry Pop-Tarts and breaking off a piece for Lucy. My phone rang as she gobbled it down.

It was my sister, Melody.

"Are you ready for this?" she asked as I scooped my skunk up and headed for the door.

"What?" I asked, digging for Ellis's front door key.

Why he insisted on locking his door was beyond me.

Well, I supposed Beau had proved his point last night.

"I asked around about that donation Fiera said she made to the library, how she had all those pictures from Jorie's house."

"And?" I asked, turning the key in the lock.

I knew Melody would come through for me on this.

"Well, the library received no donation. No photographs, letters, or anything at all. If Fiera did take anything from Jorie's, she kept it for herself."

Chapter Eighteen

"Sounds like we're going to have a word with Fiera," I told my skunk, snuggling her into a travel crate I kept in the trunk of my car. She turned in a circle and found a comfortable spot on her fleece blanket.

Lucy was calm this morning, content. She'd enjoyed our time at Ellis's house. I had too.

But it was time to get back to business. I couldn't wait around all day for Ellis to get off work. Fiera had lied to me about removing photos from Jorie's house. Then she'd lied about giving them to the library. Why?

I steered out onto Magnolia avenue. Fiera lived only a few blocks over, but I didn't think a confrontation at her house would suddenly inspire Fiera to confess to both incidents or convince her to cough up what she'd taken. If anything, it would make her dig in harder—and let her know I was onto her.

I'd have to be more clever.

In the meantime, I dropped Lucy off at my house. I sliced her a wedge of Cinnamon Banana Skunk Crumble and watched her devour it, her tail swishing with joy.

It was too chilly for her to be outside; otherwise I might feel obliged to dig out whatever had captured her interest under the porch. I didn't think my white jeans could take it. But since I'd gotten her inside the house, it could wait.

"I'll see you later, sweetie," I said, grabbing my bag on the way out the door.

When I'd met with Pastor Mike yesterday, he'd invited me to drop by the church any time to see what he had from Jorie's.

Now was the time.

I headed down the back porch steps.

I'd at least get to see some of what Jorie had saved. Hopefully it would be enough to give me an idea who might have lured her up to the bell tower, and what might have made them desperate enough to kill.

When I arrived at my car, I saw a gangster waiting in the passenger seat.

"Ha!" Frankie said when I slid onto the driver's side and deposited my bag on the floor behind me. "You're not going to take off on me today. I'm going to watch you like a hawk."

Seriously? "We're not going to intercept your brother until after dark. Wally Big Ears said so."

Frankie crossed his ankle over his knee, his foot flapping up and down like he was powering a motor. "I'm not going to sit around all day, hoping you make it back in time."

Oh, joy. I'd traded a happy skunk for an unhappy ghost.

"Fine. Hold tight," I said, leaving my keys to dangle in the ignition. "I'll go get your urn."

There was no sense arguing with Frankie when he was like this. Besides, despite the fact that he liked to dance on my last good nerve, I didn't relish the idea of him pacing the yard, alone all day, waiting for our showdown tonight. It would likely drive Lucy crazy. At least with me, he'd have something to distract him.

"Where are we going?" he asked when I'd made it back to the car.

"The Three Angels Church," I said, tucking his urn into my bag.

"That place again?" He rolled his head back. "Let's at least go to Holy Oak Cemetery, where I can score a drink with Handsome Henry."

"We don't have time to hang out with a dead hit man," I told him, pulling down on the shifter and ka-chunking my car into drive.

"He's the only guy I know whose girlfriend died hanging onto a bar cart," Frankie protested.

"Sorry." I steered down the side drive. I did like Henry's girlfriend, Rosie. She was a pistol. But we had more important things to do.

"How about we visit the police station and I strike a few deals with the dead bookie upstairs while you make kissy faces at Ellis?" he suggested.

Frankie was full of ideas this morning.

"How about you hang out in the cemetery and tell me what's going on with the ghosts at the Three Angels Church?" I countered. "Try to figure out why the place has such negative energy. Oh, and watch out for the gravedigger and the woman with the cat-eye glasses who plays the organ."

"And just like that, she puts me to work," Frankie said to nobody in particular.

At least he didn't say no.

He'd also stopped the leg twitching, which I considered a success.

We'd find answers for Frankie soon. Tonight. In the meantime, I'd be grateful if he could help me clear a few things up.

It didn't take long to reach the north side of town and the gates of the Three Angels Church.

"If I've got to see it, you've got to see it," Frankie said as the tingling sparks of his energy settled over me.

"Truly?" I asked. "You just got your leg back."

"Exactly, so let's not stay long," he ordered.

Not a problem. I didn't relish another visit to the church. "All I want to do is talk to the pastor," I assured him, and myself.

"I forgot how much this place creeps me out," Frankie said with a shudder as he noticed a woman in a bloody bathrobe standing at the entrance.

"It's ten kinds of strange," I agreed, slowing as we passed her. She stared into space, giving no indication she noticed us. "Why is she acting like we're not here?"

"Takes all kinds to make a world," Frankie muttered.

It was more than that. "You can ask her while you're waiting," I suggested. "I mean, don't most ghosts have a reason to haunt a particular building or area?"

"Your subtlety is not subtle," he informed me.

"I just don't get it," I wondered aloud. "If you had an afterlife and all eternity to live it, why not drop by the speakeasy under the flower shop?"

"You have to know the code," he said as if I were daft.

"Bad example," I said. But based on my experience so far, a good portion of the ghostly life appeared fun, or at least moderately entertaining. "If I were dead, I wouldn't mind playing cards with the Civil War guys or asking Rosie to mix me a drink. Why do all these ghosts stay here instead of going out and enjoying their afterlife?"

Frankie shrugged. "Not everybody can live like a gangster."

I was about to respond with something clever when I spotted a familiar woman up ahead, standing under a tree, staring at the ground. I slowed. "Wait. That's the organist." Her dress sagged over her thin frame, and the chains on her glasses hung low. "She's the one who attacked me the other day."

Her mop of hair blocked my view of her face. She didn't even look up as we passed.

"The organist with the knife?" Frankie asked, fidgeting

again. "You should be glad she's staring at the dirt instead of noticing you."

"Yes, but *why* is she doing that?" I prodded.

"Why not?" He threw up his hands. "You always have to know why everybody does everything, and it usually gets us in hot water."

"If you don't like the way I do things, perhaps you shouldn't have insisted on coming along," I mused.

"All I'm saying is we should mind our own business," Frankie said as we pulled into the parking area.

Because Frankie the German was an expert on staying out of trouble.

"Wander the cemetery," I suggested, retrieving my bag from the back. "Haunt a little," I added as he lowered his chin and stared at me. "Do it. See if you can figure out what's going on around here."

"Okay, fine. Better than listening to you." His voice lingered as he passed through the car door and glided toward the cemetery.

It wasn't my fault we needed answers. Besides, a ghostly investigation would be good for him. Maybe it would take his mind off Lou and our failure so far to find him.

Plus, with any luck, with a new ghost in the cemetery, the spirits would pay less attention to me.

Jorie's soul traces had all but disappeared from the grassy area underneath the bell tower. I hoped she'd found some peace as she transitioned into the afterlife.

I opened the heavy wood door of the church and stepped into the cool dark of the vestibule.

Now that I stood alone in the old church, I could feel the age and the history in a way that was impossible during a crowded fundraiser.

The heels of my boots echoed on the polished wood floors,

and I felt a sense of peace and constancy that wavered only slightly as I passed the entrance to the bell tower.

I wondered if the gravedigger lurked up there.

Pastor Mike stood at the front of the church, bent over a section of the carving of the three angels as if it were the only thing in the world.

"It's a gorgeous piece," I said, joining him.

The carving depicted two angels, a man and a woman with widespread wings and loving smiles, bending to admire a cherub resting on a bed of sunflowers. The baby raised its face to the sun shining above, which cast thick rays down over the trio.

Pastor Mike bent over one of the cherub's toes, rubbing a polishing cloth over a crack in the wood. "It's my favorite thing about this church," he mused. "Other than the people, of course," he added. He returned his attention to the piece with a small sigh. I detected more visible cracks and a chip out of the male angel's nose. "We'll fix it up," he vowed.

"You're doing a great job so far." The piece gleamed with wood polish and smelled like lemons. He'd organized several fundraisers to restore the carving. Ours with the heritage society was simply the latest.

"If only I had my grandfather's touch," Pastor Mike said, trying for levity. His regret seeped through.

"It was a different time," I assured him. Although how the original Pastor Clemens had somehow managed to finance charities and the church while weathering the effects of the depression was beyond me. Some people just had a gift.

It was no wonder so many people admired him to this day.

"Your dad showed me pictures of all the great things your grandfather did," I said, watching Pastor Mike rub a stray bit of wood polish from a ray of sunshine.

"This is his legacy," he said. "My dad's, too."

"And yours," I reminded him, smiling at the mention of his

father. I'd enjoyed my visit with Pastor Bob. "Your dad is a great guy."

"He is," Pastor Mike said, stuffing the cloth in his pocket and returning his attention to me. "Thanks for indulging him. My father couldn't stop talking about your visit."

"I always enjoy talking Sugarland history."

"Then you found a friend," he said wryly.

I'd have to stop by Pastor Bob's again sometime.

"Speaking of such, I'd be glad to show you those photos I have." He led me down toward an unassuming door behind the choir section. "I'm going to give them to Suzanne once she gets into town, but I'm sure she wouldn't mind you taking a look."

"Thanks," I said, letting him open the door for me.

I stepped into a cramped office with small stained-glass windows along the right side. Bookshelves took up the wall ahead of me and the one to the left. More bookshelves flanked the door I'd just entered.

"Is this a library?" I asked.

"The old parish office," Pastor Mike said, ducking past me to pull the tassel on a Tiffany-style lamp perched on a battered wooden desk. "The original Pastor Clemens lived in a small house behind the church and used this office." He smiled.

"There's a house in the back?" I'd never noticed.

"Oh, it's long gone. My father modernized. These days we do all of our administration out of an old barn at the pastor's residence down the road," he said, his gaze slanting over the books lining the walls. "There's more room there."

"If these walls could talk, right?" I asked.

"I'd love that," he mused. "Okay," he said, moving to a card table wedged into the corner to my right. It took up a big portion of the room. "Here are those boxes from Jorie's house. You can empty them on the table if you'd like, or if you need more space, you can use the desk. There's not much room in here."

"I'll manage," I said, glad for the chance. "On the day she died, Jorie tried to give me a picture of my grandmother at Jorie's wedding," I said wistfully. "Did she mention anything about it to you?" I added, taking a stab.

"She didn't, but I would have cherished seeing that," he said. "Your grandmother had the loveliest smile." His face lit up as a thought occurred to him. "There might be some wedding pictures in these boxes." He removed a few pictures from the top of the nearest box.

"So you haven't looked yet?" I asked, taking a few from the same box he had. The first showed a boy in front of a chalk-board, flanked by a smiling couple.

"Oh, that's the elementary school before the renovation," Pastor Mike said, excited. "No, to tell you the truth, I hadn't planned to take the time to go through these. I only wanted to help Suzanne."

"Did she tell you which ones she wanted?" I pressed.

"She didn't need to. Jorie wrote Suzanne's name on the front."

"Ah." I spotted it, on masking tape in Jorie's looping hand-writing.

He also hadn't touched a hand to his chin, which had been MayBelle's tool to know if he was lying.

I smiled. "It seems Jorie was giving a lot of memories away. I'll have to ask Fiera if she has any nice photos," I said, trying not to fish too hard.

Pastor Mike's attention had been captured by a photo of a crowd at a dance hall. "I couldn't say what Jorie wanted her friend to have." He glanced up at me. "But there were dozens of boxes at Jorie's apartment."

"There aren't anymore." I'd found only a few.

He seemed surprised at that. "No," he said, lowering the photos. "There are all kinds of boxes in a cabinet under the TV. I took the ones marked for Suzanne, but I don't think Jorie would have minded at all if you take a look at the rest of them, as long as you don't disturb anything."

Too bad someone had beat me to it.

He flipped to another photo. "The town picnic 1957," Pastor Mike gushed, as excited as I would be if I weren't distracted by a murder investigation.

Fiera must have taken almost everything.

Unless someone else had gotten a few boxes as well.

There was no way to know for sure.

MayBelle had only seen Pastor Mike and Fiera. Although, it wasn't as if she'd watched the hall twenty-four seven.

And MayBelle might not be the most reliable witness. She'd stated quite clearly that Fiera had taken her items before Mike had arrived.

"Here's a picture of Jorie's husband, Ray, with my brother, Felix." Pastor Mike said, holding it up. "Ray would play the guitar while Felix sang happy birthday to anybody at the picnic who had one." He grinned. "They sang especially loud to the ladies who wanted to forget turning a year older."

I tried to smile back. This was going to take a while with Pastor Mike.

"Oh, and here's one of the cemetery cleanup." He held it close to his face, taking in every detail. "We used to have a whole crew back in the day. The congregation could fill the church back then."

While I adored town history, I found it difficult to focus on anything but the case at hand. "What do you do to maintain the graves now?" I asked. Maybe the ghosts were upset that the cemetery had been neglected, although the grounds looked nice enough to me.

"I hire goats," Pastor Mike gushed, lowering the photo. "Cletus Barnes drives them over for me every Monday afternoon. It's eco-friendly and a hoot to watch."

"Oh my. That sounds pretty cute," I admitted.

"He puts little flower cages over the roses on Ray Davis's grave. And I leave my car at home or they'll perch on it like parrots. Come by on Monday and take a gander," he offered.

I wondered how many visitors Pastor Mike got between fundraisers, when folks didn't have an official reason to drop by.

"I've got to bring some of these pictures over to my dad's tonight," he mused, holding up a picture of a 1970s kid with an ice cream cone. "This is Grace Finch, who is now our church secretary. Ray always had that camera clicking," he clucked. "Oh, and this is MayBelle dressed as an angel for the Christmas program," he said, handing me a photo of the frowniest angel I'd ever seen, her hands folded in reluctant prayer. "That's the only time you'll see her sport a halo," he teased.

"She doesn't act like a preacher's daughter," I had to admit.

"Truth be told, she acts exactly like one," he countered. "Some see the role as a challenge and aim for perfection; others see what they can get away with." He set the picture aside. "Let's just say Grandpa Clemens knew what he was in for when MayBelle used to hang out at the five-and-dime and con old ladies into buying her lollipops. She told each of them she'd 'prayed God would send them to give her a treat.'"

"And it worked?" I asked.

"She had a whole stash under her bed." His phone rang and he pulled it out of his back pocket. "Oh, Verity, I need to take this."

"I can step out of the room," I offered.

"Oh, no. You keep at it," he told me. "I'll do a walk and talk out in the cemetery." He raised the sleeve of his shirt to display a Fitbit. "Helps me get my steps in."

"Pastor Mike," he said, answering his call. "Oh, Mrs. Danvers. How's your husband doing?"

His voice faded as he left the building, and I turned back to the photos. At least I could make a dent without hearing the story behind each one. There would be plenty of time for that. In fact, after this was over, perhaps I'd stop by and go through them one by one with Pastor Mike. His dad might even like to join.

And so I explored the contents of the boxes, placing the photos I'd seen in three stacks on the desk, to correspond with each box. It was only respectful to keep things in the order Jorie had left them.

Only I saw no pictures from Jorie and Ray's wedding. I didn't understand it. Suzanne should be the one to receive those photos. She would be the one to appreciate them.

But they were not among the pictures set aside for her. I double-checked as I placed the photos back where they belonged.

I left the office and stepped outside the church onto the stairs. Pastor Mike leaned against the sprawling old oak tree beyond the parking lot, thinking, from the looks of it.

He startled and stood upright when he saw me. "How'd you do?"

"I didn't find anything from Jorie's wedding," I confessed. "That's really the only thing I was looking for."

"I'm sorry," he said. "I know what those pictures would mean to you."

I sighed. Yes, from what I'd seen in there, he did know. "It's all right. I'll ask MayBelle who else attended the wedding. I'm sure plenty of people in town were there." This was Sugarland, after all. "Maybe someone else has a print."

"That's the attitude," he said, then his face fell. "I have to tell you, Verity. While you were inside, I made a few calls to check up on some of our members who are going through hard times." He pursed his lips. "One in the hospital has taken a turn for the worse. I'd like to stop in before visiting hours are over, so I'm afraid I have to go. You can call me or come back to chat anytime," he was quick to add.

"Don't worry about it," I assured him. "I'll be fine on my own."

Although I wondered where my ghost had gone. I didn't see Frankie among the graves on this side of the cemetery.

In fact, there might be one more person I could talk to while I was here.

"Would you mind if I stay a while?" I asked the pastor.

"That's no problem at all," he said, drawing a set of keys out of his pocket. "Are you going to try to talk to the ghosts?"

"You know this area is haunted?" I asked, walking him to a blue Ford Focus.

Not all religious people believed in ghosts. Or if they did, some didn't admit it.

He opened the door. "This is going to sound crazy," he said, turning back to me, "but the spot by the organ is oddly cold sometimes."

"That's a puzzle," I said, not quite willing to go there with him.

"Stay as long as you like," he said, resting a hand on top of the door. "And thanks for looking through some of those pictures with me. I enjoyed it."

"Me too," I said. And I meant it.

He nodded. "We're having the service here for Jorie on Saturday at three o'clock. I hope you'll be there to help us remember her."

"I wouldn't miss it," I assured him.

We said our goodbyes and I watched him drive off.

Good luck, indeed.

I'd need it, I realized as I saw the gravedigger standing next to a leaning cross near the edge of the cemetery, watching me.

Chapter Nineteen

The gravedigger leaned heavily on his shovel, staring at me as I walked past the parking lot and toward a copse of redbuds. I remembered Jorie standing out that way on the morning of the fundraiser.

She'd told me how she visited her husband's final resting place every Saturday, simply to talk, wishing he could hear her.

Truth was, Ray was probably with her more often than she realized. I had no doubt he watched over her, listened to her, loved her as much as he ever had. Couples like Jorie and Ray shared a bond that death couldn't break.

Deep down, she'd recognized it. It was what brought her back to visit him.

While I had no reason to think he'd want to hang out at his grave without the prospect of seeing his wife, I figured I'd give it a shot all the same. Ghosts often returned to places that held fond memories, and I had to assume those Saturday visits with Jorie were pleasant.

A soft breeze rattled the tree limbs above as I made my way to the moss-dotted stone bearing Ray's name. It was easy to spot. The Irish cross stood out from the others. Yet my heart sank a little when I didn't see any sign of him.

"Hey, Ray." I brushed a dried leaf off the top of the cross. "I wanted to stop by and see how you're doing." I rested my hand on the cold stone, and at that moment he seemed very far away. Still, I'd come out to talk, and if there was a chance he could hear me, I'd take it.

I glanced out over the headstones dotting the gently sloping hill, then back to Ray's final resting place. "I want to tell you how sorry I am about Jorie. She deserved so much better than what happened to her. I'm going to find justice for her. I promise."

A chill went down my back, straight to the bone. I turned and saw a ghostly lizard drop from the back of my sweater and scuttle off toward the parking lot.

"E-yikes!" I slapped at my tingling skin and shook out my sweater.

Where had that come from?

I turned back around to find the ghostly suspect sitting on his headstone, grinning at me.

"Dang it, Ray. You scared me to death!"

"You're too easy," he guffawed. "Always were."

He hadn't changed a bit. Big and beefy, with a ready smile and a bald head. "I could hire a stonemason to sharpen off that gravestone into a point," I teased, resting a hand on my hip. "You won't be sitting so pretty, then."

"Wouldn't affect me on this side." He barked out a laugh. "But that would be funny." His eyes shone, from one too many pranks or from something else, I couldn't tell. "I'm glad you came, kid."

"Me too. Despite the lizard." I'd have to get him back for that one. I shifted my weight, trying to think of an easy way to say it. Finding none, I settled on the plain truth instead. "I'm sorry about Jorie." When he simply nodded, I couldn't help but ask, "Have you...seen her? Can you tell me how she's doing?"

He hesitated. "I did see her right after she passed." He wore a small smile as he folded his hands in his lap. "It was wonderful —and it went by too fast."

I appreciated his openness. This was the first time a ghost had willingly shared with me what happened after death.

It wasn't like I could get any details out of Frankie.

He shook his head ruefully. "Maybe she'll want to come back, or maybe we'll go into the light together. It's hard to wait, but she's worth it."

I simply nodded. "Did you see what happened to her?"

He stood and shoved his hands into his pockets. "You mean who pushed her?" he asked pointedly. "Make no mistake, she didn't just fall."

My stomach fluttered. That was what I was afraid of. "What did you see?"

He closed his eyes tightly. "She came flying out of that window."

"Oh, my God." I couldn't imagine seeing that happen to someone I loved—if it was Ellis or Melody. I touched a hand to my chest, wishing I could take away some of his pain.

He looked past me, to the bell tower. With the blue sky and fluffy white clouds behind it, it was hard to imagine the horror that had happened there. "I didn't see who did it."

"I'm so, so sorry," I said, wishing I could reach out and hug him.

He cleared his throat. "Me too."

"Jorie was one in a million. She was part of so many people's lives." He of all people knew that.

He walked a few paces from his grave and looked down at the stone. "Every Saturday, I'd wait for her here," he said thickly. "Some of the dead lose track of time." He glanced toward the spirit of a woman in a flowing white nightgown as she ambled past, close to where we stood. "It's easy to do on this side, but I never lost track. I never missed a Saturday because I knew she'd be here."

"She felt close to you here," I said simply.

He nodded. He knew. "I'd watch over her during the week," he said, his eyes misting over. "Sometimes when she was paying bills or shoveling the back steps, she'd say, 'Ray, I wish you were here.'" He grazed a hand through a rose in full bloom. "I wished that, too. I wished she didn't have to figure out online bill payments or how to drill the curtain rod holders into the wall, or the million other little things I would have done for her." He shoved his hands into his pockets. "But every time she struggled, she wasn't alone. I was with her."

"It's all anyone can ask for." We couldn't control death. We just had to live with it.

"I looked forward to her visits here." He glided up to his gravestone. "I'm waiting for her now. It might take a year. It might take longer." He traced a hand over Jorie's name etched into the stone, with her birth year and the shiny, empty space where her death would be recorded. "She'll come here looking for me, and I'll be waiting for her."

Was it wise to be envious of a ghost? Because at that moment, I was.

I noticed the woman in the nightgown had stopped nearby.

"Hello?" I called to her.

She turned, and I saw her bloodied throat and the trail it left on her white gown.

She didn't speak. In fact, I wasn't sure she was all there.

"You're not going to make much headway with that one." Ray shook his head sadly. "I've about given up on the ghosts here."

Truly? "Don't you know some of them from life?" He'd been a member of this church.

"Everyone I know either went to the light or is haunting

somewhere else," he said, shaking his head. "This isn't the friendliest place. Most of the ghosts just...wander. And even if they stop for a minute, they aren't exactly sitting on their gravestones to chat."

To be fair, I wasn't sure how many ghosts did that. Except for Ray.

"Watch," he said as he approached the nightgown ghost gently and stopped a few feet short of her. "Hi," he said as if he were encountering her on the street or at a picnic. "I'm Ray. What's your name?"

She stared straight through him.

He gave me an uncomfortable shrug. "They're all like this."

It gave me the creeps.

I studied her for a moment. While she didn't seem to notice either one of us, it still felt wrong to talk with her standing so close. It was as if we were treating her like a rock or a tree instead of a person.

"Can we...walk?" I asked Ray.

"Sure," he said, putting himself between me and the other ghost.

Without agreeing on a direction or even discussing it, we set off toward the bell tower.

"Have the ghosts here always been so...dead?" I asked.

"Since I've been here," Ray said, glancing over his shoulder at the ghost we'd left behind. "I call them zombie ghosts. They don't seem to know where they are most of the time." He shook his head. "After Jorie died, I tried to see if any of them saw what had happened. I went up to every ghost I found—at least twice—and begged them to talk to me. But..." He gestured uselessly.

"No luck?" I asked.

"Denied," he said, resigned.

"Do you think it's them or the place?" I asked.

"I don't think it's the cemetery itself." We'd stopped short of the parking lot, and he glanced out over the empty space.

"When I first got here, I worried it could be contagious, but whatever it is, I'm fine."

"I sent my friend Frankie to talk to some of them. So far, he hasn't made much headway, either."

"I would have bugged out a long time ago, except that Jorie was so attached to my grave." Ray glanced back at it. "Being there makes me feel closer to her. But the rest of this place has been unsettling to say the least."

He gritted his teeth and cocked his head.

The woman in the nightgown had followed us. And she had been joined by the ghost of a bloody butcher who wielded a very large, very sharp looking cleaver.

"It's interesting," Ray said, once again maneuvering himself between me and the other ghosts. "I think they're perking up."

"That's good, right? Maybe they're becoming less zombielike." Although the ghosts' attention felt less social and more like I was being stalked in an alley. "Maybe this is our chance to ask them about Jorie."

"You read my mind," Ray murmured. I felt the chill as he drew closer. "But give it a minute. Let's see what's going on first."

"Right." I usually liked to talk first and worry about consequences later, but that didn't always work out so well.

"Let's keep moving." Ray led me across the parking lot, skirting away from the bell tower. "See if they follow us."

We stopped by a large magnolia on the left side of the church past the front steps. "Ray, when you grew up in this parish, do you remember any tragedies or anything bad happening on the property?"

"Well, let me think." He ran a hand over his bald head. "There was the time Naomi Jenkins took charge of buying the communion wine and Pastor Bob accidentally served the congregation prune juice instead of grape juice."

"Ray," I prodded. His mind would have to go that way.

"I'm sorry," he said, "I can't think of anything big and tragic. This has always been a pretty simple parish."

I skimmed my hair back from my face, thinking. I mean, this was Sugarland. If this property had a shocking or tragic history, it would have been known all around town. Wouldn't it?

Ray shifted slightly and I saw a figure behind him. The gravedigger stood at the top of the church steps, watching us.

"Um," I began.

Ray glanced over his shoulder. "Honey," he said, turning back to me, "I think we have a bigger question to answer. These ghosts weren't interested in anything before, and now they're interested in you."

"That's the one who chased me down from the bell tower," I said, although he didn't appear aggressive at the moment.

"I do see him up in the tower a lot," Ray said, nodding at him. "That could be his spot." The bloody butcher and the nightgown lady began gliding across the parking lot toward us. "I'm not sure why they're so curious," he added. "Maybe they see me talking to you and realize you can see us. Your talent is unusual."

It was Frankie's power, not mine. But, yes, I could understand where it might draw a crowd.

"It's not just that they're noticing you. They're getting more active." Ray glanced past me, to a man in a tuxedo carrying a broken champagne glass.

"Hi," I said, giving tuxedo man a little wave.

The man tilted his head toward me as if asking whether I could see him. Then he raised the glass.

"Maybe don't do that," Ray said, raising a hand to ward off the ghost.

"Oh, I'll be fine," I assured him. "I'm good with people."

"It's not that," Ray said, stiffening. "Have you noticed that most of the spirits here...their lives seem to have ended badly."

"That doesn't mean they were bad people," I insisted. I'd met plenty of ghosts who'd endured terrible deaths. Although not so many at once.

"Sure," Ray said absently, distracted by a dead preacher drifting down the road toward us. "How is word spreading?"

"I was hoping you'd know." I hadn't seen any of them talk.

"I'm not a ghost expert," Ray said. "I'm just dead."

Now he sounded like Frankie.

"I have an important question for you," I pressed, shifting a little closer to him, damn the chill. "On the day she died, Jorie tried to give me a wonderful photo of her and my grandmother on your big day. It was gorgeous." And it was gone. "Jorie had it with her when..."

I couldn't say it.

Ray drew a hand down his face as if that could blunt the pain. "I think I know where it ended up," he said gently. "I'll show you."

Chapter Twenty

Ray walked me down the side of the church. Scraggly rosebushes haphazardly climbed the walls, and those branches that hadn't the strength to cling swooned lazily. A flapper stood in our path. She wore a wire garrote like a necklace, the wooden ends dangling against her throat. Her killer had strangled her from the front. They'd watched her die.

Her bow-shaped mouth opened and closed as her unfocused eyes flitted over us, like a rifle sighting a target.

"Let's try something," Ray said under his breath, leading me straight for her. "A test. Don't look at me. Don't talk to me. Let's see if she notices you."

"Right," I said on an exhale.

I tried my best to walk casually. I hummed a little tune as we passed close enough to touch her.

I don't see anything.

Maybe if I thought it hard enough, it would be true.

The flapper turned her head to watch us pass, wheezing as if she couldn't quite draw a breath she didn't need to take.

I said a quick little prayer for her and wished I could have done more.

Usually, I went out of my way to interact with the ghosts I met while investigating. I liked to offer comfort where I could and gather any help or insights they were willing to offer.

It was my favorite part of the job.

This felt unnatural. I couldn't help but wonder if I was being overly cautious to avoid them, just because one had a knife, two had attacked me, and quite a few of them were creeping me out.

They were people, after all. Or, they had been. I liked to think I was more open minded.

I looked over my shoulder at the flapper. We locked eyes.

Oops.

Hers widened for a split second, then narrowed as she zoned in on me.

"I think I just answered our question," I murmured. She began to glide toward us.

"Yeah, you did," Ray said, picking up the pace. "I know you want to talk to them, and I do, too. But let me show you what I know about Jorie's photo before we get all chatty. You mind hoofing it?"

"Gladly," I said, breaking into an easy run as he led me to the back of the church.

"Maybe they'll lose interest if we're not right in front of them," Ray said, hurrying me past a small patio and down a short brick path.

The path opened onto a modest memorial garden, merely a circle of camellias with a pair of stone benches and a birdbath in the middle.

The bath stood dry, its bowl charred. A stick lay a few feet beyond, the end of it burnt.

Ray stopped and crouched near a grouping of spindly trunks enmeshed in dried leaves. "Here," he murmured, and I saw the charred corner of a vintage photograph caught among the leaves.

"Oh no." I squatted next to him. "It might not be the one Jorie gave me," I added, with hope disguised as logic.

I turned the remnant over with a stick, determined to preserve any potential evidence for Ellis, and my heart sank when I saw the back. A small piece of masking tape remained, with the "ity" of my name on it, written in Jorie's hand.

I closed my eyes. My photo was well and truly gone.

It seemed the person who'd pushed Jorie had wanted the wedding picture, or at least didn't want anyone else to have it. And I had no idea why. Perhaps it had something to do with the entire package she'd given me.

But what would make somebody want to kill over a rose, a picture, and a letter?

Ellis would have told me if the police had found anything significant in the letter. I mean, I'd asked him directly, and he'd said it was only a chatty piece of correspondence. I'd ask him again in light of the burned photograph.

"Thanks for the help, Ray," I said, straightening. "I wouldn't have found this without you."

"Thank you for looking closer at Jorie's death," he said. "It means a lot that you care."

I opened my mouth to tell him how much everyone cared, but then I saw something that made me lose my train of thought.

The flapper ghost stood directly behind him. A tiny rivulet of blood trickled from the corner of her mouth.

"Hi," I said to her, going for a peppiness I didn't feel. I tried not to let my gaze travel down to the garrote at her throat.

"I've seen you around," Ray chimed in. "My name is Ray Davis."

She stared at him.

"My wife, Jorie, and I grew up going to the Three Angels," he said heartily.

I felt the cold behind me and turned to see the minister from the road.

"Well, hello," I said, glad to see he wasn't even a bit bloody. "I'm Verity. Who might you be?"

Wordlessly, he reached for me.

I made a quick sidestep. "No touching," I warned, spotting the bloody butcher trailing across the grass straight for me.

This was turning into a crowd.

The preacher made another grab for me, and I sidestepped toward the butcher. "Let's all relax. There's no need to get pushy."

The butcher raised his knife and drew closer.

Okay, now I was getting a little nervous.

"Why don't you put down your cleaver and we can talk," I suggested.

"Verity," Ray warned. He gripped the preacher by the coat, holding him off as the bloody butcher closed in on me, arms extended, cleaver raised.

"Can I at least get your name?" I asked the butcher. With that vacant look and those bloodshot eyes, I wasn't sure what he wanted. "What's your favorite cut of meat?"

"I think it's time to get you to your car," Ray said. "Now," he added as the woman in the bloody nightgown surged straight through the butcher, toward me.

"Yeah, I think I'm leaving," I said, opting to go sideways, between two camellia trees, their lower branches scratching at my back and tearing at my hair as I fought my way through.

It was better than the touch of a ghost or three.

Or another encounter with a stabby one.

"You can't go the way we came," Ray's voice sounded in my ear. "There are more of them that way."

I stumbled out from the trees and started booking it down the other side of the church, toward the parking lot.

"They're gathering in the parking lot," Ray's voice warned.

Holy smokes. I nearly tripped myself skidding to a stop.

"You can still make it to your car if you hurry," he urged.

Easy for him to say.

"I'll hold them off," he pledged.

"How?" With ghost lizards and other pranks? I turned the corner. On the other side stood the gravedigger. He raised a hand to reach for me.

He'd have to catch me first.

I hightailed it for the parking lot, struggling to keep my footing on the uneven ground on this side of the church. Still, I ran full-out, trusting Ray, hoping there weren't as many ghosts waiting for me as I feared.

I made it to the front of the church and realized it was worse.

At least a dozen ghosts milled in the parking lot. Either the gathering was a huge coincidence or word had spread. One by one, they all looked up and saw me.

"Frankie!" Now would be a great time for him to take back my power.

"Frankie!" I didn't see him anywhere.

I made a dash for the car. The ghosts might be dead and creepy, but I could run like the dickens.

A child with hollow cheeks and a wicked grin dropped his shoeshine box and closed a hand around my arm. "You," he rasped. I felt the shocking chill of his grip down to my bones. I yanked my arm away from him.

Keep running!

I ran full out to my car, flung the door open, and slid into the driver's seat like it was home plate.

The bloody butcher sat in my back seat.

Sweet baby Jesus. "Really?" I demanded as the bloody nightgown woman walked straight through my hood, toward me.

"I've got you," Ray said, materializing in my passenger seat. "Move."

Fingers shaking, I dug in my bag, found my keys.

"Go, go, go!" Ray hollered as ghosts began gathering in the road in front of us, blocking my only exit.

The butcher grabbed the back of my seat with a beefy hand. The other held the bloody chopping knife.

"Ray!" I hollered. If he wanted to protect me, now was the time.

"I got it," Ray said, huffing as he scrambled onto his knees to take on the butcher.

He grappled with the ghost. I shoved the car into drive, looking for another way out, but it was all ghosts in just about every direction.

"Hold on!" I spotted a hole in the thickening ghost mob and plowed straight through it. I felt the chill of the butcher trying to climb up next to me, or maybe it was Ray fighting with him as I gunned the engine like Mario Andretti. The speedometer read forty, fifty, sixty mph. Pedal to the metal, I fled the property and whatever demented souls haunted the old churchyard.

"Good girl!" Ray said, one of his hands pressed against the butcher's face, the other holding back a beefy hand clutching a hatchet as we passed the cemetery gates.

To my astonishment and sheer relief, Ray evaporated along with the butcher the second I crossed the property line.

I sped away, putting distance between me and the mess at the cemetery. "What was that?" I was chilled and sweating at the same time, my heart fluttering like a hummingbird.

The ghosts back there didn't answer when I spoke to them. They just wanted to paw at me, and half of them came with deadly weapons. It was ten kinds of awful, and it didn't make sense.

And oh, my word—I glanced to the seat next to me, then craned my neck to the empty back seat. What happened to Frankie? He couldn't go anywhere without his urn. He should have been pulled off the property the second I left.

Unless he lay dead—again—somewhere back there.

"Frankie?" I scanned the car, not willing to slow down or take my eyes off the road for more than a split second. "Where are you, Frank?"

A long moment later—too long—Frankie materialized next to me in the passenger seat, holding his throat with both hands, gasping for breath. "Don't call me Frank."

We had bigger problems. "What happened?"

"The shoeshine kid tried to kill me!" he heaved.

"Davey?"

"He strangled me with my stolen laces. He's out of his mind!"

"I think I saw him back there. He grabbed me." It didn't make sense. "Did Davey say anything before he attacked you? Like, did you even get to talk to him?"

"Yeah," Frankie said, glaring at me. "He asked about you."

Oh my.

"I told him how I lent you my power, and he went nutso," Frankie said, both hands braced around his neck as if he feared someone might start strangling him again. "Like that kid doesn't break the rules, too."

"What exactly did you say?" I pressed. I mean, there'd been plenty of times I'd wanted to strangle Frankie.

"Nothing!" He insisted. "It took forever to get him talking, and when I did, he went for my windpipe."

It was a good thing Frankie didn't need to breathe. Although I didn't think he'd appreciate the reminder.

"I was afraid you'd gotten killed again," I said, flying past fences and cows and ponds.

"I'm hard to kill," he said, fingers shaking as he loosened his tie.

I still worried about him. "Can you take your power back?"

He ripped it away so fast I swerved and got a head rush. "Thanks," I said, ignoring the spots dancing in my vision.

"I'm never setting foot in that cemetery again," Frankie vowed.

We'd worry about that later.

He was still out of breath as he settled back in his seat. "It seems you at least learned how to use the gas pedal. Good work."

"Only because I'm fleeing." Stars. He'd missed the whole thing. "They saw me back there. The ghosts. They saw me talking to Ray and they went all *Night of the Living Dead* on my rear."

His mouth dropped open. "Are you insulting the dead? Right in front of me?"

"No." I blew out a breath. My heart hadn't stopped racing. "I'm just trying to figure it out. I mean, Davey was nice to you last time."

"He stole my laces."

"This time, he tried to kill you." I gripped the steering wheel. "Is it because of me?"

"What makes you so special?" Frankie demanded.

"You told him about giving me your power, and he tried to kill you." It was simple deduction. "Now the kind of power transfer you do with me—is it forbidden?"

"Probably," Frankie snarked. "But why would a shoeshine boy care?"

Why indeed? "And why would they go after me? The ghosts have no reason to fear or dislike me. I've barely talked to any of them." Not that getting to know me would make them homicidal or anything. I was a nice person.

"I told you. I said it when you first wanted to go to that fundraiser. Nothing good happens at that church. We're never going back, and I mean it."

I didn't see how we could avoid it. I'd promised Ray I'd learn the truth about Jorie's death. We couldn't ignore this for the year or more it took until Jorie returned to give us the scoop herself. Even then, she might not have seen who pushed her. In the meantime, the trail would go cold and the evidence would be gone.

"I'm beginning to see Ellis's point," Frankie said, flinging his hands out like an Italian grandmother. "You don't know when to stay away from things that aren't good for you."

Said the drinking, gambling, chain-smoking gangster who gave up our secret to the shoeshine boy.

"That place is a menace," Frankie insisted, holding his palms faceup. "Look at my hands. They're fading from the stress. I need to be on my game when we intercept Lou tonight."

Between his issue with Lou and the strange environment at the church, our regular ghost-hunting activity was draining Frankie of energy at an alarming rate. My ghost had a lot on his plate.

"Why don't you get some rest?" I suggested. "Maybe head off to the ether?" It was an in-between where ghosts went to recharge. I had a few things I wanted to take care of anyway.

Frankie gave me a suspicious glance and slowly faded from sight.

I steered toward town.

With any luck, I could get a little work done while he rested. Knowing someone had purposely burned the photo Jorie had tried to give me at the fundraiser made me even more eager to discover what was so special about it.

I turned on to Magnolia street and headed toward downtown.

So what did a picture of two ladies from a wedding in 1955 have to do with a modern-day death? One thing was certain. I needed to see more pictures from that wedding.

I pulled over in front of a lovely powder blue bungalow with a wide stone porch and made my call for reinforcements.

"MayBelle?" I asked, bracing a hand against the steering wheel. "I was with Pastor Mike this morning, going through

Jorie's pictures. I'd hoped to find a few of the wedding, but there weren't any. Do you know anyone who might have some?"

"Like the one I showed you?" she asked, her voice crackling over the connection.

"Exactly." Although MayBelle's photo of that day had been wonderful—and very similar to the photo that had been burned —there hadn't been anything unusual about it.

I rested my head against my arm. Maybe I was barking up the wrong tree. Maybe I wouldn't find a surprising element in any of the photos from that day, but the photo I'd almost received was the closest thing I had to a clue. I had to look to be sure.

"I smell what you're cooking," she said. "Meet me in front of the senior apartments in twenty."

"Thank you." MayBelle had come through for me before. Hopefully, she would again.

I found a parking spot across the street from the senior apartments and had almost made it to the covered entryway when I caught sight of MayBelle crossing Main Street from downtown. She wore black yoga pants with a fluttery pink wrap sweater and could have passed for a ballerina if not for her wide-brimmed straw sun hat. And the fanny pack.

"Dancing?" I asked, by way of greeting.

"Naked yoga and then lunch," she said. "Come on." She continued down the sidewalk. "I'll drive."

Wait. "You're kidding about the naked part, right?" I asked, catching up. Barely. The woman walked fast.

"Yeah," she said regretfully. "I've taught hot yoga. I've taught Hatha to Vinyasa to Senior Stretch—with cursing allowed because, face it, that's relaxing to some people." She reached into her fanny pack and drew out a cigarette case and a slim silver lighter. "But I think Sugarland would draw the line at naked."

"One would assume," I said, watching her tap out a smoke on the top of the cigarette case. "Um, is smoking allowed in yoga?" I asked as she lit up.

She took a drag and blew it away from me. "There are no rules in yoga."

Ah, well, no wonder she liked it. "So," I said as we crossed to the residents' parking lot at the side of the building, "did you find us some wedding pictures?"

"I think so," she said, pointing her smoke at me. "We'll know for sure in a few minutes." She pulled a key from her fanny pack inserted it into the door of a red 1959 Cadillac Eldorado convertible a few cars up.

"Oh, tell me this is yours," I said, admiring the taillights and the whitewall tires. My late father would have had a heart attack on the spot. He'd always wanted one of those cars.

"Been driving it since it rolled off the line," she said, balancing her smoke on her lip and tossing her hat into the back. She grabbed a purple silk wrap skirt and fastened it around her waist. "It's my baby."

"I have my Grandma's 1978 Cadillac," I told her. "We should start a vintage car club."

"Sure," she said, with manufactured enthusiasm. Maybe she wasn't a joiner.

Too bad for her it would take a jackhammer to get me out of her passenger seat. I slid onto the springy white leather seat. "I love this car."

"That makes two of us, babe." She pulled a few pins from her hair, her black bob swinging as she settled into the driver's seat. "Buckle up," she ordered, stubbing out the cigarette in the car's ashtray before whipping the black wig right off her head.

She was bald! As bald as Ray.

I tried not to stare as MayBelle tossed her wig into the back seat and began to pull the car out.

"It'll blow off when I drive," she said as if it were obvious.

I had a million questions, but my manners were too good to ask any of them as she pulled out of the lot and began hurtling down Second Street toward Main. "Where are we going?" I asked, settling on a safe one.

"The Sugarland Heritage Society," she yelled above the engine and the wind. "Five years ago, they had a bunch of the pictures you want as part of a display on wedding dress styles over the years."

But that was five years ago.

"Archived," she said as if she could see the question swirling. "Trust me."

I did. At least on this. MayBelle had been in the Sugarland Heritage Society for longer than I'd been alive.

We drove west through town and then out Wilson's Creek Road and past the old Southern Spirits distillery. Ellis had recently opened a small restaurant in the historic building and he'd been picking up extra shifts at the police station to help afford a chef and a manager. Business was growing, slowly but surely. I'd have to treat Lauralee to lunch once little Hiram recovered.

About a mile down the road, we reached the two-story clapboard headquarters for the heritage society.

It was originally a home for widows and orphans, or so the story went. I'd learned an entirely new, very unofficial history of the house on an earlier adventure.

While MayBelle retrieved her wig from the back, I admired the woodland hyacinths out front. If I still had Frankie's powers, I might have even sought out a ghost. Molly had provided valuable assistance on a murder case I'd solved here, and she'd fallen for Frankie at the same time. She used to come around often, and I credited her relationship with Frankie for keeping up the ghostly energy I relied on to do my work. He hadn't experienced much energy drain since they became an item, and I was beginning to wonder whether they were on the outs. I hadn't seen her at the house in a while, and he had been dealing with an energy lag lately. Maybe it didn't have everything to do with Lou.

"Ready?" MayBelle asked, straightening her hair.

"Always," I said, heading up to the white painted porch and opening the door for her. "Was your mother in the society?"

"It was practically a requirement, seeing as my grandfather set up the foundation that runs this place."

Of course he did.

She breezed on in, and we were greeted rather sweetly by Eudora Louise Markam, one of the ladies I'd seen at the fundraiser where Jorie had died.

"How are you doing?" she asked, giving me a big hug. "I heard you made Lowell Sanders's one-man-show last night. How awful was it?"

"It was different," I admitted.

"For the man whose claim to fame is being an extra in a "We Are the World" video, he sure is high and mighty," she said. "He could even be lying. He knows there's no way we can tell if that little dot is him."

MayBelle inserted herself between us. "Hi. We came to the heritage society because we'd like to look at a collection."

"Right," Eudora said brightly. "We're not just here to chitchat."

"You could have fooled me," MayBelle said, then sent Eudora off to fetch the wedding display archives.

"Found them!" Eudora said a few minutes later, wheeling in a small cart with museum-quality albums. "Come on. Let's set you two up." She ushered us to a table in the society president's office off the main lobby.

"You do pull some weight here," I said to my companion. A

large wooden desk stood in the center of the room in front of an original fireplace.

"Actually, I'm just nice," Eudora said, lingering in the doorway.

We took seats in white dining chairs at the heavy round table. Several glass pitchers crowded the table, one decorated with a pink polka-dot design, another in bubbled glass with a thick green handle, both etched to commemorate various years of tea-themed luncheons.

"My mother never joined the heritage society," I said, folding my hands in my lap as Eudora carried the albums over. "She's outgoing but prefers small groups. I suppose your mother didn't have that luxury, as a pastor's wife, I mean."

MayBelle gave me the side-eye.

"Yes, I'm fishing," I admitted. "Rather clumsily, I might add. But I just want to know more about you," I said quite honestly. "Pastor Bob wouldn't stop going on about your father the other night. I was just curious what kind of lady stood with him."

"My mother," she said wryly, "was the exact opposite of me."

Before I could think of what to say about that, Eudora carefully opened a white leather photo album on the table in front of me. "All of our 1955 brides are in this one," she said. "Preserved on acid-free paper. I've brought you gloves, although we ask that you do not touch the photographs directly."

"Thank you," I said, taking a pair of white silk gloves and handing the other pair to MayBelle.

Eudora stood at a polite distance, watching us as we handled the album.

No doubt ready to listen as well.

I glanced back, flustering her.

"I'm sorry," she said, "I'm not allowed to let that album out of my sight."

It was awfully inconvenient, but at the same time, it heartened me to know they were taking such good care of the collection.

We paged through dozens of giddy, happy, nervous brides. Some things never changed. They wore sweetheart necklines, full skirts, and I even saw a hat made to look like a bow. "I could definitely get married in the '50s," I gushed.

"I couldn't," MayBelle countered.

"Check out the pearls," Eudora stage-whispered before making a show of silently buttoning her lip.

Only I knew better than to think the lips in Sugarland could stay zipped for long.

MayBelle turned the page, and there it was—a photo of Jorie and my grandmother smiling together outside the church near the old oak tree, their eyes dancing with happiness.

And in a split second, I saw exactly what the killer had wanted to hide.

Chapter Twenty-One

❦

I've never had a good poker face. MayBelle knew right away I'd found something.

"So," she prodded, the lines on her face deepening, "tell me. What do you see?"

The picture before me captured Jorie and my grandmother in a moment of radiant happiness. Unfortunately, I'd caught a glimpse of some people I recognized in the background. People I didn't expect to see at the wedding of my grandmother's friend.

The Three Angels gravedigger.

I'd met that man's ghost in the bell tower.

The gravedigger stood dour faced, shovel at the ready, as he watched Pastor Delmore Clemens in a frantic discussion with the mobster I'd met in the back of the flower shop—Mr. Peony himself.

A few other guys in suits stood in a separate cluster nearby, smoking cigarettes and eyeing the ground in front of the trio.

I flipped to the next page to see if there were any more like it, if any other mobsters might have enjoyed an acquaintance with the saintly Pastor Delmore Clemens.

But the next spread in the book featured a different pair of smiling newlyweds posing on the courthouse steps.

"Verity," MayBelle pressed.

"I'm still trying to figure out what this means," I murmured, turning the page again. More wedding pictures. More smiling faces. None at the Three Angels. I barely noticed the rest of them.

"Did you find the one of Fannie Brewster releasing doves?" Eudora asked before zipping her lip again.

We definitely had an audience.

"You're hiding something," MayBelle insisted, subtle as an ox. She snatched the album from me and turned back to the page in question. "What is it?" She studied the photo. "Jorie and Delia, my dad, a worker, and some wedding guests. What?"

I watched the woman who had called Jorie and Delia her friends scan the photograph, not recognizing what was now so plain to me.

Although perhaps that was the issue—MayBelle had focused on the radiant, smiling women in the foreground.

And to be fair, she didn't hang out with Frankie like I did.

I wished I could share my find with MayBelle. She'd led me here, after all. Perhaps she regretted it now, or if not now, then she would. Because from what I saw, I had a feeling I shouldn't trust her anymore.

"I think that wraps it up," I said, pushing back from the table. "Thanks so much for your time, Eudora, but we ought to be getting back."

"No." MayBelle stared at the page that had changed everything for me. "Not until I figure this out."

Eudora bent over her shoulder. "Oh, what a lovely picture of Jorie."

"Can it, sister." She waved off Eudora before looking to me. "Dang it, Verity. Help me on this."

"There's nothing to help with." Not anymore. "I told you, I need to get back. Lucy has an appointment," I fibbed.

"I'll bet," she said, reluctantly pushing back from the table.

I closed the album and handed it to a smiling Eudora to be placed back in the archives.

"But you did find what you were looking for?" she asked sweetly.

"Unfortunately, no," I told her, "but at least we've scratched something off our list."

"Good," she said, smiling. I could see why she'd been elected Hospitality Chair.

MayBelle practically bored a hole in the side of my head with her stare as we exited. "Are you going to tell me what just happened in there? You ought to thank me for not making a scene."

If that was her holding back, I didn't want to see her go for the gusto.

"Thank you," I said, holding the door open for her.

I realized I was acting out of character. My default tended to be talking, sharing—and if Frankie were to be believed, overexplaining. But if I told MayBelle what the photograph led me to believe about her father's past, not to mention the motive for Jorie's murder, the evidence might vanish before Ellis arrived with the police.

For the time being, it would be relatively safe in the archives.

We couldn't afford for another photograph to be destroyed. This could be the only one left with the evidence I needed.

"She was my friend, too," MayBelle said, sliding into the driver's seat.

"I'd been hoping to see something in the photographs, and I didn't," I told her. Well, it had been missing from all but one.

MayBelle whipped off her wig and tossed it into the back seat. "And I'm Stella McCartney." She clenched her jaw as she started the engine. "So what's next?"

Ellis and the police station.

"I'll have to think about it," I told her. "Thanks for driving me out."

She rolled her eyes and set off for home.

I didn't chat much on the way back. The convertible made it hard to talk, anyway. MayBelle wanted some sort of explanation. Unfortunately, I didn't have one for her. I'd have to work on that part of my investigation technique—the cover-up.

"I think I'm going to streak the town square," MayBelle said as we pulled up to the boulevard stop at Second Street and Main. "Want to come?"

"Maybe next time," I said, not really listening. "Have fun."

"Um-hum," she said, crossing the four-way intersection.

Soon I'd be back at my car and on the phone with Ellis.

MayBelle and I said our polite goodbyes, and I could feel her stare on my back as I crossed the street to where I'd parked the land yacht. I slid inside, locked the door behind me, and dialed up Ellis.

He didn't answer.

I left him an urgent message to call me back.

He was working today, so I drove south on Main and over a few blocks to the Sugarland Police Department. It stood on the corner of a commercial block, across from Roan's Hardware.

The Sugarland PD was housed in the same quaint two-story brick building it had occupied for the last fifty years at least, and I could probably say the same about more than half of the businesses in that section of town.

There was plenty of street parking. I found a spot just down from the hardware store, in front of J&B Meat, the butcher shop I'd loved as a kid because Mr. Bates kept a giant roll of candy buttons for us kids. He'd tear off a strip and it was like a lottery to see if I got pink or yellow or teal or blue. My favorites were the one with the mix as the dot colors changed.

It was a special bonus surprise to get the fun dots, as my sister and I had called them.

I wished adulthood came with more fun surprises.

I shut off the car and retrieved my bag with Frankie's urn. Perhaps the gangster had been right when he told me I needed to learn how to lie. I didn't think I'd ever be the type to want to mislead anyone else, but MayBelle's suspicion earlier was dangerous.

But why would she have brought me to the place where I could find the key to the mystery, if she didn't want me to solve it?

Unless she hadn't expected me to find anything in those photographs.

I passed the hardware store and absently waved to the gray-haired men playing chess in the window of Roan's, before crossing the street and pushing through the front door of the Sugarland PD.

The place smelled like old bricks and coffee.

I made my way to a big wooden desk that had to have been there since the '50s. Joshua Carter, who was taking a year off after his sixth year of college, sat on a tall chair behind the desk, absorbed in his phone.

"Hi," I said to him while he frantically hit a button that made explosion sounds. "I need to see Ellis Wydell. It's important."

"Okay." His tan uniform shirt gaped at the buttons as he worked hard to blow up more imaginary objects.

I planted my elbows on the long wooden desk. It looked ancient, scarred and sanded and scarred again so many times the surface had a permanent tilt in places.

"I'm on a schedule here, Josh." MayBelle could very well be heading back to the heritage society to take another look at that photograph. It was what I would do if I had questions someone wasn't willing to answer.

Worse, MayBelle said herself that she had a good poker face.

Her confusion could have been her way of tricking me into tipping my hand to reveal what I'd do next.

"Officer Wydell is out of the office on a case," Josh said. A dramatic warning sounded in his game and he doubled down on the button pushing.

I snatched the phone out of his hand.

"Hey—"

That got his attention.

"You need to call Ellis on the police emergency line and tell him I need him."

Josh made a grab for his phone.

"Now," I said. Too bad for him, he was slower in real life than he was as a—I glanced at his phone—space captain in the outer territories.

"That's theft," Josh protested, making another grab for his phone.

"Arrest me," I told him.

Duranja walked in from the back room, papers in hand. His mouth tightened when he saw me. "Ellis is out on a case."

"So I heard." Josh took advantage of my momentary distraction to make another grab for space supremacy. He failed. "I found evidence that will blow our case wide open."

"*Our* case?" Duranja raised a brow.

"It's really quite remarkable," I added, glancing at the sulking Josh, hoping he was trustworthy. "I mean, who'd have thought a wedding picture from 1955 would be the key to solving the mystery of Jorie's death?"

"I don't," Duranja snarked.

"Ha." Not funny. "We're on a timetable here. The photo is at the Sugarland Heritage Society, and I'm afraid someone will get to the archives before me and destroy it if we don't hurry."

Duranja looked askance at me. "You're serious. You're looking in old records for evidence on an accidental death from two days ago."

"It wasn't accidental, or you wouldn't have been so mad when I took that letter I found in the bell tower," I said, not making the point as well as I'd have liked. "But I'm sorry about that," I added, glad at least for the chance to apologize. "You have to understand I was being chased by the ghost of a gravedigger and I wasn't thinking straight."

"She also stole my phone," Josh said.

Duranja's face had grown progressively darker. "Listen, sweetheart," he said, depositing his folder on the desk and looking down at me, "I don't want to hear about your ghosts or your excuses. I don't want to hear about what you found in a dusty archive that has anything to do with a woman falling out of a tower two days ago."

"Pushed," I interjected. "Her husband said she was pushed."

"Her dead husband is a witness?" he asked, a little snarkier than I'd have preferred.

"He didn't actually see anyone push her—" I corrected.

"Of course not," Duranja snapped. "Just like you didn't really see him. You may have half the town suckered into believing you chat with the dead over sweet tea—"

"Frankie prefers Cutty Sark and water," I countered.

"But I don't believe in ghosts or your so-called gift. I'm nice to you because Ellis would kick my ass if I wasn't, but I don't like you, and I don't want you bothering Ellis."

"I'm his girlfriend," I shot back. "I can bother him all I want."

"Go for it," he said, raising his hands as if to wash them of me. "Go nuts. Talk his ear off. Just not when he's on the job."

"Because solving a murder's not his job?" I said to Duranja's back as he turned to leave.

"And give Josh his phone back," he tossed over his shoulder right before he walked out.

Well, that was...annoying.

I fought off a wave of disappointment as I watched Duranja leave.

Ellis would take me seriously, if I could just locate him.

Sniveling Josh was back on his phone. I placed a hand between him and the space federation. "Promise me. If you get an emergency call from the heritage society, you make sure they send a team right over."

"Because we don't already rush for emergencies," Josh drawled.

"Bless your heart," I said to him before I left to figure out how to protect that picture on my own.

When I returned to the car, Frankie sat waiting in my passenger seat.

"How's the fuzz?" he asked as I tossed my bag into the back.

"Frustrating," I said, running my hands through my hair.

"Some things never change," he agreed, and we pulled out.

Still, I wondered where I went wrong in there. Or if I'd had no chance from the start. Even Ellis wouldn't be happy to know I'd been investigating.

"You realize we're two blocks away from tonight's stakeout," Frankie said as I stopped at a crosswalk to let a woman pass with two grade-school-age girls and a shopping trolley. I wondered if they were going to J&B Meat.

"Lou's not supposed to arrive until midnight, right?" I asked, giving the woman a small wave. I didn't know her. They must be new to town.

"Let's run by really quick and case the property," Frankie said, drumming his fingers against his leg. "I got to get the lay of the land for my guys. I can't do proper surveillance while you've got me grounded."

"I'd rather go back to the heritage society and keep watch over that photo," I told him. "You can visit with Molly," I added, sweetening the pot.

"Uhhhh," Frankie cringed. "Let me get this fixed with my brother before I worry about Molly."

"She's your girlfriend, not an afterthought," I said, steering past the clock shop and watch repair. "If you're having issues, you need to communicate."

"And I should take advice from you because your love life is going so well," Frankie groused.

"Do you want to talk about it?" I asked.

"No," he practically shouted. "Let's just"—he waved a hand —"just drive me past the target property. Please. It's on Sycamore Street, just north of Seventh."

"Okay." But after that, we were going to guard that photograph. "Ellis is going to call back any time. And when he does, we're going to break Jorie's case wide open."

"Oh, sure," Frankie said, "because her death is way more important than mine."

"I didn't say that." In fact, I thought I'd done a pretty decent job of pleasing everyone. "We'll make it work."

"You seem to think you're always in control of everything that happens around here," he snarked.

I ignored it because the poor gangster was in pain. And even more, he had a point. While I wanted to make everything right for every soul—living, dead, and...recently dead—I could only do my best. I hoped it would be good enough.

We drove down Sycamore Street, past a series of original 1920s-era storefronts anchored by the YMCA building.

"This is the supper club right here," Frankie said, directing me to a cheery green and pink painted Groomingdales Pet Salon storefront.

I'd heard about this place. It was new. And it stood next to a traditional barbershop. "Oh, how precious." I parked in front and was about to shut off the car when Frankie gasped and shrank into a tiny flame.

"Drive!" he ordered.

Holy smokes. I checked my rearview mirror for ghosts with guns, or any traffic, and pulled out fast.

"What's going on?" I demanded. I didn't see anything. I didn't hear anything.

"Lou was hunkered down by the barber shop," Frankie said. "If he spots me, he's going to run again!"

I looked, but I didn't see anything.

Oh, wait, I didn't have Frankie's power.

And just like that, we were half a block away.

"Turn around," Frankie said, taking form again. "Go around the block. I want to see what he's doing. I swear I saw Lou hiding behind a newspaper."

"Well, how are you going to hide from him and also see what he's doing?" I made a right and started to circle the block.

"You're going to tell me," he ordered as his power settled over me. I winced as it prickled through my skin, down to my bones. He had to stop doing these power exchanges while I was driving.

I also had a question. "Why would Lou be hiding out on the street by the place he's going for supper tonight?"

"Yeah, I know. It's eight hours before Wally Big Ears said." Frankie drummed his fingers on his leg. "But that was him."

"I think there's more to this story than we know," I said, a flicker of hope blooming. "Maybe you and Lou can work this out."

"And maybe Lou is auditioning for the barbershop quartet," Frankie shot back. He slouched in his seat. "Just...don't get your hopes up."

"I won't," I told him.

But that didn't mean I was ready to give up on him.

We came up on the block again. This time, Frankie was prepared. He sank down through the passenger seat so that only his eyes, forehead, and hat were above the window ledge. Only the most recognizable parts of him. Although I didn't feel he'd appreciate it if I pointed that out.

I just hoped he wouldn't blow his cover because I didn't feel like trying to track down Lou to yet another hideout.

I stopped a few stores down from Groomingdales Pet Salon and found a parking spot in front of a pickup truck, with a clear view of the sidewalk.

"There," Frankie said, pointing to a ghost leaning on a wall next to a swirling red, white, and blue barber pole. He wore a fedora pulled low, his face and upper body blocked by a newspaper.

"It could be anybody."

"It's him," Frankie muttered. "I know how he leans."

The man lowered his paper, and I still couldn't identify him. He seemed to be scoping out the upper windows of a building across the street, the Pastry Box bakery.

If that was Lou, he was up to something. "That bakery isn't another mob front, is it?"

"Not every business in town is a mob front," Frankie snipped, tense. "And, no—that's not one of ours, or anybody else's for all I know."

We'd just have to see.

A shadowy figure of a woman moved behind the window. I couldn't see her well enough to determine if she was a ghost or a real-life person. It seemed good enough for our man on the street, however.

"Look," I said as he quickly folded his paper. "It is Lou." He tucked it under his arm and scurried across the street.

"He's going into the bakery," Frankie said as Lou passed through the glass window displaying fresh pies, mounds of cookies, and cakes on stands. "But...but...that's just a bakery," he protested, trying to figure it out.

It appeared so—both in his world and mine. Still, I knew better than to take it for granted. "Let's check it out." I grabbed my bag.

We hurried across the street, and moments later, Frankie passed through the same window as Lou.

I settled for the door.

A bell jingled as I stepped onto the white and teal tile floor that had been here for a few generations.

"Be right with you," called a dark-haired woman with dreadlocks tied into a ponytail. Maya Anderson had been two years ahead of me in high school, and she probably didn't remember it, but she'd directed me to my locker freshman year.

"No worries," I said, glad to see her attention diverted as she focused on a tween boy standing in front of a huge glass display case of cookies, candies, and cake bites.

"I can't decide," he lamented.

"Well, you do always get the cinnamon roll," she said patiently.

"He can take all the time he wants. I'm just browsing," I said. He could take an hour for all I cared.

Meanwhile, Frankie backed Lou into a corner behind a wooden bookshelf display of local honey and homemade jellies. "I have a question for you, brother." He spat the last word.

Be kind. I willed the thought at Frankie as I took a gander at a jar of Miss Jean's Rhubarb Jam. This was the only brother, the only family, Frankie had.

"What are you doing here?" Lou demanded as if Frankie had just walked in on him taking a shower. "Get out!"

"I need answers," Frankie hissed, blocking him in.

"You're messing me up." Lou's gaze darted past Frankie to the stairwell at the back of the store. "Don't make me shoot you again."

Frankie whipped a gun out of his jacket and pressed it to Lou's forehead. "I'd give you a matching bullet hole if I could."

Oh no. Not a promising reunion.

Lou held up his hands. "Don't shoot," he pleaded, nervous. "I can't get knocked out. I haven't been this close in years."

"What is he talking about?" I whispered as Frankie cocked the revolver. "Hold up, Frank."

"Don't call him Frank," Lou pleaded. "Everybody calm down." His eyes darted from his brother to me and back again. "I've got a person I'm tracking. I've got one chance at this."

He sounded desperate. "We'll help you," I murmured, hoping Maya was sufficiently distracted.

"What?" Frankie demanded. "No, we won't. I'm here for answers and revenge. In that order."

I'd seen Lou watching the shadow of a woman in the upper window. "Lou's tracking a lady, to the second floor of this building if I'm not mistaken." The look on his face told me I was right. "We'll do this with you," I pledged.

"I think we need to argue more," Frankie countered, but he lowered his gun.

And at that moment, Lou disappeared.

Frankie let out a stream of cuss words that would make a drill sergeant blush.

"He's headed upstairs," I told him. Lou wouldn't leave. Not when he was so close.

The bell on the door tinkled. "I can help you now, Verity," Maya called.

The boy had left with his cinnamon roll, just as she'd called it.

"Erm." Think fast. "I need to go upstairs."

Yeah, that was smooth. But I was desperate. I had a feeling I knew who Lou hoped to find upstairs in the bakery, although I wanted to know more about why.

And I definitely didn't want Frankie shooting either one of them.

I expected Maya to frown or be confused at my desire to wander upstairs in her shop, but instead, she broke out into a wide grin. "Congratulations!" She bustled out from behind the glass case. "Oh, this is wonderful news," she said, giving me a hug.

She smelled delicious, like sugar and frosting, and I was so confused.

"We have all the basic wedding cake styles upstairs on display, but I can make anything you like. Just bring a picture in."

"Oh," I said, surprised. "Oh!" Of course. She used the upstairs space to meet with couples who needed wedding cakes. She thought Ellis and I... uh-oh. Stars. News of our "engagement" would be all over Sugarland before suppertime.

At least that might get Ellis to call me back right away.

"We're not saying anything publicly," I stammered. Because we weren't saying anything at all. Because there wasn't anything to say. Just last night, he'd as soon have arrested me as kissed me.

Maya gave me a wink and a smile. "I'll keep your secret." She squeezed my arm and dragged me into a side-hug. "I'm so happy for you."

"Me too," I said, not quite ready to believe what had just happened.

The bell jingled and a pair of giggling girls rolled in.

"I think I'll go up now," I said to Maya.

"Sure! Have a look around. Let me know when you want a tasting," she called after me.

Sakes alive. What I did for my job.

I hurried up the stairs to find Frankie with his gun drawn, stalking between pedestals topped with simple round stacked wedding cakes, cakes with flowers, cakes with pillars and fountains.

"Where is he?" I asked. Framed portraits on the walls displayed happy brides and grooms cutting even more of Maya's creations.

"We lost him," Frankie said, eyes wild, finger on the trigger. "I can't believe we lost him!"

"Maybe not." Lou had seen his target in the upstairs window, but this room had none. "Look." A folding bistro table leaned against the wall, and behind it, painted the same pink as the walls, stood a door.

I moved the table while Frankie passed through the wall. "Wait up," I said, walking into a narrow storage area lined with shelves and running the length of the store.

This didn't count as breaking and entering, did it?

I'd worry about it later.

I passed shelves lined with bins of plastic cake tiers, display trays, free-standing pedestals, and pretty much every cake topper known to man. The hallway opened up on a small work-room with two windows facing the street. Spare folding chairs lay stacked against the wall between the windows, and to the right, a pink painted bookshelf held sample binders and books like *The Wilton Wedding Guide* and *Simply Modern Wedding Cakes*.

I also detected the faint scent of violet and vanilla.

"You've got to talk to me." Lou stood near the window nearest the bookcase, holding the hand of the woman we'd seen in the apartment above the speakeasy.

"It's her." Frankie's voice went up an octave. His gun never wavered.

The woman let out a small cry, her gaze darting like a trapped mouse. I recognized her smoky eyes, the curl of her dark hair.

"Tell the girl to wait outside," he ordered. "We have more important things to talk about."

"Get out of here, Frank," Lou demanded, tightening his grip on the woman, who was about to faint or run. I doubt even she knew which.

"You know I hate that." Frankie advanced on them. His

brother looked ready to chew nails. "You shot me, and now you don't even have time to talk about what happened?"

"Stop it," Lou ordered, putting himself between Frankie and the woman. "You're scaring her."

"Who the hell is she to you, anyway?" He pointed the gun at his brother.

Lou didn't flinch. In fact, he looked ready to strangle Frankie with his bare hands. "She's my wife."

Chapter Twenty-Two

❧❧

F rankie nearly dropped his gun. "You're not married," he
said to his brother.

I couldn't believe it, either. Yet the pretty brunette
behind Lou didn't look surprised in the least when he said it.
Her fingers dug hard against Lou's suit jacket as she peered at
my housemate, her lower lip quivering with fright.

Frankie took aim at the couple. "Who are you really?" he
demanded of the woman.

She clutched Lou's shoulder, her polka-dot day dress
swirling at her knees. "Ch-Chastity Winkelmann."

Frankie gaped at her.

"Sorry." Lou shrugged.

"What's he going to do to us?" Chastity asked, starting to
panic.

"Nothing," Lou assured her. "I'm just thinking this is a lousy
way to tell my brother we ran off and got married."

"Congratulations?" I ventured. I mean, this sounded like a
happy thing.

Frankie looked as if he'd been slapped. "So not only did you shoot me in the head, but you didn't invite me to your wedding?"

He would have to look at it that way.

Lou's jaw tightened. "It was for your own good."

"He's going to kill us," Chastity declared.

"No, he's not," Lou assured her.

"I think I am," Frankie countered.

"Lou's already dead," I reminded Frankie. Killing him again wouldn't solve anything.

"I'm not safe here," she whispered, her image beginning to fade. "I have to go."

"Wait." Lou turned to her, presenting his back to Frankie, which was a terrible move six ways to Sunday. "Don't go," he pleaded with his wife. "Not again. Please. Stay with me. Trust me," he added on a whisper. "It's going to be okay this time."

"We won't hurt you," I promised.

"Speak for yourself!" Frankie said.

"My brother's just crazy," Lou coaxed.

"Only when I get double-crossed," Frankie muttered.

"Let's start over," I said, dredging up a perkiness I didn't feel. "Chastity, this is your brother-in-law, Frankie. Frankie, this is Chastity, who loves your brother as much as Molly loves you."

Frankie's features tightened. "The way Molly *used* to love me. Now she thinks I obsess about the mob too much."

I'd forgotten about his issues with Molly. That might not have been the best pep talk, now that I thought about it.

"Lou worries about the mob, too." Chastity's soft voice emerged from behind her husband. "He worries about letting people down."

"Babe," he grumped as she aired his business.

"It's all right," she assured him. I was pleased to see she didn't run, like some might have when they realized they had a Frankie in the family. Instead, she emerged slowly from behind her husband. "I have a brother-in-law," she said shyly. Lou slipped his hand into hers as she sized up my housemate. "He appears a trifle unstable."

"He's always like that," Lou said, with grudging affection.

I mean, this was the guy who still held a gun on her groom. "Hey, Frankie," I said. He seemed frozen in place. "You might want to put that down," I suggested.

He looked blankly at me. "Too soon to tell." He kept his eye on Lou. "We're getting way sidetracked on the revenge thing here."

"I'd rather know what has her running, and Lou chasing," I told my housemate. "Wouldn't you?" I'd bet there was more to the story than Frankie or I realized. Shooting Lou wouldn't give us answers. Talking to him would.

Lou had begun to stroke his wife on her back, soothing her.

"For the love of Pete." Frankie wrinkled his nose, clearly not used to seeing his brother like this.

"Oh, come on," I said. "Give your brother a break. Remember the time you made Molly a crown of dandelions?"

"You're kind of ruining my image here," he snapped.

I leaned close. "What about the time I caught you in a smoking jacket with a sketch pad, drawing her *Titanic*-style?" I muttered in his ear.

"I don't want to think about that right now," he growled.

And I'd wanted to bleach my eyeballs. "You need to remember that a good woman can do a lot for a man." And I had a feeling Chastity was central to the story Frankie was trying to uncover. "You need to offer your sister-in-law a little reassurance," I said. "Show her we're on her side."

Frankie looked at me like I'd sprouted horns. "I'm on *my* side."

Maybe that was his problem.

"How's that working out for you?" I asked. Lately, it seemed his power drain had everything to do with him pulling away from Molly and obsessing about his brother.

He had a chance to confront at least one of those issues right now.

Elbow bent, he pointed his gun up toward the ceiling. "Can I just shoot Lou in the knee or something? I could stand to blow off some steam."

Steps echoed on the stairs up to the second floor.

"Do you hear that?" I asked. "Footsteps."

Lou drew his gun.

Chastity's eyes went wide. "It could be them. Did anyone follow you?"

"I wasn't watching," I admitted. We'd been too busy tracking Lou.

"I'll check," Frankie promised, gun at the ready as he slipped through the wall toward the stairs.

Lou followed.

"Frankie's keyed up," I said to Chastity, who clutched the skirt of her dress. "Lou hurt him, but deep down, he loves his brother. We'll help keep you safe."

They were family.

She wrung her hands. "I'm not the best at knowing who to trust."

I glanced to the wall separating us from the intruder on the stairs. "We tracked down Lou because Frankie needs answers about the night he died," I explained. "The guys have some things they need to work out." Some serious issues, actually. But Lou had raised Frankie, sacrificed for him. That had to count for something.

Frankie's focus on revenge was only hurting him.

Chastity's eyes glazed with fresh tears. "I'm sorry," she said, wiping them away. "I'm just scared."

"I've been there," I assured her.

She touched a hand to her chest. "I don't have much experience with the living. Not since I was one of them."

"It's just a dame with a slice of cake and a lemonade," Frankie said, coming back through the wall. "She's looking for you."

Maya. I sure hoped she didn't find me in her storage room.

"You stayed," Lou said, rushing to Chastity. He embraced her. "You need to stop running."

She buried herself in his arms. "I'm trying."

Lou rested his chin on the top of her head. "Since we've been dead, I've been chasing my wife from safe house to safe house." He held on tight. "This is the first time I've caught up to her."

She drew away from him, wiping her tears. "I need to find a safe place for our baby."

Lou's jaw clenched.

This time, Frankie did drop his gun. "Baby?"

Chastity nodded, eyes glistening. "They have our baby."

"I'm an uncle?" Frankie said, one step behind.

No wonder she was frightened. Someone had taken their child. "Who has your baby?" I pressed.

Chastity swallowed hard. "My father took her. I'm afraid he might hurt her." She clutched Lou's hands. "I'm going to get her back. Once I have a safe place."

"How awful," I said. Ghosts had a tendency to get stuck in the last strong emotion that they felt before they died. Poor Chastity must have been both terrified and desperate in her last moments.

"You need to let me help," Lou urged. "We can stop running. I'm not with the gang anymore."

"Yes, he i—" Frankie began and I poked him. "Ow!" He doubled over and so did I, the touch shocking me to the core.

"What'd you do that for?" Frankie demanded.

Because he had no tact.

Lou kissed Chastity on the forehead. "He's not going to hurt our child. I paid his price to keep our baby safe. I've been trying to find you to tell you."

She ran her hands over his suit coat nervously. "What price? What did he make you do?"

Lou didn't respond. In fact, he appeared physically sick as he stilled her hands in his.

"You can't clam up on us now," Frankie prodded. "What's the going rate for babies these days?"

Chastity gasped. Lou clutched his wife tighter as he looked at his tactless brother.

Meanwhile, my stomach dropped as I put the pieces together. Chastity was on the run from someone who wanted to kill her. She was desperate to save her baby. Whoever got to Chastity must have offered Lou a chance to save his child for a price—a blood price...

And I was pretty sure the deal had gotten my housemate killed.

Frankie's eyes went cold as he made the same connection. "I think you'd better start talking, Lou."

"Lou?" Charity furrowed her brow and looked to him.

Frankie's brother hesitated, then swallowed hard. He held onto his wife like a drowning man with a life preserver. "I knew from the first day on the job that getting involved in the mob would cost me my life. I accepted that. I was okay with that."

"I don't buy it," Frankie said. "You never liked the rules."

"And you do?" I balked.

"Mob rules," Frankie corrected.

Lou's wife sobbed, and he wrapped a protective arm around her. "I might have been willing to bite it, but I wasn't going to let it hurt the girl I loved. I wanted out."

"It doesn't work like that," Frankie stated as if Lou were asking him to trade his revolver in for a squirt gun. "Once you're in, you're in. You can't just leave. Gangsters retire six feet under."

"You're right," Lou said, resigned. "I couldn't leave." He wet his lips. "But I could make a change." He looked to his brother, as if willing Frankie to understand.

"Like when you called in sick for the Spiro job," Frankie mustered.

"As part of the South Town Boys, me and Frankie handled business down this way for your daddy," he said, bringing Chastity along.

"Who's her dad?" I asked.

Lou didn't answer, but she did. "Salvatore Spiro."

"Bloody Sal Spiro?" Frankie threw his hands up. "Oh my God, Lou, you know the rules!" He dragged both hands down his face. "You're not supposed to look at Sal's daughters. You don't talk to them. You don't ask them about the weather. You don't even look at their pictures in the paper."

"We were in the society pages a lot," she admitted.

"How could I ignore this beauty?" Lou asked, gazing down at her.

"You did more than look," Frankie declared. "You were the one who deserved to get shot between the eyes the second you thought about maybe saying hello. You deserved a bag over the head, cement shoes, and a trip to the bottom of the river. Not me. You."

Lou still hadn't taken his eyes off her. "I fell in love."

"I don't care if you fell on top of her," Frankie said. "You don't talk to her!"

She stroked his cheek. "We snuck down here to get married in secret."

Frankie spun a circle. "That's why Sal's guys were looking for you!"

"I thought we could disappear here," Lou said. "Other guys did it."

"Well, sure," Frankie admitted. "Nobody rats out the home-town guy. It's not our problem if you owe somebody money or if you maybe drove off with a truck that wasn't yours. It was tough times. But you? You stole a crown jewel."

"Nobody in Sugarland gave me up," Lou insisted.

Yet somehow, they'd been discovered. "Somebody must have seen you," I reasoned. It was hard to do anything in Sugarland without your neighbors noticing. Plus, the safe house in the flower shop stood above a speakeasy. It wasn't exactly a shack way out in the middle of nowhere.

"The town stuck together. Even regular people," Lou insisted.

"It's what you did back then," Frankie said as if reluctant to admit Lou could be right. He looked at Chastity. "Nobody said anything about a girl. Not even to me."

"I didn't go out," Chastity insisted. Her face fell. "I didn't see anyone. It was awful."

"I didn't think you'd have to hide that long," Lou told her. "I had no idea your dad would go so nuts."

Frankie snorted.

"I mean, we were married," Charity reasoned. "I wrote my mother and told her so."

"That might not have been the best idea," I told her.

"Pastor Delmore Clemens married us," Lou said. "He kept our secret, too. He wrote our names in the marriage book as Mr. and Mrs. Smith."

"Clemens?" Frankie dragged a hand over his chin. "That guy was straight as an arrow, never touched the business. Why him?"

"Because he was straight as an arrow," Lou stated. "We wanted a proper wedding, and he swore he wouldn't tell nobody."

"Well, somebody told," I pointed out. "It could have been Pastor Clemens. It could have been your mother," I said to Chastity.

Her mouth dropped open. "It wasn't!"

"Well, I don't think it was Pastor Clemens," Lou countered.

"It wasn't me because I was busy doing all the dirty work while you ran off with the mob princess." Frankie threw up his hands.

If he wasn't careful, I was going to poke him again, and to heck with the shock.

"So what happened after you were married?" I asked the couple, trying to keep the conversation on track.

Lou gazed down at his wife. "We had it great for a while," he said, wrapping his arms around her. "The best year of my life. I had been so wrapped up in Chicago business for so long, I didn't think they would look for me here."

Beside me, Frankie stiffened. "But then Sal and his enforcers came down from Chicago to do that deal. I wondered why Sal bothered to come."

"He was sniffing out his daughter," Lou admitted.

Chastity held on tight. "One day I ran out to get some milk for the baby and spotted a man across the street, my father's enforcer, Vinny." She paled at the memory.

"Yeah, I know him," Frankie said, balling his fists in his pockets. "Ugly mug, even without that one busted eye sitting lower than the other one. I heard he killed his own grandma."

Chastity's lips formed a thin, determined line. "I knew I had to hide. There was no time to tell anyone. I didn't even take the baby back to the apartment. Bonnie and I went underground, to another safe house, the one by the river." Her eyes dulled. "But Vinny caught up with me. He brought us back to my father. As soon as he saw me, Daddy went purple with rage."

Lou took both of his wife's hands in his. "I'm sorry I never told you the danger we were in when we eloped. We should have never come back to Sugarland. We should have run out to the middle of nowhere. I thought this was nowhere enough. I'm sorry, sweetheart."

"I was his perfect little girl. I think he would have come

around eventually," she assured her husband before lowering her head. A tear dripped down her cheek.

"You could have told us," Frankie said. "The South Town Boys would have stood by you."

"I wanted to keep my family separate from the job," Lou said quietly, his attention on his wife.

"The South Town Boys were your family," Frankie insisted.

"No," Lou said simply.

"I was your family," Frankie shouted.

"No," Lou thundered. "*They* were your family. I was nothing to you anymore!"

"Whose fault was that?" Frankie demanded, tossing his arms up. "I invited you to go to Memphis to bust some heads. You said you had a wedding to go to." His eyes widened when he realized whose wedding. "I asked you to help Suds and me fix a horse race. You said you had a dinner."

"I was trying to get out, and you dived straight in," Lou shouted.

Frankie looked ready to shoot his brother again. "They talked to me. They listened to me," Frankie spat. "They actually gave a damn!"

Lou looked like the weight of the world had just been dropped onto his shoulders. "I just couldn't do it anymore. I never wanted to do it in the first place."

For the first time in his life, Frankie stood speechless.

Chastity held on tight to Lou's arm. "You're a good man. That's one of the things I love about you."

"I didn't protect you," he said quietly.

"It wasn't your fault, Lou," she insisted. "Daddy wanted to annul the marriage. He dragged me back to Pastor Clemens and demanded the preacher undo the marriage at gunpoint."

"He can't do that," I insisted. "It wouldn't be legal, even if it was moral." Which it was not.

"You don't understand—when Daddy didn't get his way, he'd

go crazy. Still, I was his angel girl. He'd never hurt me, not in my whole life," she insisted. "I thought when he saw the baby, he might come around." Her expression hardened. "But he wanted me back under his thumb. I refused to sign the annulment papers Daddy brought with him from Chicago. That's when he killed me.

My heart sped up. "In front of your baby?"

Her eyes glistened with tears. "I stood up to him. No one ever stood up to him. He said, 'No one leaves the family.'" She hung her head. "Our baby was in my arms. I didn't let go of her."

Sal was a monster. No wonder Chastity kept running from him, even after he killed her.

Lou stared into space. "Sal had Bonnie when he found me," he said quietly. He looked down at his wife. "I thought he had you locked up. I didn't know you were dead."

Lou closed his eyes briefly. "Sal said I'd stolen from him, that I had to pay him back, blood for blood."

"That is the code," Frankie said grimly. "But it don't extend to family matters."

At least for Sal, it seemed that the business was his family, and he ran his family like the business. Mob rules all around.

Lou looked to Frankie. "I had to kill my own brother to spare my child."

I gasped. I couldn't imagine living with that kind of choice.

For once, Frankie had nothing to say.

Chastity's father had been a cold-blooded killer. One with a sadistic streak a mile wide. He punished his daughter by killing her. And he took his revenge by making Lou murder his own brother at point-blank range, the brother he'd joined the mob to protect.

"You knew I'd be at the rendezvous point the night the big deal went down," Frankie said, looking at his brother with new eyes.

Lou held his gaze. "I shot you before you even knew it was me," he said softly. "I made it quick."

Right between the eyes.

Frankie didn't react, not even when his hat rode up and exposed the raw wound in his forehead. "Did I save the baby?"

Chastity's eyes filled with tears. "I don't know what happened to her."

Lou looked down at the floor. "Sal was holding Bonnie when he gave me the orders. He sent one of his guys along with me, to make sure I did you in."

"Did it work?" Frankie demanded. "You did your job. What happened to the baby?"

Lou cleared his throat. "Sal told me to meet him in the doorway of the church. Said he'd give Bonnie to me out there." He flicked his eyes up to Frankie. "Instead, he shot me in the chest and tossed me into the river. The bullet hole is still in the old wood archway."

"I'm so sorry," Chastity sobbed.

"Did he hurt Bonnie?" Frankie pressed. "Did he kill her?"

"I don't know what happened to her," Lou said, looking completely and utterly lost.

Chastity buried her head in his chest and cried.

I exchanged a glance with my increasingly frantic house-mate. "We know the last place anyone saw her was the church. And I'm not buying the idea that Pastor Clemens was as squeaky clean as everyone thinks."

"Not if people are getting shot outside his church," Frankie said.

"I told you something bad happened on that property," I said. "And it gets worse. When I went to the heritage society this afternoon, I saw a wedding picture from 1955."

"That's almost twenty years too late to make a difference here." Frankie deflated.

"The church gravedigger stood in the background," I told

him, "along with the mobster that we met in the back of the flower shop."

That got Frankie thinking. "Hold up. The gravedigger didn't work for any of the gangs. Nobody at the church did. Clemens didn't allow it."

"The photo I saw showed the gravedigger and the original Pastor Clemens with a mobster, burying something in the churchyard." And he wasn't alone. "There were also a few other guys standing around in suits, looking at the ground."

"I'll be damned." Frankie exchanged glances with Lou.

"I don't know the entire story, but I'd like to check out that grave," I told them. "I'd also like to talk to the gravedigger." If he could talk. "He might have seen what happened to little Bonnie."

"I'll talk to him," Lou snarled, drawing a revolver out of his jacket.

"Hold up," Frankie ordered, shooting me a sideways glance. "If I know Sal, he's already gotten to any witnesses. Clammed them up. Verity is an outsider, and alive. She might be our only shot."

"But what can Verity do?" Chastity protested. "No offense," she said to me, "but we're on an entirely different plane."

I understood her doubt. "I admit, I've had trouble getting the gravedigger to talk to me."

"That's when you didn't know what to say to him," Frankie countered.

I still didn't. "I can't exactly walk up and say, 'Hi, I heard you might have witnessed a murder and buried the body.'" Many bodies, possibly. Or other illegal objects. "Besides, I'm afraid Sal took Bonnie back to Chicago with him. Would the gravedigger know if he did?"

"Sal always kept his plans close to the vest," Lou said.

"He liked control," Frankie agreed.

"If you find her, I'll never let her out of my sight again," Chastity promised, gliding toward me.

"Please find my baby," she urged.

"I'll try," I promised. I'd do everything I could.

"Come on," Lou said, holding out a hand to her. "I'll take you back to our apartment."

"It's not safe," Chastity said, avoiding his touch, glancing at us. "Those two found me there."

"I've got a shed you can use," Frankie offered.

Pride warmed my heart as he gave them my address.

"What?" Frankie muttered in my direction as the couple thanked him and disappeared.

"You're a good brother." I smiled at his shock. "You helped him instead of shooting him."

He shoved his hands into his pockets. "It's not going to be a habit." He stared at the wall. "Besides, I got to take care of my niece's parents. I'm an uncle now." He looked to me, as serious as I'd ever seen him. "We need to learn what happened to little Bonnie."

"We do." Lou and Chastity were reunited now, but they needed their child with them to make them whole. "Are you ready to go back to that graveyard?" I asked.

Frankie gritted his jaw and gave a sharp nod. "Are you?"

Chapter Twenty-Three

I tried Ellis again on the way to the church.

"Why do you always want to get the cops involved?" Frankie asked, digging for a cigarette. "What have they ever done for you?"

"Let's see," I said, tapping my fingers on the steering wheel, "Ellis has saved me from a haunted tub, camped out with me in a cursed bedroom, he's a heck of a kisser..."

"Okay. Stop," Frankie said, lighting up.

"I shot Frankie a slanted look. "The truth is, I don't want any old police officer." I needed someone who believed in me. "I want Ellis. I just don't know where he could be." I'd left another message. I knew he wouldn't be thrilled to know I was running around investigating, but he should want to call just to lecture me on it.

Besides, I'd told him in my messages that it was important.

"You'll do fine without him," Frankie said, taking a deep drag of his smoke. "I'll cut your power if the ghosts in the cemetery get out of hand."

"Be sure you're close by to do it this time," I said, steering up the hill toward the gates of the old church. "Davey has it out for you, and there could be more."

"You're the one who wanted me to be friendly," Frankie said as if it were the silliest thing he'd ever done. He leaned forward to get a better look out the window. "I told you from the start there was something wrong with this place." Frankie wrinkled his nose, wisps of smoke trailing from it, as we passed the woman in the bloody bathrobe standing at the gate.

"We'll get to the bottom of it," I vowed. "And we'll learn what happened to Bonnie."

For Bonnie's sake and for Frankie's. He was starting to put his family back together, and I wouldn't let him down.

I paused to let a man clad in long underwear and sporting a bullet hole in his back stumble aimlessly across the road.

The sky had gone cloudy, and a single raindrop smacked my windshield.

I steered past the dead preacher standing in the middle of the road. He stared blankly, not seeing, which was great by me.

I'd be quite happy to attract as little attention as possible. Last time, the ghosts had noticed me only when I began talking to Ray. The time before that, my morning had started going sideways when I approached the ghost of the organist.

"Stick close, but try not to talk to me," I warned him.

"Oh, I can be subtle," he said, leaning a hand out the window of my car and ashing his cigarette.

"If there are any living people at the church, we'll leave and come back later," I pledged. I needed room to work, and the ability to go places I maybe shouldn't. "If the ghosts get unruly, you'll turn my power off, and we'll escape and come back later."

"Piece of cake," Frankie declared.

"Famous last words," I said, pulling into the empty lot.

"Actually, my last words were, 'What are you gonna do? Stab me?'"

Frankie took a drag from his dwindling cigarette, slipped out of the car, and stubbed it out on the ground.

The church stood lonely under a gray sky, and the air had gone chilly. I slammed the car door behind me and dragged my bag over my shoulder.

This was it.

I wasn't sure where to find little Bonnie, but I'd start with getting my bearings set and my facts straight. Frankie drew his gun and held it low at his side while I started up the front steps of the church.

The arched entryway took on an entirely new meaning when I noticed the round bullet hole about shoulder-high on the right side. The hole had been filled by putty or some other substance that had sunken in over the years. It had been painted over. But the scar remained. Exactly where Lou said it would be.

I stood at the top of the stairs and surveyed the grounds. Ray's grave appeared peacefully abandoned. Beyond it stood the flapper staring at the ground. The bloody butcher ambled about in the distance. On the other side of the road, past my gangster, I saw the oak tree that Jorie had posed under on her wedding day.

The space around it appeared blessedly ghost-free, for now at least.

I hurried down the steps and pretended not to notice Frankie as I walked past him out to the old oak.

This was the same tree that the gravedigger had stood under in the background of the photo from the heritage society, accompanied by the gangster from the flower shop and other shady-looking characters. The tree had grown taller in the intervening years; the branches sprawled wider. Still, I recognized it.

I kept an eye out for the ghost of the gravedigger as I approached. He had to be somewhere nearby. I'd seen him on all of my visits to the church recently.

The trunk of the tree stood twice as thick around as me. I stepped carefully to avoid tripping over any exposed roots as I made my way to the very spot where my grandmother and Jorie had stood together all those years ago.

There were no gravestones under the tree. It was simply a quiet, peaceful place. A gentle wind rustled the branches.

So what were those guys doing over here, in the middle of a wedding no less?

"I didn't think I'd see you again so soon," Ray said over my shoulder. When I turned, he quickly added, "Don't look at me."

"I won't," I said under my breath, trying to appear as if I were looking through him, at a bird in the distance or a squirrel.

Anything.

"But I do have a very important question for you," I murmured. "Did you invite any gangsters to your wedding? Specifically, anybody who worked for Connor O'Malley or any Italians from Chicago who worked in a flower shop?"

"My." He furrowed his brow. "That is specific. But no—we had a small wedding. No mobsters allowed."

"I figured," I said, nudging a rock with my boot. At least about the mob. The men standing with the old Pastor Clemens and the gravedigger hadn't looked like they were posing for a wedding photo, as guests would do.

No question about it, the original Pastor Clemens had been caught up in something. I didn't care what Lou and Frankie thought. Just because he hadn't worked with the South Town Boys didn't mean he hadn't mixed himself up with somebody else.

"What's going on, Verity?" Ray pressed.

I kept my eyes carefully trained away from the ghost. "Have you seen the ghost of an infant on these grounds?"

"What? No. That would be terrible," he said. "A tragedy."

I couldn't agree more. But I needed to figure out what had happened to her, and it wouldn't do to make assumptions.

"What about the old Pastor Clemens?" I hadn't seen him, but Ray had spent a lot more time here.

"Delmore Clemens?" Ray asked. "No. He's not here."

Shoot. "I'm also looking for the gravedigger."

"Ah, Verity...I'm not sure that's such a great idea," Ray hedged. "In fact, I think we need to cut this short."

"What?" I looked up, ready to gaze straight through him, when I saw the flapper gliding across the parking lot, eyeing me with interest. The dead preacher stumbled up the road toward us.

"How did they—?" Dang it. "We were careful just now." At least I'd thought so.

"You've also got bloody-bathrobe lady coming in at six o'clock," Ray warned.

I turned and caught her in a dead stare.

"Bye, Ray. Thanks," I said, scurrying for my car. Curses. I'd wanted to talk to the gravedigger. At least if he ran me out of there, I knew I was doing my job.

Frankie eyed me as I headed for him and the car.

"Don't look at me," I warned.

"Want me to cut your power?" he asked.

"If they get out of hand, yes," I said, trying not to make eye contact with him as I said it. "But I want a shot at talking with the gravedigger first."

My stomach clenched at the thought of going home and breaking it to Lou and Chastity that I hadn't learned a thing about what might have happened to their baby.

I didn't know where she was. Or how they could hold her again.

I glanced behind me.

Bloody-bathrobe lady milled under the oak tree, confused. It seemed she'd lost her bearings. Maybe I'd been quicker this time.

I held my breath as the flapper wandered past.

Maybe I could still pull this off.

Slowly, casually, I edged around the front of the car. If the gravedigger wasn't outside, he could be in the church.

If I caught him in the church, I could talk to him with more privacy than Ray and I had enjoyed under the tree. As long as he didn't attack me.

I at least had to try.

"Nothing to it," Frankie murmured, because he wasn't the one who had to hurry casually up the steps and slip inside.

The arched door boomed closed behind me, and I quickly crossed the vestibule into the main church. The place held an air of quiet reverence. Shadows fell over the empty pews, and I stood for a moment, listening for any sounds, any trace of another soul—living or dead.

I'd seen the gravedigger in two places, in the churchyard and in the bell tower. He hadn't been among the ghosts roaming the churchyard today, so whether I liked it or not, it was time to visit the bell tower. I glanced to my right and toward the open doorway that led to those narrow stairs.

I could do this, I reminded myself. The scent of freshly cut wood tickled my nose as I began my ascent up the tower. I'd done it before, when I couldn't even touch the banister due to it being a crime scene.

Daylight illuminated the cut in the tower floor above.

I'd done it before I knew what might lay ahead, waiting.

Still, I wasn't quite prepared for what I saw when I stepped up into the small bell tower.

Out the arched window ahead, dozens of ghosts crowded a section of cemetery far beyond Ray's grave.

I rushed to the window and saw a shop girl clutching her neck, a waitress in a frilly apron streaked with blood, and a man in a suit, stumbling around without a head.

"Oh my God."

I'd seen ghosts before, but never this much carnage.

Out the front window, where Jorie had fallen, I saw more. They streamed past Ray's grave; they fanned out toward the church.

They surrounded my car.

Dead hookers, dead flappers, a trio of dead railroad workers. It didn't make sense.

And then it hit me.

I gasped and drew a hand to my mouth.

They'd all been murdered. None of them had gone peacefully. I saw a man rise up from under the parking lot.

My heart thudded in my chest. Ray had mentioned that these ghosts weren't exactly sitting on their gravestones.

They couldn't.

"They don't have gravestones," I murmured. This was a mob dumping ground, a place to get rid of evidence. That was what was going on in the background of the wedding picture. They were plotting to bury someone in an unmarked grave.

No doubt the gravedigger knew where all the bodies were buried.

Because he'd done the work himself.

I turned away from the window and saw the ghostly shovel, rusted at the top and clumped with dirt, leaning against the corner to the right.

He was here.

The faint smell of earth and sweat lingered in the air.

If he'd been watching me, he probably knew I'd learned his secret.

"Hello?" I called.

The handle of the shovel quivered.

"I don't mean any harm," I assured him. "I'd just like to talk."

The air was deathly still.

The heavy footsteps of a living person creaked on the bottom of the stairs, and I nearly jumped out of my skin. Heart pounding, I listened to them scrape the newly installed safety pads on the stairs as they made their way up, up, up.

"I need your help," I said to the ghost.

I glanced out the window, at the mass of dead gathering below.

It couldn't be Ellis on the stairs. Mine was the only car in the lot.

I searched the tiny room for a weapon, frantic. But there was only the ghostly shovel.

I braced myself as my visitor stepped up into the bell tower.

Chapter Twenty-Four

Pastor Mike filled the space between me and the stairs.

The only safe way down.

I backed up against the window Jorie had fallen from.

"I didn't see you when I came in," I said, forcing a smile, trying to act casual.

He had an odd look about him, stiff and unnatural. Like he'd forced himself into a role he didn't like. "I saw you drive up and walked over from the rectory."

"Oh!" I said, a little too excitedly. "That's great. I came here because"—I thought fast—"I have something for your father, and I know you see him almost every night."

It seemed reasonable.

Plausible.

He hadn't moved from where he stood, blocking me. He simply watched me, as if getting his nerve up.

"What do you have for my father?" he asked in an odd tone of voice that didn't comfort me in the slightest.

"Um…" All thoughts escaped me. My instincts told me to flee. Now. "It's down in my car. I'll go get it." And drive away.

I'd come back another time. With Ellis, no matter how much trouble he'd give me. "If you'll excuse me," I added, scurrying a bit to the left to get around the pastor.

I'd have to face the ghosts outside once I got out of there, but I'd worry about that later.

Pastor Mike stepped in front of me, blocking my way. "We need to talk," he said, deadly serious.

I didn't like the sound of that. I looked for a way past him. "You know, now isn't really good for me. Maybe some other time."

"Indulge me," he said, cutting me off, maneuvering so I had no choice but to back up toward the arched window above the hard lawn at the front of the church. "Eudora Louise said you were at the heritage society this afternoon."

"That didn't take long." Even for Sugarland.

He gave a brief, empty smile. "She's handling hospitality for the Save the Bell Tower Bake Sale next month. We had some important matters to discuss." His gaze flicked over me. "I don't know what I'd do without her."

Right then, I wanted to toss her through a window.

"Okay, listen," I said, deciding to level with him. Maybe I could distract him. Maybe he could even help. It was clear he wasn't letting me go until we had some sort of conversation, hopefully one that didn't leave me crushed like a grape. "A mobster was killed at the church door in 1938," I began, giving him part of the story. "A man by the name of Lou Winkelmann."

Pastor Mike gave a sanctimonious sniff. "There's never been a murder at this church," he said, cutting me off. "We are on holy ground."

"I hate to tell you, but this cemetery is littered with unmarked graves," I said, glancing out the window to the name-less ghosts below. "I think the original Pastor Clemens might have been a little too friendly with some gangsters. I mean, have you ever thought about where he got the money for all those soup kitchens and community programs?"

"Donations," Pastor Mike stated as if daring me to contradict him.

"I'm sure that's what the mob would have called it." They never liked to make things sound messy. "Your grandfather renovated the church in the aftermath of the depression. He commissioned the three angels carving. He supported the town. I'm not saying he didn't do some great deeds, but he might also have seen some unsavory things along the way." Including Lou's murder. "I mean, he lived here. He worked here. He knew where the bodies were buried."

Pastor Mike looked past me, out the window. I followed his gaze, and as if on cue, the ghost of a man wearing an old-timey baseball uniform rose up from underneath the parking lot.

The pastor began to speak and then stopped, shaken. But I could see in his eyes that he believed me. "Am I to assume you found proof at the heritage society?" he demanded.

"I found an important piece of the puzzle." I needed him to go with me on this. And to realize tossing me out the window, if he were so inclined, wouldn't solve his problem. "I can show you where, if you tell me what you know."

He rubbed the back of his neck. "You wouldn't be the worst person to tell," he said reluctantly. He dropped his hand. "We found something during the renovation of the pastor's room last year, in the office at the front of the church. There's a book that lists burials."

"That isn't unusual," I admitted. "It makes sense to have a book."

"Not the main records. I have those at the office in the barn. These are...other burials." He looked at me hard. "Meticulous notes kept by my grandfather. Entries like: young man, two paces down the path from the steps. Josephus the butcher, front yard." He shoved his hands into his pockets. "Below this tower, in fact."

Wow. That was…disturbing. "But why would they bury people so close to the church? Why not in the corner of the cemetery somewhere?"

"My grandfather was a merciful man," he said as if it were the most natural thing in the world. "He didn't need to write it down. Most men would want to forget." He huffed. "I did when I read it. But I think Granddad did it to…remember them. Honor them in any way he could." He looked at me, raw. "I think whoever made him take on these poor souls enjoyed watching him suffer."

I didn't doubt it, at least from what I'd heard about Chastity's father, Sal.

"I found a picture from Jorie's wedding," I said, the words spilling out. "It shows the church gravedigger and at least one mobster in the background. I think they were digging a hole to bury a body."

In the middle of a wedding.

"It appears your grandfather went out to stop them," I added. Or at least hold them off until a more convenient time.

He inhaled sharply. "The last burial in my grandfather's book happened in 1957."

Two years after Jorie's wedding.

They'd been doing this for a while, then. "How long did your grandfather serve?"

"Until 1957," he said grimly.

And there it was.

"He lived here until then. And after? My father didn't like living on the property, so we moved down the road."

My heart hammered in my chest when I asked, "Did you see the mobster in the picture Jorie tried to give me?"

"Yes," he whispered. His eyes met mine. "I recognized him

immediately when Jorie showed me her picture. I knew others would too."

I hadn't. "Who was it?"

"Marty the Rat." He ran a hand down the side of his face. "He was one of the big guys in Chicago. Joe Pesci played him in that movie," he said, as if I watched gangster movies. Half the time, I felt like I was living in one. "There are those artsy T-shirts of him where they take his old picture and add bright colors everywhere. The kids wear them."

"Not familiar," I said honestly.

"If that picture of him at the Three Angels got around, people would also want to know why there's no marked grave under the old oak tree."

"Jorie's picture showed an open grave," I said on an exhale.

I'd been too busy looking at my grandmother.

"It might as well have shown a body," he admitted.

"You destroyed the picture." He'd burned it out back.

"Yes," he said simply. He took a step toward me, then another. "You have to understand, my father is frail. News like this could kill him."

"He seemed all right enough to me," I said, backing up. Sure, Pastor Bob didn't leave his apartment much, but he did get out for dinner sometimes, and his mind was still sharp.

"Worse," he continued, "it could cause the demise of the church—my father's life's work. My grandfather's life's work." He stopped directly in front of me. "And then where would I go?"

I stepped away from the window and kept the wooden wall of the bell tower at my back. "Did you lure Jorie up here?"

He stood silent for a moment. "Lure isn't the right word."

"Tell me," I urged, inching sideways, away from the window. The gravedigger's shovel lay in the corner, but it would pass straight through the very alive Pastor Mike.

In a second, he would realize he was as trapped as I was.

"Is this supposed to be a confession?" he asked. "I'm not Catholic."

"Sometimes it's good to unburden the soul," I said breathlessly.

He gave me a small smile. "I didn't murder her. I'm not a killer."

"Of course not," I said as he slipped his hands out of his pockets.

He took a deep breath. "I asked her if I could have the picture. This all could have been avoided if she'd let me take it and be done with it."

"But she kept it for me."

"She tried," he corrected. "I needed to convince her in private. So I brought her up here during a break in the tours." He glanced out the window. "I said it was urgent, that it would only take a minute."

"How did you get past me?" I'd been in the parking lot, placing the pressed rose in a book. They would have had to walk right by my car to get inside.

"There's a hidden door behind the rosebush, near the place where Jorie fell."

I gasped. "I never saw it."

"Ellis Wydell did. He even found my prints." He cocked his head to the side. "But that's not so unusual." He drew close. "She didn't have to die."

"But she did," I whispered.

"I gave her plenty of chances." He stepped away from me. "When she refused to give me the photo, I confessed to Jorie the real reason I needed it. I trusted her. I told her why she had to destroy that picture and any like it, for the good of the church she loved so much."

"She refused?" I asked.

He tossed up his hands. "She didn't understand at all. This church, this sanctuary of God, is a piece of Sugarland history, and it's in more trouble than people realize. These days, people don't want to drive out to the country. People don't want a simple experience. They go to the big mega churches or strip-mall churches with rock bands and Bible plays and glitzy carnival committees while this house of the Lord rots!" A lock of his perfect hair flopped in his face and he scraped it back. "The only thing that keeps our doors open is the donations from the Eudora Louise Markams and the Ovis Dupres and the Virginia Wydells of the world. They care about the church's historical reputation. If that were sullied, they would stop supporting it. Us."

"I have to admit, you're right about that." It made me sad, but not enough to kill.

He took a deep breath and exhaled. "The first Pastor Clemens established a reputation for this church. From 1910 to 1957, he was an institution, revered and respected, his legacy to be preserved as a point of town pride." Pastor Mike stood tall, in full preacher mode. "The word of God teaches us: If the church isn't blessed, clearly we're not favored by God. So, through the church's blessings, through these donations, and through our favored heritage, we are blessed and worthy."

"But your blessings came from gangsters," I said slowly, trying to understand.

"You will not speak of it again," he ordered.

That wouldn't make it any less true.

I understood he wanted to believe in this perfect, anointed image, but how realistic was that? "You can make mistakes and still be blessed." It couldn't be all or nothing.

"Nonsense." He brushed it aside. "I know the law of the Lord, not you." He towered over me. "And let one thing be clear; I never hurt Jorie. She hurt herself."

Stars above. "How?"

He stiffened. "I tried to take the picture from her. That wasn't wrong. I was protecting my father and this church. She pulled back too hard." His voice cracked. "She lost her balance. She fell."

He buried his face in his hands and let out a sob. "It was an accident, a terrible accident. But who would believe that?" He lowered his hands, his skin blotched and his eyes red. "Rage is a sin. She died in sin, and it's my fault."

"You need to tell Ellis that." The police had to be made aware, and Ellis would understand.

"I can't tell anyone." He gulped. "In order to tell people what happened, I'd have to tell them what was in the picture." He looked out the window to the ground where Jorie had lain. "She clutched it in her hand as she fell. And after she...landed, the wind caught it. I stood right here and watched it get tangled in the copse of redbud trees. It was the will of God. He kept it safe for me." His eyes were red-rimmed and wild. "Everything happens for a reason."

I inched toward the stairs.

"Do you forgive me?" he asked. With catlike speed he grabbed my shoulders, his grip hard and bruising. "You must keep my confidence in this," he added, turning me toward the window. "It is the will of God."

"I'll be quiet," I promised, my boots slipping on the freshly stained floor, frantic to escape.

"Yes, you will," he said as the cold breeze tickled my cheeks. "God has seen to it. He has delivered you to me."

Chapter Twenty-Five

I stared up at him, wide-eyed, like a sweet Southern belle. Then I kicked him in the shin.

He doubled over, and I ran for the stairs.

The gravedigger stood just behind the hole in the floor, arms outstretched.

Sweet heaven. Not him, too!

I dropped down on to the stairs, bracing my hands on the walls, stumbling down, down, down, as fast as I could go.

Above me, the pastor shrieked. "Cold!" Then he fell so hard it rattled the walls under my fingertips.

"*Go,*" a raspy voice sounded in my ears.

The pastor cursed as he came tumbling down after me.

I swung out the doorway, hanging onto the frame as the pastor toppled out after. We both landed on the hardwood floor of the church. Pastor Mike curled in on himself, bleeding from the head.

The gravedigger stood behind him, his large hands braced against the arched doorway to the bell tower.

I gasped, pain streaking through my right knee as I struggled to stand.

"Run," he urged.

"Thank you," I warbled, trying to find my voice.

"Now," he ordered.

I'd paused a few seconds too long. The pastor wore a vicious sneer as he staggered to his feet.

The gravedigger tried to grab him by the throat, passing right through. Pastor Mike shrieked and flailed at the unseen chill.

I ran.

Out through the vestibule, out of the church. I started down the stairs.

The butcher waited at the bottom.

"Frankie!" I hollered, backtracking several steps. He needed to turn my power off.

Now.

Ghosts rose from the parking lot, from underneath my car, from the road. They surged up everywhere from unmarked graves—desperate, angry, murdered spirits.

"Frankie!" The butcher tracked me up the front steps toward the church, wielding his bloody cleaver.

The organist with the knife waited inside my car. I couldn't go that way. I felt a chill at my back. The woman in the bloody bathrobe stood directly behind me. She reached for me.

Pastor Mike emerged from the doorway behind her.

I was out of time, out of options, and missing the one ghost who could turn off my power.

"Frankie!" I leapt off the side of the steps, landing on the soft earth as a ghostly hand erupted from the ground and grabbed my ankle.

I screamed. It was cold; it was wet. And it had a strong grip.

Then I saw Frankie by my car, splayed out spread eagle on the ground. He was out cold. His head lolled to the side, staring blankly. An ugly gray bullet hole cut through the skin and bone right above his original bullet hole. He'd been shot. Again. In the forehead. It would be hours before he woke up and could take his power back.

Ohmygod. I was on my own.

And desperately outmatched.

I stomped on the hand that gripped me. I stomped again and again. It had to hurt to touch me. It had to hurt just as bad as it hurt me, the singeing, stinging, bone-deep chill. But this ghost didn't care. Or maybe it was already in so much pain, it didn't notice.

A bald, bloody man's head poked from the soil, screaming.

I screamed too as a ghostly grip closed under my arms and dragged me straight up.

"I've got you!" Ray hollered, breaking me free. "Argh!" he cried at the pain of touching me. He dropped me onto the ground the second I cleared the grasping hands.

I rolled away from the tortured head sliced nearly free of the bloody shoulders emerging from the soil.

Ray stood over me, wild eyed. "What the hell?"

"You can't touch me." He couldn't even save me for long. I scrambled to my feet. I couldn't get to my car. I couldn't outrun a pack of ghosts. And I had no idea where Pastor Mike was, but I had a feeling he'd be on me in a heartbeat.

"Find Ellis," I ordered Ray. "Tell him I'm here."

"Are you nuts?" He tossed out an arm and clotheslined the organist, stunning her. While she was down, he knocked the knife out of her hand. "You need me here."

I did. But he could only protect me from the dead, not the living.

There was no time to explain the ghost app on Ellis's phone, which he might not have handy anyway.

"Trust me. Talk to Ellis like he can hear you." And I'd pray that he could. "I'll hide," I promised. Or I'd get ripped to shreds trying. But my one chance, my only chance, to survive both the living and the dead was plain. "Tell Ellis I need help!"

"Verity," he protested.

"Go!" I ordered.

Ray looked at me, torn. Then he disappeared.

Thank goodness. I was alone.

With a mass of angry, murdered souls and a pastor who wanted me to join them.

Chapter Twenty-Six

⚜

I had to get to my car. The organist with the knife now lay beside me, out cold, so the land yacht might be unguarded. I grabbed her knife, ignoring the slice of pain as the chill of it radiated down my arm.

It was a weapon, for as long as it lasted. And beggars couldn't be choosers.

A trio of flappers stood between me and my car. So did a shop girl. And a gangster. I gripped my ice-cold knife as the woman in the bloody bathrobe blocked my path to the parking lot. I turned toward the stairs to find the butcher.

I could stab one, but I couldn't get them all.

And as the tip of my knife began to disappear, the bloody butcher took the lead. He towered over me, his meat hatchet raised. His lip curled, and in a rusty voice he hissed, "You..." He pointed the cleaver dead at my heart. "Tell them we are here."

I stared into his bloodshot eyes, not quite able to process what he said. The hatchet hadn't fallen. I was still in one piece. He could have killed me by now...if he'd wanted to.

I cleared my throat. "Excuse me. What?"

"We are lost," he said urgently. "Trapped," he added as if the words didn't come easily. "We need out."

A chill wound through me that had nothing to do with the clash of my world and theirs. I dropped the knife.

"You need me to help you," I said, hoping, praying I understood right.

The woman in the bloody bathrobe next to him mouthed words I didn't understand. Her voice came out as a gurgle, but I barely made out, "Please."

Pastor Mike stumbled from the church.

I dug for my keys, my only real weapon, as he staggered down the stairs. The ghosts formed a tight circle around me. I wouldn't make it far, but Mike could certainly target me. I braced myself.

He'd have to come to me.

Instead, he dropped down and sat on the bottom step, his head in his hands. "I think I have a concussion."

I approached him slowly, careful not to get too close. "That's what you get for trying to kill me." I clutched my car keys. If he tried to get the jump on me, he'd be sorry.

He raised his head slightly. "I wasn't trying to kill you. I wanted to explain." He winced and braced his head again. "I need you to believe me. Jorie's death was an accident. I feel terrible about it."

"Not bad enough to confess to the police," I reminded him.

We'd fix that soon enough.

A few minutes later, Ellis's police cruiser blazed down the drive, sirens on. He launched himself out of the car.

"I'm fine!" I called to him, glad when he ran straight for me and hugged me tight.

"What's going on?" he demanded, looking at the forlorn pastor, who raised his head once more.

"I'll give him the chance to tell you. Mike?" I prodded.

The pastor looked like he might be sick, but he cleared his throat and stood. "I have a confession to make."

~

Duranja pulled up a few minutes later, followed by the police chief.

Ellis kept the pastor inside the church for questioning.

Meanwhile, a line of ghosts had formed, waiting to talk to me. I started by simply taking everyone's names on one of the fast-food napkins I kept in the glove box of my car.

It was a start.

The gravedigger stood at the edge of the cemetery, where the graves gave way to trees, watching me.

I took it as an invitation and walked out to him, careful to avoid the other ghosts, wishing I could sidestep their graves as easily. But we'd work on that. We'd lay them to rest in a way that allowed them to truly find peace.

He clutched his shovel tightly, fidgeting nervously as I approached.

"Hi." I stopped several feet from him, not wishing to cause him any more anxiety. "Thank you," I added. "You saved me back there." Despite what Pastor Mike had claimed about meaning no harm, he'd proven himself more than capable of it. I was glad I'd run. And grateful for the gravedigger's help.

He scratched his head and shuffled his feet. "You're trying to make things right. It's more than I ever did."

"It took courage to help." He needed to recognize that. I felt the corner of my mouth turn up. "I know it doesn't feel so good to touch a live person."

He barked out a laugh, then quickly stifled it. "Maybe I wouldn't have done it if I'd known."

"You would have." I had no doubt. After all, he'd done it twice—once at the top of the stairs and once below. Even if all he could offer was a horrid cold spot, it had taken a sacrifice on his part. I appreciated that.

"I'm Verity, by the way."

He stood quietly as the breeze rustled the trees behind him.

"Carl," he grunted out as if this sort of interaction were foreign to him.

"What's your last name?" I asked. "I might know your kin."

He appeared startled by the question, and it took him a moment to answer. "Hodges. My people are long dead." He cleared his throat. "I'm a felon, but you're safe with me," he added quickly.

"You've proven it," I told him.

He ran an uncomfortable hand over his unshaven jaw and eyed me as if he wasn't quite sure why I'd taken the time to speak with him directly.

"You were right about Lou Winkelmann," Carl blurted out.

"He died here at the church, right out front," I said. Carl didn't need to confirm. I knew it was true.

"The pastor and I saw him get shot." Carl planted his shovel in the ground between us. "The mob boss ordered me to dump the body in the river. I didn't want to. I didn't want to hide any of them, but I needed this job." He gripped his shovel tighter. "The boss took his daughter's body back to Chicago with him."

"Did you bury the baby?" I asked, breathless, not wanting to know the answer if it was bad.

"Little Bonnie Winkelmann?" He fiddled nervously with his shovel. "They didn't kill her. The mob boss gave her to the pastor. He and his wife kept the baby as their own, fudged some papers to adopt her. They called her MayBelle."

Chapter Twenty-Seven

※❀❁❀※

More people arrived at the church as word in Sugarland spread. Spoiler alert: it didn't take long.

I studiously avoided the reporter for the *Sugarland Gazette* and instead approached Pastor Bob as he finished a brief chat with Duranja.

"How are you holding up?" I asked.

"Well enough," he said. "I wish I could say the same about my son. I'm sorry if he scared you."

"He thought he was protecting you." It might have been wrong, but I could see at least some good in that.

He nodded tightly and gave a small sigh. "Walk with me."

I nodded.

"And go slow," he added. "I'm not the sprinter I was in high school."

We struck out down the road, where it was easier to walk. "I should have been honest with Mike from the start," he said, shaking his head. "Our generation. We used to think there was honor in keeping these things quiet, a stiff upper lip and all."

"So you knew about your dad's mob connections?" He'd talked about his dad with such pride.

"My dad was as clean as they came." He held up a hand when I tried to protest. "Yes, he was. Dad helped anyone who needed him spiritually, regardless of whether or not he considered them 'good.' In fact, he believed it was more important to minister to those who were struggling. He called them his lost sheep."

I stopped walking. "We're talking about killers."

Pastor Bob glanced out over the graveyard. "Dad learned that when Salvatore Spiro came to town." He brought his gaze back to me. "Sal killed his own daughter in cold blood. Then he killed his son-in-law. Dad was afraid for the baby. He begged Sal to spare the child. My dad would adopt it, raise it. Sal agreed, but for a price." A car came trundling down the drive, and Bob steadied himself on my arm as we moved to the side. "At first, Sal wanted to store guns in the church office. Then he wanted to park hearses outside the cemetery, filled with God knew what."

"Then he started burying bodies," I said, looking out over the grassy cemetery.

"Yes," Bob said. "The deal kept getting worse and worse. But what could Dad do? If Salvatore Spiro would kill his own daughter, who knew what he'd do to MayBelle?" Bob dropped my arm as we stood at the edge of the cemetery. "Dad said blessings over the graves after the gangsters did their work. He tried to do his best for those people." He held his chin high. "It was the only way to keep my sister safe. Sal threatened her life whenever my dad tried to refuse him."

"But they paid him. That's how he funded the church renovation and the social projects."

"They paid him," Bob said stiffly. "They tried to act like it was normal. *Business*, they said. Dad didn't want their blood money. He was also afraid to refuse it. So he spent it all on the town, helping as many people as he could. He renovated the church. Those three angels behind the altar—that's the couple who died. The mother and the father. And their baby that dad saved. He renamed the church after them. He never let himself forget."

Lou, Chastity, and MayBelle.

He wiped a hand over his eyes. "Sal died in 1957. That's when Dad let me take over." Pastor Bob sniffed. "Dad was used up long before then, but he didn't want me to ever deal with Sal." His voice caught. "He didn't want anyone else to suffer the guilt he had."

"Your dad died shortly after, didn't he?" I asked gently.

"Mid-sermon at the pulpit," Bob said, cracking a weak smile. "We buried him in the rectory churchyard. He held on until he knew it was all over."

"Does MayBelle know about any of this?" I pressed.

"No," he said quickly. "We kept her separated from it. We tread carefully around her. I think Mom and Dad—they were scared to death they'd lose her if she knew."

MayBelle had told me plain she'd never felt like part of the family. But she didn't realize it wasn't because she was different —though she was very different—or that they didn't love her. They'd thought they were protecting her.

That was the moment she chose to come strolling out from the back of the church, cigarette in hand.

"She's here," I said, surprised.

"She had to drive me," Bob said. "And she's as worried as I am about Mike," he said, sobering.

"You need to tell her the truth." It was past time.

"I do," he agreed. "My father was insistent that we protect her, but I think I'm realizing secrets hurt more than they help." He clasped my hand. "Thank you, Verity. I feel lighter than I have in ages."

"I'm glad," I said as we walked together back toward the church. "Just be gentle with your sister. She's a sensitive soul, whether she'll admit it or not."

"I'll take your word for that." He laughed. "Oh, after you left the other night, I looked through some more of my photo albums. I found a picture of your great-grandma Ida Jane. She looked a lot like you."

"So I've heard." I'd met her hometown beau on a past adventure. "I'd love to see it."

"Stop by for dinner some night and I'll give it to you," he offered.

"Thank you," I said. "It'll be my treat." The chipotle chicken and waffle sliders from my friend Lauralee's food truck would knock his socks off.

"I'm looking forward to it," Bob said as we neared his sister. "Wish me luck," he said as he kept walking and approached MayBelle.

But he didn't need luck. He had a sister who loved him.

I left them on the path and headed back to the parking lot, where Frankie still lay unresponsive on the ground. The poor gangster had probably been shot by Davey or one of the other cemetery ghosts. My housemate shouldn't have told anyone that he was the one who could turn off my power. They'd wanted to talk to me quite badly.

As I drew near, I caught Frankie stirring. He blinked furiously and brought a tentative hand to the fading second bullet hole in his forehead.

At least that one would go away.

"Dang, that stings," he said, sitting up. "I didn't even see who shot me. Why do I never see it coming?"

"You need fewer enemies," I said, wishing I could help him up.

"What's the fun in that?" He frowned when he looked at me. "Why are you smiling?"

I told him what he'd missed. And where he could find his niece.

He stumbled to his feet on hearing the news. "That's my

niece?" he asked, watching her smoking at the side of the church, embracing Bob and then pushing him away with a laugh.

"You don't see the resemblance?" I asked.

She had the same dark eyebrows, same angular features. Same annoying smoking habit. Although I supposed that last one didn't count.

"I have a living niece," Frankie marveled. "I have family!"

"Actual living family," I agreed. As well as a reconciled brother and newfound sister-in-law.

Frankie's eyes widened. "Lou and Chastity are in the ether. Wait until they get out and hear about this!"

It would feel good to reunite them with their little girl, even if she was all grown up now.

I settled for Frankie's joy as he glided to where MayBelle stood at the side of the church, eager to connect with his niece.

A few moments later, Duranja exited with Pastor Mike, and Ellis stood talking to the chief as they loaded Mike into Duranja's cruiser.

Ellis spotted me soon after and walked over.

"You're going to let him drive away with all the glory?" I asked as Duranja headed down the drive.

"I wanted to talk to you," he said, stopping short of me. "I'm glad you're okay."

"So I take it you got my message."

"Oh, you mean when my ghost app started yelling, 'Murder, murder, church, murder.'"

"I'm sorry," I said, hating the distance between us. "You were right. I let my blind faith in my abilities lead me into a situation I couldn't get out of." If the ghosts had been out to kill me, I'd be dead.

He huffed out a breath. "I'm sorry, too. I—" He threw up a hand. "I should have been honest with you when I first started worrying. I know you're careful, and I know you're good at what you do. I think I just got so defensive because I hadn't said anything for so long, and then you found out anyway."

"Oh." I wasn't sure what to think about that.

"And you've got to start treating the law like the law, and not like a set of guidelines."

"I'll work on that," I promised. Although, Frankie wasn't the best influence.

He closed the distance between us and took my hands. "I protect people. It's my job. But I know I can't wrap you in bubble wrap and keep you on a shelf."

"That's weird, Ellis."

He laughed. "You know I suck at talking." He squeezed my hands. "I'm awkward and I worry too much. I'm a stickler for the rules, and I try to fix problems you don't even know you have. I get bossy about it."

"You threatened to arrest me," I added.

"And I would have done it, too," he joked.

"Remind me why I'm dating you again," I teased.

He didn't take the bait. "Because I love you," he said simply. "I'd do anything for you, and I always want what's best for you. Even if I act like an idiot about it sometimes."

"I love you, too," I told him. "And I promise I'll try not to get defensive when you worry about me. I'll make sure to obey the laws." Whenever I could. "And I respect you enough to always tell you the truth."

"Right back at you." He winked.

He was so...not smooth. "I did try to tell you about this trip back to the church," I reminded him. "Multiple times. I even stopped by the Sugarland PD to let Duranja mock me."

Ellis shook his head. "Five minutes after I got off this afternoon, my mom called me with a plant emergency."

"Sounds serious."

"She didn't like the way her landscaper spaced her hostas."

He held up a hand. "Don't even say it. I'd like to believe it's her excuse to spend time with me."

Free labor was more like it.

But I was a good girlfriend and didn't say anything.

"Anyway," he continued, "I didn't realize she'd taken my phone and turned the volume off until my ghost app started going crazy."

"That's awful. And dangerous. What if the police needed you?"

"You needed me," he pointed out. "I was too busy running here to tell her off, but it's on my list. I'm not going to bury things and let them explode. I'm not doing that anymore."

"It'll be good to talk about our worries instead of letting them get the best of us," I agreed.

"We'll both work at it until we get it right," he promised. Then he dragged me into his arms. "So I hear we're getting married."

"What?" I sputtered up at him.

"Word around town is that you were at the Pastry Box, picking out a wedding cake. Did you tell them I like chocolate?"

"No," I said, extricating myself from his grip. "I was investigating. I had to get upstairs where the cakes were. And wedding cake is supposed to be white."

He laughed. "I think we should do what we want."

"Why are you teasing me like this?" I asked, placing my hands on my hips.

I mean, yes, we were dating. And we were getting more serious all the time. Especially now that I knew I could trust him to work on our problems instead of brushing them aside. Even if we got angry with each other sometimes. And I really loved the fact that he was mature and thoughtful and he never left me feeling like an argument meant the end of the relationship...

"Verity?" he asked.

"What?" I'd been woolgathering.

"You do know I'm going to marry you someday."

He said it as if it were the most natural thing in the world. I like my coffee black. My cake chocolate. And oh, by the way, I'm going to marry you someday.

I felt my mouth drop open right before my face went numb.

"Where else did you think this was heading?" He laughed as if he didn't quite understand my surprise. Or lack of ability to speak.

"Not today," I reasoned.

"No," he said, drawing me back into his arms. "Not today."

He kissed me slow and sweet. And I decided I liked this new "tell it like it is all the time" Ellis. He might not be perfect. He might not be smooth. But I loved him, and he was mine.

Chapter Twenty-Eight

that night, I took Lucy out onto the back porch and we shared a bowl of strawberries while I told her about my amazing, shocking, and ultimately satisfying day.

She didn't say much. She never did. But I knew she listened. And when the strawberries were gone, she hightailed it down the stairs and out into the yard.

I was perfectly fine with her adventuring—she needed it as much as I did. But I wasn't as thrilled when she circled around the apple tree and scurried under the porch.

Darn it. There was something stinky under there, and I hadn't quite gotten around to removing it.

"Lucy," I called, standing, knowing full well she'd pretend she couldn't hear me.

She'd be a mess if I didn't fish her out. And fast. Lucy loved stinky things. "You come out or I'm coming in after you," I said, my boots echoing off the wooden stairs.

She'd best learn now that ignoring me wouldn't get her off the hook.

The sun hung low in the sky as I bent over and located the

shadow of my skunk about half-way under, eating something she no doubt oughtn't. Oh, my.

"Lucille Désirée Long. I just fed you!" I got low on my stomach and scuttled past a loose section of white-painted lattice. And then I smelled it full-on, a pungent sulfur-like odor that made my eyes water.

Something was definitely rotten in the state of Denmark.

Or at least under my porch in Sugarland.

Lucy began to eat faster.

"That could hurt you," I warned, closing a hand around her warm little tummy and pulling her away. She bit down on her bounty and dragged it with her.

Once I'd secured my skunk, I grabbed her prize and found a rotting head of broccoli.

"Naughty girl. Have you been raiding Mr. Morris's garden?" I hadn't bought broccoli in weeks.

Lucy blinked up at me with her wide, button eyes, all innocence. She definitely had the look down pat.

"I know he feeds you carrots, but that doesn't mean you should help yourself."

She snuggled against my chest, as if that made everything right. Darn my weakness, it did warm my heart.

I ran a hand over her soft little head. "We'll make better choices next time," I promised her. And perhaps the next time I made cookies, I'd make a few extra for Mr. Morris.

I held her and stroked her under the ear, the way she liked it, enjoying the moment, even if we did both happen to be filthy and under the porch.

We were just about ready to scoot out and start talking about a bath when I saw a familiar pair of black wing tips shimmer into existence outside on the grass.

"You made it back," Frankie said, and I thought he was talking to me until I saw the lower half of a ghostly couple appear directly across from him.

"We couldn't rest," Chastity said.

"Not with our little girl missing," Lou said, his voice strained with worry.

"That's why I found her," Frankie said, his voice warmer than I'd ever heard it. "Me and Verity, anyway."

Chastity let out a shriek and hugged Frankie while Lou gave a gut-deep exhale. "Thank God."

"Where is she?" Chastity prodded. "Where's my baby? Is she safe?"

"She's alive," Frankie said, as if he still couldn't quite believe it himself. "She's in perfect health, and she lives on the fourth floor of the Sugarland Grand Hotel."

"She's safe?" Chastity asked, as if she couldn't quite believe it.

"The pastor raised her," Frankie said. "Her name is MayBelle Clemens now. We can all go meet her tomorrow if you want. Me and Verity will help everybody talk."

"I'm going to go see her right now," Chastity said, disappearing.

"I'll be there in a minute," Lou called after her before turning back to his brother. "Thanks, Frankie. I don't deserve your help after what I did to you, but I want you to know you've given me my life back."

Frankie let out a low huff. "I never thought I could forgive you for plugging me, but I do."

"Thanks," Lou said, his voice rough.

Frankie cleared his throat. "Yeah, well, I understand why you did it and I'm glad. I wouldn't have a family right now if you hadn't." He shifted uncomfortably. "Not that I'm expecting you to stick around."

"I'd like to," Lou said, his voice going hoarse. "If you'd like me to."

"We can try that," Frankie said, noncommittal and fast as if he had to get it out before he lost his courage.

"I'm going to go see my kid," Lou said, backing away. "You're a pretty good brother."

"You're not so bad yourself," Frankie said, as Lou disappeared.

A few days later, we gathered at the Three Angels Church to say goodbye to my grandmother's dear friend.

Pastor Bob had turned over his father's record book, the one that contained all the names of the dead and the burial locations the original Pastor Clemens was able to gather.

I'd helped by recording the names of the ghosts I encountered and matching them to the notes, which were sometimes incomplete.

The coroner's office hired extra hands in the form of University of Tennessee forensics graduate students. They dotted the cemetery in small groups, marking suspected grave sites and preparing them for exhumation.

Each group was watched over by a ghost, recognized at last.

These people had been forgotten for too long, buried and left to rot. Just noticing them, remembering their names—recognizing they'd existed at all—it seemed to give many of the ghosts a touch of their humanity back.

Even the woman in the bloody bathrobe didn't seem as lost.

She stood near the front steps of the church and nodded to me as I approached.

I was so focused on her, I barely noticed Beau Wydell approaching.

"Hey," he said, "where's Ellis?"

"Oh," I said, turning. "He's waiting for me inside."

Beau grinned. "Glad you two made up. And that Ellis got his head out of his ass."

"Yes, well, he's inside with your mother," I clarified.

He'd arrived early with Virginia Wydell, who'd claimed amnesia about the entire cell phone incident. When Ellis didn't let her off the hook, she'd confessed a burning desire to have him accompany her to the funeral, lest she faint at the shock of having Pastor Mike in custody rather than at the altar.

In short, honest talk worked on some people better than others.

"I'll go take that bullet," Beau pledged. "He'll be out in five."

"You'd do that for me?" I asked, warming.

"I stood down a gangster for you," he said, with typical bravado. "For you and for my brother."

"Thanks," I said. And I meant it.

"Just make sure you sit far enough away from us," Beau said. "Or else my sacrifice will be in vain."

"I'll remember you fondly," I called after him as he took the church steps two at a time and left me with a salute.

While I gave him a minute, Fiera crossed the parking lot toward me. She wore her gray hair in a French twist that went well with her black dress.

"I'm sorry, Verity," she said before I could greet her. "I lied to you."

"About the pictures for the library." Melody had already told me that the boxes of photos Fiera had taken weren't for the donation she'd claimed.

She clutched the purse strap dangling from her shoulder. "Jorie's daughter, Suzanne, asked me for a special favor. She wanted me to remove some...personal things." She sighed. "Not just the photos, but a lot of private correspondence. Military life can be tough, and maybe it's best not to have anyone else judging the family for things that are best kept private."

A plump redhead approached us. She had Jorie's eyes and Ray's nose, and she wore a hesitant smile as she stood next to Fiera. "I'm sorry for the confusion," she said to Fiera as much as me. "It's just that you don't lock your doors enough in Sugarland."

"I'll give you that," I said. As far as I was concerned, that was a good thing.

It seemed Fiera had tried to do right by too many people. I knew the feeling and was certainly glad she'd done her best for poor Suzanne. "I'm so sorry for your loss," I told Jorie's only daughter.

"Oh, come here." Suzanne gave me a hug, in true Southern style, before accompanying Fiera into the church.

Ray stood a few feet behind her, watching her go. "She's so grown up." He smiled fondly.

"How are you doing?" I asked. This had to be so hard for him.

"I'll watch the eulogies. It'll be fun to hear people's stories about her. But that's just talk. The best part happens later, when she comes back here to find me."

"How long do you think it'll take?" I asked him, promising myself I'd have to make regular visits in the meantime.

"Could be a year, could be two," he said with the shrug of a shoulder. "Time doesn't matter much to me anymore. The important thing is she's coming." He started up the stairs. "Are you going in?"

"I'm waiting for someone."

He smiled at that and continued on his way.

I looked to the place where Jorie died, where I'd seen her soul traces rise up from the ground. I said a silent, private goodbye and gave thanks, knowing she was loved and protected.

The gravedigger stood just beyond, next to the rosebush that concealed the hidden door.

I walked to him, seeing him tense at my approach. "Hi, Carl."

He gripped his shovel and grunted an acknowledgment as he averted his eyes.

"I was just wondering how you're doing." I smiled at him as he shifted in place.

"Nobody usually notices me," he said as if embarrassed by a simple hello, a minor acknowledgment. "But I watch," he insisted. "I watched you, and I knew you were good."

"So are you," I told him.

His cheeks flushed, and he ducked his head. I also caught the hint of a smile before he disappeared.

"Look at you, walking on the lawn," a gravelly voice called out behind me. I turned and saw a bare-headed MayBelle getting out of her convertible.

"Don't forget your hair," I called.

She reached into the back seat and pulled out a dark wig with tight Betty Boop curls. She slipped it onto her head with a grin.

"So I hear you're related to the mob," I said as she approached. "Are you scandalized?"

"Yes, and it's fantastic," she said, adjusting her hair. It really did look good on her. "Ellis explained to me about your ghosts. I'd like to invite them for a cocktail at my place. You're welcome too, of course."

It would be interesting to translate that conversation. "We'll be there," I told her. "In fact, they're here right now." She'd arrived with Lou and Chastity in the back seat. Frankie had joined them as soon as MayBelle pulled up.

MayBelle leaned close. "The night Mike was arrested, my apartment smelled like violets, and I don't have any in the house."

"That's your mother," I told her.

Ellis descended the front steps of the church. "My brother is a miracle worker," he said, joining us. "Not to mention pushy."

"Glad to see he's using his powers for good," I said as he offered me his arm.

"Would you like to sit with us, MayBelle?" he asked. "The service is starting soon."

"I'd be glad to walk in with you," she said, accepting his other arm. "But I promised my family I'd sit with them."

She said that last part with a heaping dose of satisfaction.

I couldn't have been happier for her.

～

The service was beautiful and funny and touching, the perfect send-off for a woman who had touched so many lives.

When Ellis and I returned to my home after the reception, I found two things waiting for me on the back porch; an ecstatic skunk, which was not at all a surprise, and a plain manila envelope, which was. It stood propped up outside my back door, with no return address, no note. No...nothing.

Ellis took care of Lucy while I handled the package. I slipped a finger under the seal, and inside, I found the letter Jorie had tried to give me the day she'd died.

"Look!" I said, drawing it out, holding it like the precious artifact it was.

"Ah, yes. They released it when they dropped the charges against Pastor Mike," Ellis said, cuddling my skunk. "I asked Duranja to run it by as soon as he could."

For once, Duranja had done something nice. The officer didn't like me much, but perhaps he did have a good heart after all.

We took the show inside, where Ellis cut bananas and washed blueberries for Lucy—he didn't like her eating junk— while I sat on the couch and read the letter my grandmother had written to Jorie. It was dated three days after I'd been born.

I read about how exciting she found all ten of my fingers and toes, how she looked forward to making cute dresses for me and teaching me to sew. Well, one of those things had taken. I did like dresses. She wrote how she couldn't wait to bake with me. I let out a hearty laugh, thinking of the last point.

"What?" Ellis asked, raising his head from his banana chopping.

"I just wonder what Grandma would think of me baking skunk treats."

"She loved animals, didn't she?" he asked, flipping a slice of banana to Lucy, who gobbled it up.

"Yes, she did." I smiled. Grandma would have loved Lucy. And Ellis. And the life I'd made for myself here in Sugarland, in this house that she'd cherished for so many years.

"Speaking of happy surprises, I have another one for you," Ellis said, setting Lucy's bowl down for her. She promptly attacked it, crashing it into his feet. "I like the enthusiasm," he said to her. "Wait right there," he added to me.

Oh my. I hoped my misadventure on the second floor of the Pastry Box hadn't put any premature thoughts into his head. I mean, I loved Ellis and thought it wonderful he'd said he wanted to marry me someday. But he was the careful sort, and so was I—even if that didn't always translate to ghost hunting.

It seemed too soon.

He returned with a flat, wrapped package a foot and a half wide and at least two feet high.

"What on earth?" I asked as he handed it to me.

"Open it," he said, taking a seat next to me on the couch.

I tore at the magnolia flowered paper to reveal a framed photograph of my grandmother and Jorie on her wedding day.

"It's the one from the heritage society. I tracked it down and had a copy made."

"It's wonderful," I said, fighting back tears. "It's perfect." And I knew just where it would hang.

Ellis measured for the nail, and I hung the photo above the fireplace mantel in my parlor, right next to the trash can with the rosebush where I kept Frankie's urn. We stepped back to admire the two friends smiling, ready to face the world, never mind the mobsters in the background.

They'd braved life's ups and downs. They'd made memories. They'd lived life to the fullest.

Together.

So would we.

Note from Angie Fox

Thank you so much for dropping in on Verity, Ellis, Frankie, and the rest of the gang. Southern Bred and Dead *was such a joy to write— it was a kick to explore Frankie's past and his world in a whole new way. I can't tell you how many books I've spent trying to get that ghost to open up a bit. I mean, is it so hard? Don't let him answer that.*

The next book is a light-hearted romp through Sugarland, called The Haunted Homecoming *In it, Verity and Ellis are growing closer by the day, when Verity's mother rolls into town in her RV, excited to visit some of her favorite local haunts. Too bad the discovery of a dead body interrupts the fun. Meanwhile, Frankie has no shortage of ideas on how to get his relationship with Molly back on track—all of them guaranteed to drive Verity crazy. And if that's not enough, I have two words for you: 1980's ghosts.*

If you like these mysteries, and want to know when new ones come out, sign up for my newsletter at www.angiefox.com.

Thanks again for reading!
Angie

Don't miss the next
Southern Ghost Hunter mystery
The Haunted Homecoming

Apple cider, bonfires, football, and—ghosts.

It's homecoming weekend in Sugarland, Tennessee and ghost hunter Verity Long is tickled to see so many souls—living and dead—back in town to celebrate. But not all reunions are happy ones, and when Verity stumbles upon a dead body by the football field, it appears someone has already evened the score.

Coming August, 2021!

About the Author

New York Times and *USA Today* bestselling author Angie Fox writes sweet, fun, action-packed mysteries. Her characters are clever and fearless, but in real life, Angie is afraid of basements, bees, and going up stairs when it's dark behind her. Let's face it: Angie wouldn't last five minutes in one of her books.

Angie earned a journalism degree from the University of Missouri. During that time, she also skipped class for an entire week so she could read Anne Rice's vampire series straight through. Angie has always loved books and is shocked, honored and tickled pink that she now gets to write books for a living. Although, she did skip writing for a week this past fall so she could read Victoria Laurie's Abby Cooper psychic eye mysteries straight through.

Angie makes her home in St. Louis, Missouri with a football-addicted husband, two kids, and Moxie the dog.

If you are interested in receiving an email each time Angie releases a new book, please sign up at www.angiefox.com.

Connect with Angie Fox online:
www.angiefox.com
angie@angiefox.com

CPSIA information can be obtained
at www.ICGtesting.com
Printed in the USA
BVHW040229300623
666611BV00006B/74